FIVE DEAD MEN

RACHEL GREEN

ALSO BY RACHEL GREEN

Madame Renard Investigates:

Body on the Rocks

Five Dead Men

No Tears for Sandrine

Five Dead Men

Copyright © Rachel Green 2022

The right of Rachel Green to be identified as the author of this work has been asserted in accordance with the Copyright, Designs and Patents Act 1988.

All rights reserved. No part of this publication may be reproduced, stored in or transmitted into any retrieval system, in any form, or by any means (electronic, mechanical, photocopying, recording or otherwise) without the prior written permission of the publisher. Any person who does any unauthorised act in relation to this publication may be liable to criminal prosecution and civil claims for damages.

This is a work of fiction. Names, characters, businesses, places, events and incidents are either the products of the author's imagination or used in a fictitious manner. Any resemblance to actual persons, living or dead, or actual events is purely coincidental.

To find out more about Rachel Green visit: www.rachelgreenauthor.com

PROLOGUE

The snap of breaking wood was loud enough to cut through the drone of the digger's engine. Watching the bucket pull something unexpected from the ground, the foreman threw up his hands in alarm.

"Stop!"

The driver promptly killed the engine. Leaning out through the side door of his cab he jutted his chin. "What?"

Hanging from the teeth of the digger's bucket was what looked like a timber gate. A tangle of briar ensnared it, and the broken ends of half the boards remained firmly stuck in the ground. A ripe, loamy smell rose up from the freshly-loosened earth.

The foreman grabbed a spade. He hacked through the vegetation to get to the edge of the patch they'd been clearing and then climbed onto the mound of soil. Too much debris had fallen in to see clearly, but it was obvious the gate had been covering a hole. The driver jumped down from his cab.

"What is it?"

"Not sure." The foreman pointed.

They both stooped to peer in. The sides of the hole were

beginning to crumble so they took a step back. Rubbing the stubble on his chin, the driver straightened. "An old land drain, maybe?"

The foreman shook his head. There had been nothing on the plans, and given they were halfway up a hillside, on the edge the woods, a land drain made no sense, particularly as it would have been heading directly towards the rear of the villa. He carefully stepped down into one side of the hole, and once he'd found a firm footing chipped away at the sides. Soon his spade connected with something solid, and as more earth fell away an area of masonry was quickly revealed, much too elaborate to be any kind of drain.

The foreman climbed back out. He and the driver shared a worried look. Fifty metres below them, the rest of the crew were still at work, busily clearing the overgrown vegetation from the land to the side of the villa. The mid-morning sun was intense so they moved into the shade of the trees while they decided what to do. They still had half a hectare to clear and they were already behind schedule, but curiosity had got the better of both men. The foreman made up his mind.

"Let's pull out the rest. And carefully this time."

The driver returned to his cab.

The excavator made short work of clearing the loosened soil, and a few indelicate scrapes pulled away most of the vines. As soon as he'd made an easier way through, the driver turned off his engine and got down for a second time. Now a clearly-defined hole was revealed, perhaps two metres deep. The brickwork was an arch, framing the entrance to a tunnel, almost big enough to stand up in. The foreman took out his handkerchief and wiped the sweat from the back of his neck.

"Do you have a flashlight?"

"There's one in the cab."

The fact they would be going in didn't seem in doubt.

The passage was little more than a metre and half in height, meaning they had to stoop. The foreman went first, cutting the air ahead of him with his beam of light. The tunnel had a pronounced curve to it, giving them no clue what they might be heading into. The fact that some considerable work had gone into its construction was evident from the start where the first few metres were lined in brick. After that, the brickwork gave way to timber, but still the planks had been joined and filled with care. As the gradient steepened, steps cut into the dirt made the going a little easier. When the foreman paused to look back, the outside world had shrunk to a tiny white circle. The air had turned noticeably cooler, the earth around them heavy with the smell of damp and decay.

Given the fact they'd been descending a hill it was difficult to tell how deep underground they were, but something told him they were far from the surface. As the tunnel levelled out, the light reached a little further, revealing a cave of some kind. A more pungent aroma began to cut through the earthiness: the smell of an animal that had died, perhaps. A hand grabbed the foreman's arm, giving him a start. Turning sharply, he found the wide white eyes of the digger driver staring back at him.

"Perhaps we should go back." There was fear in his voice.

But the foreman shook his head. "We can't just leave it." They couldn't complete the job without knowing what was down here. A tunnel or a cave like this might be unstable. There was no point restoring the gardens to their former glory only to have the ground beneath them start sinking. And besides, another thought was creeping into the back of his mind. There might be buried treasure: family heirlooms hidden during the war, a hoard of jewellery stashed by bandits. How could they resist?

Soon they were entering a larger space, only this was no cave. The tunnel came to an end in a small chamber, high enough to stand up in. Its walls were made from dressed stone; the ceiling formed into a barrel arch. Whatever its purpose, some thought had clearly gone into its construction. The foreman's imagination once again lit up as he eagerly searched the space with the flashlight. A place like this was sure to have an illicit purpose. They might find wealth beyond their wildest dreams. They could split the profits fifty-fifty, not let on to the others, put an end to all their money worries. But his hopes of instant riches were promptly dashed as his light moved to the farthest corner of the cold dark vault.

Lying in a heap on the floor were the blackened remains of five dead men.

1

Six years later

Standing beneath a palm tree in the strip of garden at the rear of the harbour in Argents-sur-Mer, Margot studied her canvas. It was a poor representation of the scene in front of her. The proportions were all wrong. The old stone turret at the mouth of the harbour looked more like an ice cream cone than a fortification, the masts on the yachts in the marina more like birch trees in a forest. She put down her paintbrush and sighed, sunk with frustration. Why was it so difficult? It seemed impossible to get every element right: proportion, line, colour. There wasn't a white in her palette bright enough to capture the way the sun sparkled on the surface of the Mediterranean, glistening serenely beyond the harbour walls. Or a blue rich enough to match the depth of the sky. As for the terracotta rooftops ... she'd turned her palette into a muddy mess in an attempt to mix a satisfying hue. She'd been working on it for two days now and all she wanted to do at that moment was douse the canvas in white spirit and set light to it.

"That's very good, Madame."

Margot turned sharply. An elderly gent was standing close by, having evidently been watching from over her shoulder. Margot forced a polite smile. "It's just a silly hobby."

He appeared shocked. "Not at all. You should show it to one of the galleries."

"I really don't think so."

She unscrewed the big wooden clamp on top of the easel and quickly stowed the atrocity in her portfolio.

Walking home she continued to stew. She'd been going to art class for three weeks but didn't seem to be making any progress. The teacher had started them on watercolours, but Margot was drawn to oils. She wanted to let loose her imagination, go wild on the canvas, do something abstract. She loved the smell of linseed oil, and the way you could layer up the paint. Impatient as she was, she'd gone ahead and started her first oil landscape, though given the results perhaps the teacher had been right.

Florian was standing outside her front door. As Judge Deveraux's assistant it was unusual to see him away from his office in the *Palais de Justice*, though the untidy bundle of papers he had tucked under his arm was very much the norm. Spotting her, he came to the gate, pushing his spectacles up the bridge of his nose.

"Sorry to bother you at home, Madame Renard," he said. "There was no answer from your mobile."

Burdened as they both were, they opened the gate between them, comically dropping a number of things in the process.

"I keep it switched off when I'm painting. Sorry. Would you like to come in?"

"No, I can't stop. I'm on my way to the post office." He indicated the papers under his arm. "Célia wanted to know if you could drop by and see her today."

"Of course. What time?"

"Two o'clock?"

Margot glanced at her watch – eleven-fifteen. She had no plans for the rest of the day. Or the week, for that matter.

"Two's fine."

"But not at the office," he added cryptically. "She wants you to go to her home. Shall I send the car?"

Margot blinked. She'd never been invited to the judge's house before and was intrigued. "Where does she live?"

The address he gave was on the other side of town but it was only a few kilometres on foot. "No need. I'll walk."

"Are you sure?"

"I could do with the exercise." Margot patted her hip. Too many cakes, not enough swimming.

But two hours later she regretted her decision. The August heat was intense and she was hot and sweaty even before she reached the top of Rue Voltaire. At least it was downhill from there, and a narrow winding lane took her to the cliffs on the northern edge of town where a brand-new pair of apartment buildings sat serenely above a rocky beach.

The air-conditioned lobby was bliss. On the way up in the mirrored elevator, Margot adjusted her clothing. The cool air had left a thin film of sweat on her back, making her glad she'd worn her linen rather than silk. Not to mention her Chloé mules. Increasingly these days she found herself drawn to the more comfortable shoes in her wardrobe, though she wasn't quite ready for the trainers and a dress look.

On the top floor, she rounded a corner into a sleek corridor, a single door at its end. Célia answered promptly and showed Margot into a space that was bright and modern, all travertine and glass; a far cry from the grand old office at the *Palais de Justice* where they usually met.

"What a wonderful apartment."

"Thank you. I only moved in a month ago. I'm still getting used to where everything is."

Célia gave her the tour. The accommodation was arranged over several levels with a split staircase going down to three bedrooms and a straight flight leading up to a solarium. Climbing the last few steps brought them onto the roof where nothing but glass balustrades separated them from views of the sea. Yet more steps took them up to a higher level, screened by low green hedges and complete with a hot-tub.

Margot put on her sunglasses as she took in the view. Most of the town was visible from the top deck, even the turret at the entrance to the harbour that she'd been attempting to paint just a few hours earlier. When Célia came to her side, they were both smiling brightly.

"That's an incredible view."

"If you lean out far enough you can just about see your house."

"Can you?"

It must have been there somewhere, tucked in amongst the jumble of old stone buildings that made up the lower half of the town. Margot's eyes traced the coastline back towards the cove where she went swimming every morning, but it was hidden behind a bluff.

"Where did you live before?"

"Oh, a stuffy old house in Perpignan. I've always liked the modern style but for one reason or another never took the plunge. I'm not getting any younger, so I thought, why not?"

"You only live once."

"Exactly."

It was a sentiment Margot admired, though it still seemed a surprising choice given the fact Célia must have been approaching retirement and, as far as Margot was aware, had only one son. Why would she want to rattle around in a place as big as this?

If anything, the sun was a little too intense so they retreated to the lower deck where a canvas sail provided a welcome triangle of shade. Célia wheeled over a drinks trolley from the outdoor kitchen. "What can I get you?"

Margot took off her sunglasses. "Ooh, something nice and cold."

"Sangria?"

"Why not?"

She garnished two highball glasses with a fresh fruit melange and then filled them with a jug she took from the fridge. Margot made herself comfortable on a big floppy sofa, the frustration of her painting session quickly melting away.

"Much as I'd like to spend the rest of the day relaxing with you," the judge said, "I suppose we'd better get down to business." She had a quick suck on her straw and then set down her glass. She crossed her legs, the split in her gown riding up over a pale white knee. "I imagine you're wondering why I asked you to come to my home."

Margot mirrored her actions and took a generous mouthful before setting her own glass down on the table. "It did seem rather unusual."

"There's a case I would like you to look into. Only this one has a rather personal connection."

It had been three months since Margot had accepted the judge's offer to work as an advisor but so far the job had been nothing but paperwork. Margot had been itching to sink her teeth into something more solid. "You can count on me to be discrete."

"Do you remember the case of the five men found dead in a villa in the Pyrenees? A village called Saint-Clair-de-l'Ouillat?"

Margot shook her head.

"It's been six years now but it was big news at the time."

Margot searched her memory. She and Hugo had bought the house in Argents-sur-Mer five years ago and for the most part had used it as a holiday home. It was only after Hugo's premature death that she'd made it her full-time home. "We would have been living in Paris at that time."

"Not to worry. The villa in question used to belong to my cousin, Amélie. Prior to that it had been in the Deveraux family for generations. It was built by one of my ancestors, General Deveraux, a Napoleonic duke no less." In the few months that Margot had known her, Célia had made no secret of her noble ancestry. She sought no glory from it; neither was she embarrassed by it. She continued, "It was conceived as a winter retreat, but when the family estate got broken up the villa became the main home. My great grandfather was very fond of the place. He was the one who created the gardens and gave it its present name – the villa Belle Époque. Finally, my cousin, Amélie, came to inherit. She and her husband, Louis, moved in around thirty years ago. They had two children there, Pascal and Roselyn. But unfortunately, it didn't turn out to be the country idyll they'd hoped. After a series of family tragedies they ran into money troubles and were forced to sell up."

"How sad."

"It was bought by a couple from London. They wanted to turn the place into a boutique B&B." She spoke the word 'boutique' as if it left an unpleasant taste in her mouth – what would the Napoleonic duke have thought? "By that stage, the grounds had become rather neglected so the new owners brought in a contractor to tidy up. And it was as they were clearing the site that they uncovered the entrance to an underground passage."

Margot raised her eyebrows. "What kind of passage?"

"A tunnel. It started from a hole in the ground on the edge of the woods and led down to a chamber at the back of the villa. Some local historians believe it was built by smugglers who used it for storing contraband. The villa's only a few kilometres from the Spanish border, and there's a whole network of smugglers' trails across that part of the Pyrenees. But the truth of how it came to be is still a mystery."

"I'm guessing they didn't find any buried treasure."

"No. Just the bodies of five men."

"That must have been a shock."

"Quite. And you can imagine what a blow it was for the new owners. Naturally, their redevelopment plans had to be put on hold. The police investigation dragged on for well over a year, and when it finally wound up they decided to put the villa back up for sale. Sadly, they had no takers. You can imagine how off-putting a history like that would be to potential buyers."

"So who were the victims?"

Célia paused to clear her throat. She had a little cough, and then went on.

"We've never found out. Whoever killed them went to great lengths to prevent them from being identified. All five had had their teeth extracted, and it's likely acid had been used to remove any identifiable marks. They were all male, the youngest in his early twenties, the eldest mid-fifties."

"Were they able to recover any DNA?"

"Yes, but nothing they found matched anything on police records. They'd all been tortured. The injuries they'd sustained were really quite horrific: multiple stab wounds, broken limbs, amputations ... the pathologist's report makes for grim reading."

Margot shifted on her seat. "Was there a consistent pattern to the injuries?"

"The pathologist concluded not. The police did look into the possibility of there being more than one killer, but ultimately that was ruled out. The working hypothesis was that it had been the work of a cold and calculating psychopath."

"Were they murdered in the chamber?"

"It's thought they were drugged first and then taken down there to be killed."

"How long had they been down there?"

"Between one and three years."

"And was there any sexual motive?"

"Apparently not. The bodies had not been sexually interfered with. That's not to say the perpetrator gained no sexual gratification from killing them, of course." She leaned forward and placed a hand on Margot's knee. "If any of this is too disturbing please do say."

Margot shook her head. "My husband dealt with some extreme cases in his time."

"I can imagine."

Hugo had always been reluctant to discuss the more gruesome aspects of his cases, but Margot had usually managed to prise some details out of him. Not because she enjoyed hearing it; far from it. But if you wanted to fully understand the human mind then you really needed to know what one *homo sapien* was capable of doing to another.

"Were there any suspects?"

Célia switched the crossing of her legs, looking a little uncomfortable. "Yes, and this is where the matter cuts close to the bone."

"I see."

"There was only one plausible suspect and that was Amélie's son, Pascal. He had a difficult childhood. When he was six years old he witnessed his father's suicide."

"Oh my."

"One Sunday morning, he and Roselyn went into the dining room to find him strung up from a beam. Apparently, he'd just climbed up onto the dining table and stepped off the edge."

"How awful."

"One can only imagine the effect it must have had upon their developing minds. Although, even before that he was a troubled young boy. He rarely mixed with other children, and always seemed lost in a world of his own. After his father's suicide, he got into trouble at school. He used to play some terrible tricks on his teachers. In the end Amélie had to pay for him to be tutored at home. Later on, he did seem to settle down. In his early twenties he won a place in a theatre school and found his natural habitat on the stage. He was quite successful. He worked at the Comédie-Française for over a year. Then there were a few films, a couple of roles on television. He'd been born into a life of privilege, but success as an actor meant he could have it all – women, drugs, whatever he wished for. And he certainly made the most of it."

Margot reached for her glass. As Mae West had once said: *Too much of a good thing can be wonderful.*

"Inevitably the acting work dried up, along with the money. Instead of modifying his lifestyle to suit, however, he carried on living the highlife. His gambling debts built up. When the banks stopped lending him money he turned to loan sharks. At one point I recall Amélie telling me he owed over a hundred thousand euros. And it was Pascal's debts that ultimately forced her to sell the villa."

"Why was he a suspect?"

"Well, for one thing, he grew up there and knew the ins and outs of the house as well as anyone. It's hard to believe that a young boy living in a place like that wouldn't know of the existence of a secret underground passage. For another, he did once confess."

Margot raised an eyebrow. "To murdering them?"

"In a way. The police carried out an intensive investigation. Amélie often complained what an ordeal it was. The whole thing became so exhausting she eventually holed herself up in their apartment in Paris. But at one point during the *instruction* she revealed to the *juge* that Pascal had boasted of killing a man."

"What did the *juge* make of that?"

"He re-interviewed Pascal. His explanation was that he'd been drunk at the time and had made it up. He said he'd only told his mother to try and rile her."

"And he believed that?"

"Yes."

"What about you?"

"Do I believe he actually killed someone?" Célia gave it some thought. "It's hard to say. Amélie certainly took it seriously. I've only met Pascal a few times as an adult and he's always come across as rather enigmatic. He has a vivid imagination so the idea of him concocting a story like that wouldn't surprise me. But equally, he's moved in some dubious circles, and frankly I don't think I would put anything past him. Of course, without knowing the identities of the victims it's impossible to say whether or not he had a motive."

"But presumably he had the opportunity, seeing as though he lived in the villa?"

"Quite. But as no evidence was found to implicate him, the *juge* dropped him as a person of interest."

"Did they employ any staff?"

"They had a groundsman and a housekeeper. I believe Gaston, the caretaker, still lives on the grounds."

"And neither of them knew of the existence of the chamber?"

"Apparently not. The discovery of the bodies came as a surprise to everyone."

Margot mulled that over while she took another sip of Sangria. It was certainly shaping up to be an interesting case. After clearing her throat, Célia went on,

"It's been almost two years since the *instruction* was paused and in all that time not a single new line of enquiry has been opened. It's time for a fresh pair of eyes."

"Indeed."

The judge leaned forward and looked at her with renewed intensity. "My main concern, and the reason I would like you personally to look at it, is that I want to ensure the investigation was carried out without bias. It wasn't my case, of course. The family connection ruled out any possibility of me being involved, but the *juge* who supervised the investigation was a close friend. I would hate to think he showed any leniency out of respect for me. It pains me to believe that Pascal might have committed such terrible crimes but if he did, if he is guilty, then justice must be done."

Margot nodded. If she were in Célia's position she was certain she would have felt exactly the same way.

"The *juge* concerned died a few months ago which is how I came to see the dossier. I've been through all the evidence with a fine-tooth comb and everything appears to be in order, but I would like a second opinion, if only for my own peace of mind."

Margot straightened her back. She was certainly intrigued, and keen to get started. She downed the remainder of her Sangria, and returned the glass to the table.

"Where would you like me to begin?"

"Firstly, I thought you might like to go to the villa. Stay in the area for a few days and have a good look around."

"Will the new owners mind?"

"I very much doubt it. They never actually moved in so you won't be disturbing anyone. I'll contact them to check, of course, but I imagine they'll be as keen as anyone to see the mystery cleared up."

"Do the *gendarmerie* cover that area?"

"Yes, but there's an excellent municipal police station in Saint-Clair-de-l'Ouillat. I'll ask for their assistance."

"And Pascal?" Margot let the question hang in the air for a moment. "Would you like me to speak to him?"

Célia briefly shifted her gaze out to sea before bringing it back to Margot, and nodding. "I think it would be useful, assuming he'll agree. He got so irritated by the investigation that he lodged a formal complaint of harassment with the *Procureur de la République*. But I'll call him and see if he's amenable."

"Thank you."

Célia's tone hardened. "However, if he does agree to see you, I must warn you to remain on your guard. Pascal can be quite the charmer when he wants to be. Like most actors, he craves attention. But there's a darkness to him. Don't be taken in."

Margot inclined her head. "I'll bear that in mind."

2

According to *The Illustrated Guide to Post Mortem Techniques*, a pathologist routinely used rib cutters, bone saws, even pruning shears to remove the rib cage when performing an autopsy. Alia Leon contemplated this fact as she gazed out at the garden through the open front door of the Saint-Clair-de-l'Ouillat police house. Imagine if that were her job: going into the mortuary on a Monday morning and cutting up someone's body with a selection of power tools and gardening equipment. She'd watched an autopsy live at university once and, unlike several of her peers, hadn't passed out. She'd watched with interest as, one by one, the surgeon had removed the organs from the chest cavity and weighed them on the scales. Could that be her calling? In her idle moments she'd always assumed she would one day move on from the municipal police force and join the *Police Nationale*, become an *officier de police juidiciaire*, investigating crime in some big city. But perhaps she could become a police surgeon instead. Go back to university and retrain, though the prospect of studying for another five years to gain a medical degree was far from appealing.

She turned the page in her textbook. *Chapter 3: Procedures for Dissecting a Brain*

A familiar tapping sound made her look up. Henrietta, having just wandered in from the kitchen, was pecking at something on the floor. Alia sighed in annoyance, then sprang out from behind the counter and squared up the bird. She pulled an imaginary gun from her hip and shot it three times with invisible bullets. The dumb bird barely batted an eyelid.

"I see. Playing hardball, are we?"

Changing tack, Alia flapped her arms and clucked like a chicken on speed as she chased it through the kitchen and out into the yard. "Papa," she called out. "The hens have got loose again."

Busy in the side garden, her father grumbled something back.

Chicken-wrangling complete, Alia picked up a peach from the fruit bowl and wandered back to the office. She paused on the front doorstep while she bit into the peach. The garden was a soul-warming sight at this time of year, a riot of cosmos and beeblossom, teeming with insect life. It was impossible to walk down the front path without disturbing a small flock of butterflies, feasting on the overgrown stems of the verbena. Of course, the downside to becoming an *officier de police juidiciaire,* investigating crime in some big city, was that she was unlikely to have a view like this to gaze upon each morning. Or, if she became a police surgeon instead, would she be able to stop for five minutes to eat a ripe and juicy peach? Unlikely, unless she became one of those pathologists you see on TV who merrily eat their cheese and tomato sandwiches after pulling the heavily-scarred liver from some poor soul's cadaver, hands still covered in blood. Alia wiped the peach juice from her chin and then lobbed the stone into the woods on the far side of the track. For now, she would have to be content as a *policière municipale* in sleepy old Saint-Clair-de-l'Ouillat.

At ten o'clock she received her first visitor. A shadow entering the hallway preceded the arrival of farmer Lémieux. Seeing Alia seated at the desk he hesitated in the doorway, apparently surprised to find her there even though she'd been in charge of the police station for over nine months now. Most of the elderly men in the village reacted the same way. On good days, Alia would give them the benefit of the doubt and believe that it was her age rather than the colour of her skin that made them pause on the threshold, looking like little lost schoolboys. On bad days, she would find some other way of getting back at them.

"Bonjour, Monsieur Lémieux. How can I help you this fine day?" She closed her textbook and slid it to one side, giving him her warmest smile. He was in luck – today was shaping up to be a good day.

Lémieux's eyes searched the corners of the empty hallway, no doubt hoping her father would appear and put him out of his misery. "Is Didier not in?"

"My father is in but he retired as a police officer almost a year ago. I told you that the last time you were here." *And the time before*, Alia added in her head.

Lémieux grumpily took off his cap. He mumbled something, seemingly on the verge of going away.

"What is it this time?" Alia prompted. "A tiger on the loose? Aliens in the haybarn?"

The sarcasm was lost on him.

"Blasted bears again." His reticence evaporated now that he'd got onto his pet bugbear and he strode up to the reception desk. "Nine sheep I've lost this week. Nine!' – though for some reason he was only holding up five fingers – "And sixteen more the month before that. Something needs to be done."

Alia sighed in resignation. The history of brown bears in the Pyrenees was a story that trod a familiar path. Hunted to near extinction in the latter part of the 20th Century, they'd been re-introduced in the mid-1990s since when their numbers had increased. But more bears meant more conflict with livestock, and reports of apparent attacks had risen sharply. Actual attacks were rare; usually the bear's scent would be enough to scare the sheep into jumping off a cliff. But Lémieux farmed fifty hectares on the lower slopes of the Albères, and although in summer he would let his flock graze on the high mountain pasture, there were no bears in that region. Alia opened her notebook and clicked the end of her pen.

"When did this happen?"

"Last night. I went up to check on them first thing this morning and there they were."

Alia pretended to write something down in her notebook but doodled a picture of a bear instead, devouring a stick man, his bony feet sticking out of the bear's mouth. She maintained a serious face.

"Did you see any bears?"

"Of course I didn't see them. They're far too cunning."

"What about tracks? Did you see any pawprints, or droppings?"

"You really think I've got nothing better to do than go crawling around on the ground, sniffing bear shit?"

"It was probably a wolf."

He shook his head. "I know a wolf attack when I see one. It's bears, I tell you."

"There are no bears in the Albères, Monsieur Lémieux."

"Oh really? And how do you know that?"

"Because the mayor sent out a ranger last year."

"That man was an idiot."

"Nevertheless. He found no bear tracks."

"Pah! It's getting out of control." He jabbed the desk with his forefinger. "Next time I'll go up there with my gun."

Alia made a point of clicking her pen shut. She sat back in her seat, arms folded. "I really wouldn't advise that."

"Oh, wouldn't you now?"

"Shooting bears is illegal."

"Who said anything about shooting them?"

"You're not allowed to fire warning shots, either."

"What?"

"Bears are a protected species."

"And what about my sheep? Who's going to protect them?" He jutted his chin.

Alia was just about to send him on his way when her father came in through the kitchen. Lémieux's eyes lit up, having seen his salvation.

"Didier – have you heard this nonsense? Your daughter's telling me I'm not allowed to fire shots to warn off bears. What is the world coming to?"

Didier calmly approached the desk and the two men shook hands. "Bonjour, Lémieux. The bears again?"

"Damn right it is. Three more sheep last night."

"I've already told h—"

"It's all right, Alia. I'll deal with this."

"But—"

"The hen is still loose in the yard. Could you see to it, please?"

Alia smouldered. If her eyes could shoot laser beams her father would not be a happy man right now. She got up out of her seat and marched into the kitchen, and then carried on out into the yard where she turned her laser beams upon the errant bird instead, prompting a worried reassessment from Henrietta, surprised that her daily escapology act was being met with such annoyance. In no mood for playing games, Alia grabbed the hen from behind and flung her into the run.

"Next time—*pfft*." She drew a finger across her own throat.

The hen retreated to the sanctuary of the nesting box, looking most put out.

Alia pulled up her trousers. What irony the fact she didn't even have a uniform of her own, the one she was wearing being her father's hand-me-down. She'd asked the mayor on at least two occasions if he might possibly consider getting her a new one (preferably one with a more feminine cut) but he'd merely added it to the long list of items that were never going to get done.

The telephone began ringing inside the house. Alia went back into the kitchen and searched for the handset amongst the clutter on the table. She could hear her father still out in reception, talking to Lémieux. "Papa, what have you done with the phone?"

She found it hiding under a tea towel, next to the cheese board.

"What?"

"It doesn't matter."

She wiped it clean of dirty finger-marks before raising it to her ear. "Bonjour. Saint-Clair-de-l'Ouillat police station."

"Could I speak to officer Didier Leon, please?"

Alia rolled back her eyes. She had half a mind to make her response a recorded message: "I'm Alia Leon, Didier's daughter. I'm the village officer now. How can I help?"

From the other end of the line came a scrunching of papers. "Ah … Yes … I see now. Please accept my apologies."

"Apologies accepted."

"My name's … erm, Florian Legrand."

"Are you quite sure?"

The voice seemed surprised. "Yes."

"Continue."

"I'm calling on behalf of Judge Deveraux."

Alia had no idea who that was but they sounded rather important. She straightened her tie, adjusted her trousers, wondered if she should put on her cap; it was around here somewhere ...

"It's in connection with a case involving your village," Florian Legrand went on. "The bodies that were found at the villa Belle Époque."

Alia gulped. "The Belle Époque?"

"Yes. Are you familiar with it?"

There was unlikely to be a resident of Saint-Clair-de-l'Ouillat who was not familiar with the case, it being the biggest thing to have happened in the area in living memory. Alia was more familiar with it than most having spent many hours studying the files.

"Hello? Are you still there?"

"Yes, I'm here." Alia pressed the phone closer to her ear. "How would you like me to help?"

"Judge Deveraux has called for a review of the case. She's asked one of her advisors to come over and see you. Her name's Margot Renard. She has the owner's permission to go to the villa, but if there's any way you can assist with her enquiries the judge would be most grateful."

"Of course. When is she coming?"

"Tomorrow. In the morning."

Alia leaned to the side to cast a glance into the hall. Her father was on the doorstep, saying goodbye to Lémieux.

"Okay. I'll make a note in the diary. Thank you."

Alia was still holding onto the handset when her father came in. He picked up on her state of surprise and regarded her more closely. "Who was that?"

She came to her senses. "Someone named Florian Legrand, from Judge Deveraux's office."

"What did he want?"

"They're sending someone to review the villa Belle Époque case."

Didier's eyes widened. "The Belle Époque?"

"Yes."

"What for?"

Alia shrugged. "I've no idea."

He sat down, and then immediately stood up again. Why was he looking so worried?

"That is all right, isn't it?" Alia said.

Her father stayed lost in thought for a while but finally he nodded. "Yes, yes, of course," he said and went out into the garden, rubbing his chin.

3

Célia was full of surprises.

The following morning, at exactly nine o'clock, a shiny new Bentley appeared in the lane outside Margot's house. It moved along the street as if borne on a cushion of warm air and briefly came to a halt outside next-door's, before reversing. Margot watched from her salon window as a tall blonde chauffeuse came to the door, lipstick a perfect match for the car's candy red bodywork.

"Madame Renard?"

"Yes."

"I'm Célia's driver. I've come to take you to Saint-Clair-de-l'Ouillat."

Wow. So this was how *la noblesse* lived.

Cocooned in cream leather upholstery just a few minutes later, Margot felt like a million dollars. She was tempted to go back in and put on something rather more elegant than her washed denim jeans and gladiator sandals, but the seat was just too comfortable to get out of. "No, the car doesn't come with the job," the chauffeuse would explain later when they were en route. "I work for Célia in a private capacity."

When she grew up, Margot decided she was going to be rich. Doubly so when she discovered the illuminated, glass-fronted chiller integrated between the two rear seats, a bottle of vintage Pol Roger offering itself up like a gift from the gods. The chauffeuse offered to uncork it, but Margot said no. Her days of drinking champagne at nine o'clock in the morning were both behind and ahead of her.

A thirty-minute drive along the highway passed like a breeze. Skirting Perpignan, they took a D-road into the mountains. The snow was long gone at this time of year, but the Pyrenees were an impressive sight at any time – ghost mountains, Margot often thought of them, the way they appeared to hover just above the landscape. The Bentley swept effortlessly along the curving road as they climbed into the foothills, and for a while Margot became lost in idle thought, imagining herself a countess being whisked away to her winter retreat. The fact it was thirty degrees outside did little to dispel the illusion.

As the road climbed higher, the view through the windows changed from citrus, gorse and olive trees to forests of ash, birch and hazel. Arriving at a break in the trees, the driver pulled up in a small lay-by. When she lowered Margot's window, the air outside was just as unruffled as the cosseted interior.

"If you look down that slope," the chauffeuse stretched as she pointed, "you can just about see the villa Belle Époque."

Margot sat forward. Woodland covered most of the slope, but a hundred metres down, a series of slate rooftops were visible in the gaps. The villa's full size was difficult to appreciate, obscured by trees as it was, but it was clearly a substantial construction. An area of formal garden jutted out to one side before giving way to grassland and then gently undulating forested hills. It was hard to believe they were looking at the scene of horrible crimes.

Margot raised the window and they continued on.

Saint-Clair-de-l'Ouillat was only a short drive away. Basking in sunshine, a sign declared it to be a *Village Fleuri*, but they didn't see much of the village itself – just after passing the sign, the driver turned onto a steep narrow lane that plunged down to a wooded river. She squeezed the Bentley across a petite stone bridge and pulled up on the far side. This time when Margot lowered her window all she could hear was the sound of running water.

"The police house should be just down there." The chauffeuse pointed to a dirt track that appeared to run parallel with the river. "I don't think it's far. Will you be okay to walk?"

There was no sign of a house but Margot assured her she would be fine.

"The auberge you'll be staying in is back up on the main street. It's the only one in the village so you can't miss it."

"Would you mind dropping off my bags?"

"Of course not."

The Bentley drove away, and with it went her fantasy. Oh well, it had been nice while it lasted.

Margot turned to face the empty track. There was no one around. When she took off her sunglasses and looked up at the trees, a chattering magpie was her only companion. The lush green vegetation prevented her from seeing the river but as she set off in search of the police house she could still hear it, babbling away. It had been thirty degrees out in the sun, but down here in the shade the air felt five degrees cooler.

The police house was a two-storey building, its walls covered in creepers. The front elevation was perfectly symmetrical apart from an off-centre porch and a blocked-up doorway suggesting it had once been a pair of semis. The house was fronted by a beautiful garden with a short path leading to the door, but Margot was distracted by a noise to her left. She moved along a neatly-clipped hedge to a small wooden gate on the other side of which a man was tilling the ground with a hoe.

"Bonjour," she called cheerily.

The man looked up. The area of the garden he was in appeared to be one of the few spots not in shade and he squinted into the sun. "Bonjour."

"I'm looking for Alia Leon."

"And you are?"

"Margot Renard."

"Ah!" A smile took over his face. "Madame Renard, of course." He set down his hoe and came to the gate. "Come on through. Alia's been expecting you."

The garden was bigger than it had looked from the gate, and once inside it opened into a sunny haven of colour. So many species were crammed into its overflowing borders that Margot didn't know where to look first. Vegetables rubbed shoulders with flowering plants, climbers and small woody shrubs. In the short time she had to look, her eyes picked out giant alliums, cabbages, leeks, purple kale, not to mention some enormous globe artichokes that she had to brush out of the way to get by. They passed a chicken coop before arriving in a small yard. At the back door, Margot wiped her feet on the mat and then followed him into a charming old-fashioned kitchen.

"Please excuse the mess." He indicated a big pine table covered in clutter, though practically every flat surface Margot laid eyes on had something spread over it. "I'm Didier, by the way. Alia's father." He paused to shake her hand.

"Of course. You used to be the village officer."

"That's right. Twenty-five years, man and boy," he chuckled.

As Margot had surmised, the building was two former cottages knocked into one. From the kitchen, an open door led into a hallway, half of which housed the staircase and half the reception area for the police station. On the other side of a wide wooden counter a young woman rose from her seat.

"Alia," Didier called out. "This is Margot Renard."

Alia was already on her way over. She smiled shyly as they met in the middle.

"I hope you don't mind me parachuting in on you like this," Margot said, gently shaking her hand.

"No, of course not."

"I'll do my best to stay out of your way."

"We'll help in whatever way we can."

She was an attractive young woman with an infectious smile, though there was no familial resemblance: Alia had short curly black hair and dark skin whereas Didier was hook-nosed and Gallic. The poor girl looked lost in her ill-fitting uniform, her trousers at least two sizes too big for her; a fact of which she seemed only too aware.

"Let me get you a drink," Didier said. "Coffee? Wine?"

"Any chance of a cup of tea?"

"Tea? Yes ... I'm sure we have some somewhere."

He led them back to the kitchen. Didier went to the sink to fill a kettle while Alia cleared some space on the table. Margot pulled out a chair and sat down. Over the hiss of running water, Didier said,

"You're here about the Belle Époque case, I understand."

"That's right."

"Well, I hope it won't be a wasted trip." He put the kettle on the stove. "The *brigade criminelle* did a very thorough job. I doubt you'll find anything was missed."

"Were you in charge here at the time?"

"I was the first officer on the scene."

"You went down into the chamber?"

"Oh yes." He joined them at the table though remained standing, hands on the back of a chair while he waited for the kettle to boil. "I went up there as soon as the call came in. The contractors who'd found it showed me the entrance. They didn't want to go back in so I went down alone. Saw it all." He shook his head. "I've seen dead bodies before but nothing prepared me for that. All shrunken and blackened, and just piled in a heap."

"You had no idea who any of them were?"

"None whatsoever," Didier said. "And the state they were in there was no chance of anyone recognising them."

"They'd all been mutilated," Alia put in. "Some of them had been tortured for days."

Margot nodded. "I've seen the crime scene photos." The pathologist had estimated the most recent victim had met his end around a year before the grim discovery had been made, the others having been down there a year or two longer.

The kettle started to whistle so Didier went back to the stove. Alia found some tea in a wall cupboard, spooned some into a pot, and then brought it to the table with three cups. They moved around the kitchen with the choreographed finesse of an old married couple, each of them instinctively knowing what the other was doing. Didier was below average height with a pronounced paunch, and like many men of his age didn't seem embarrassed by it. He arranged some pastries on a plate and offered it to Margot, but she declined, having already eaten a large breakfast.

"Were you here when this happened, Alia?"

Alia finished arranging the tea things. "Some of the time. The year the bodies were found was my first year at uni."

"Oh, where did you study?"

"Toulouse."

"She came home every weekend, though," Didier said. "Too fond of her father's cooking, weren't you, my dear?" He slid an arm around her shoulder and gave her a squeeze. He pulled out a chair and sat down, a little way back from the table. "I retired from the police force shortly after Alia finished her degree."

"Did you help in the investigation?"

Didier shook his head as he picked up one of the pastries. "The *Police Nationale* didn't want us getting involved. You've had access to their files, I presume?"

"I have."

"How anyone could have done such terrible things is beyond me," Didier went on. "No sane man could have committed those crimes."

"Or woman?" Margot suggested.

Didier firmly shook his head. "Two of them had been tied up with barbed wire. Can you see a woman doing that?"

It was unlikely but not unheard of. Hugo had once dealt with a case involving a violent female killer in the suburbs of Paris; the crimes she'd committed had broken every stereotype. Margot sipped her tea.

"What was your opinion of Pascal Deveraux?"

Didier had his mouth full of pastry and so chewed for a while before answering. "Honest opinion?"

"Of course."

"He's an over-privileged layabout with no concern for his fellow man." He shared a little smile with himself before reconsidering. "Perhaps I'm being unfair, given what happened with his father."

"Did you have many dealings with them?"

"Oh yes. Pascal rarely came down to the village but I often went up to the villa for one reason or another."

"Were you surprised when they treated him as a suspect?"

"Not especially. He's always been a bit of an oddball. Sometimes I would go up to see Louis, and Pascal would be there in the background. He had this way of looking at you, like he knew things you didn't. It's hard to explain without actually meeting him. Did you read what the newspapers said about him?"

"No."

" 'Movie-star's house of horrors' – that kind of thing. They dug up all sorts of dirt. When they were older, and Amélie was away, they often used to have parties. We'd get complaints, and when you consider the nearest house is well over a kilometre away you can imagine how noisy they were. Even if half of what they said is true he lived a pretty wild life."

"And the rest of the family? How were they viewed by the villagers?"

Didier finished eating his pastry. He wiped his fingers with a tissue and downed another mouthful of tea, sitting back in his chair with his arms folded. He was clearly a man who liked to talk. "Louis was a fine man. He wasn't a Deveraux by birth, of course. His family hailed from the Vendée and his father was a blacksmith, I believe. It can't have been easy for him, marrying into nobility, but you never heard him complain. He did a great deal for the village. He often brought Amélie down to the church on Sundays. And he helped people financially. He was a well-liked man."

"So his suicide must have come as a shock."

"It did indeed. Amélie became very withdrawn. And you're aware the children witnessed it?"

Margot nodded.

"Pascal was the one in everyone's thoughts, but of the two I'd say it was Roselyn who was affected the most. She spent most of her childhood in and out of various institutions. I remember one time she put a piece of broken glass into her mouth. The housekeeper found her sitting on the lawn with blood pouring down her chin. She'd didn't seem to realise what a foolish thing she'd done."

"I saw a note on the file about an incident in their swimming pool. A man who nearly drowned."

"That's right. That would have been, what – twenty years ago now."

"What happened?"

"A boy from one of the neighbouring villages apparently fell in. Pascal and Roselyn were having one of their parties. Gaston, he's the caretaker, called me and said I should go up. When I got there, people were sitting around, looking shocked. I'd heard this boy had been trying to get friendly with Roselyn. They said it was an accident: a bottle had got smashed, the boy had stepped onto a piece of broken glass. In his panic, he'd slipped and fallen into the pool. They'd all been drinking, of course.

"When the ambulance came, they found a shard of glass in his foot. And there was a bruise on his forehead consistent with the kind of fall they'd described."

"But you have your doubts?"

He rocked his head. "It seemed suspicious that they all told the same story, like they'd rehearsed it. And the way they kept looking at one another, it was obvious something wasn't right. The glass had severed an artery so there was an awful lot of blood. Roselyn was hysterical."

"What was the boy's version?"

"He didn't say much. A few months later he and his family moved overseas so nothing more was said of it."

"They did have a pretty weird relationship," Alia commented.

"Who?"

"Pascal and Roselyn."

Margot's interest was piqued. "In what way?"

"They used to go skinny-dipping in the river. Just the two of them."

"I once heard they had a mock marriage ceremony in the

local graveyard," Didier said. "But don't believe all the rumours you'll hear. In a small village like this people like to talk."

"When Pascal got into movies they were always going to parties together."

"They were like a perfect celebrity couple, weren't they, Alia?"

Alia nodded. "They were very beautiful. Actually, I think I've got some pictures on my phone." She took it out of her pocket and rapidly swiped through. Finding what she was looking for, she turned the phone around and handed it to Margot. "This was in *Cahiers du Cinéma*."

It was a photo of a two-page spread, dated ten years ago. Margot pinched out to zoom in. The photos had been taken at a party thrown by some famous movie producer. Roselyn was indeed a beauty; had the cheekbones of a top model, a figure to match. Pascal had the face of a Hollywood great. "It's a shame they were brother and sister," Margot said, handing back the phone.

"They were inseparable as kids," Didier said. "You would think they were twins."

"I suppose seeing their father kill himself must have forged a close bond."

"No doubt."

Didier got up to refill the teapot, but Margot used it as an excuse to rise from her seat. She suddenly had an urge to see the villa.

"I'd like to go up there."

Didier turned in surprise. "Right now?"

"If you don't mind."

He gave it a little thought, and then nodded. "Okay. That's no problem."

"Can we walk there?"

"It's possible to walk across the fields but it's much easier by car. Will you be wanting to go down into the chamber?"

"If I can."

He looked her up and down. "You may want to change your clothes."

The jeans she had on were the most practical thing she'd brought, however, and the sandals were nothing special. "They'll wash."

"Are you sure?"

"I'm sure."

"Very well. I'll just give Gaston a call. Let him know we're on our way over."

4

The dirt track at the side of the house continued down to an old timber garage, half hidden in trees. A white and blue police car was tucked into the space at the side, but the vegetation was so overgrown that Margot and Didier had to wait by the gate while Alia drove up to meet them. At the end of the track she indicated left and headed away from the village.

The road followed the course of the river for half a kilometre before turning uphill and entering a landscape of heavily wooded hills. The villa Belle Époque stood beyond a huge pair of wrought-iron gates, though nothing of the house could be seen from the road. When Alia pulled up, Didier got out, took a big iron key from his pocket and unlocked the gates. He locked them again when Alia drove through.

"We have to keep the place secured," he explained, getting back in. "This place is a magnet for ghouls."

The driveway passed an informal lake on its meandering route up to the villa. Through gaps in the trees, Margot caught glimpses of the formal gardens she'd seen when they'd parked up at the top. The villa itself was every bit as impressive as she'd expected. Originally a three-storey construction complete with a turret, more recent additions, finished in painted white render, had been tacked onto both sides. The feature that impressed Margot the most, however, was the huge veranda on the western elevation, its ornate ironwork giving that wing the look of an Italianate mansion.

Didier was the first one out. He stood on the gravel and looked up at the façade with his hands on his hips, almost proud. "A remarkable building, don't you think?"

"Not bad for a winter retreat."

"The limestone they used was brought all the way down from Burgundy. And see the detail in the gargoyles? They were designed by Eugène Viollet-le-Duc – the architect who worked on Notre Dame."

Margot paused to take it all in. Behind them, a lawn the size of a football pitch led down to the lake they'd passed on the way in. There was no sign of the road; in fact, not a single house or farm could be seen from where they stood. She turned back to the villa. It was in an excellent state of repair, despite the fact it had stood empty for the past six years.

"Who maintains it?"

"Gaston takes care of the grounds; Madame Baudet comes in three times a week to clean inside."

"And the owners – do they never come down?"

Didier shook his head. "They've barely set foot in the place since the bodies were found."

Perhaps that wasn't surprising. Imagine trying to sleep in there, knowing its history.

"Can we go inside?"

"Of course. We'll just need to get the key from Gaston."

Didier took them along a footpath that skirted the east wing. At the rear, terraces stepped up to a wild area which eventually gave way to forest and then mountain, but Didier detoured onto a grass path which took them through a parterre of clipped box. They passed an ornamental pond, its surface smothered with large pink waterlilies, before following the path through to a walled garden. Beyond that lay a working area where three large greenhouses occupied most of the space. A small stone cottage stood on what appeared to be the boundary.

A tapping noise brought Margot up sharp. Inside one of the greenhouses a pigeon was flapping against the glass, having got caught up in some netting. The weight of the net kept pulling it to the ground where it lay on its side, beak open, close to exhaustion.

"Gaston."

Margot turned at the sound of Didier's voice. A grey-haired old man was approaching from the direction of the cottage. He shook Didier's hand, nodded at Alia, took in Margot with rather unfriendly eyes. Didier went to say something but Margot beat him to it:

"There's a pigeon trapped inside, Monsieur." She indicated the open door of the greenhouse. When they listened they could hear it flapping. Margot turned to go in, but Gaston quickly moved past her.

"Wait here."

They watched from the door as the caretaker caught hold of the bird. He extricated it from the netting and carefully brought it out, holding it in both hands. It looked like a racing pigeon, though its racing days were long over: its eyes were already turning milky, and when the two men examined its wings it was clear that at least one of them was badly broken.

"It must have got lost," Didier said.

"Shame," Gaston replied.

"Poor thing," Margot added. She was going to suggest putting it in the shade, getting it some water, seeing if it might recover, but before she could speak Gaston tore off one of its legs. Margot watched in alarm as Didier flattened his palm to accept the two tiny rings that slid from the bloodied stalk.

"I'll contact the owner," he said while Gaston tossed the dead bird onto a compost heap.

Gaston accompanied them up to the front door, but after turning the key he left them alone.

"Does he work here full-time?" Margot asked, her eyes trailing as the caretaker walked back to the walled garden. The incident with the pigeon had left her feeling a little bit sick in her stomach.

"He lives in that cottage we just saw," Didier said. And then, seeming to read her thoughts: "Don't worry about Gaston. He might come across a little uncouth but he's a good man."

Stepping inside the villa was like entering a museum: all the trappings of life were there but it lacked any kind of soul. The hall rose to the full height of the building and at the top a domed lantern flooded the space with natural light. Immediately to their left, a pair of double doors opened into a grand salon which was furnished so exquisitely it would have happily graced the pages of a glossy magazine. Didier watched from the door as Margot and Alia moved around the room, curiously taking it all in.

"I think our entire house would fit inside this one room," Alia said, looking around in wonder.

"You've not been inside before?" Margot queried.

"No. Imagine what it must have been like, growing up here."

"There are six bedrooms upstairs," Didier commented. "And two more in the turret."

Margot ran a hand over the soft-sheen wallpaper. Furnishing a house to this standard in the present day would have cost a small fortune. She cast her eyes over some vintage bronze sculptures, then at some huge glass vases. "Did the new owners bring in this furniture?"

"The Deverauxs sold it 'as is'. Everything you see here used to belong to them. Louis was a bit of a hoarder. There's so much stuff inside this house I doubt anyone knows what's actually here."

Yet none of it had brought happiness to the people who'd lived there, Margot reflected: father dead, mother a recluse, two psychologically damaged children. They moved on.

The next room was evidently a music room, complete with a Rococo-style antique piano, and beyond that was a study. All four walls were lined with bookcases, each one stuffed with leather tomes. The few titles that caught Margot's eye were pretty obscure. Books provided one of the more direct connections with the past, she'd always felt; to think that, centuries ago, General Deveraux himself would have stood in this same space, turned the pages of those very books.

"The dining room's through here."

Didier called them back across the hall. He opened a cubby hole concealed in the wooden panelling and took out a key. He inserted it into a heavy brass rim-lock and then opened the door.

The room was in darkness. When he switched on the light, it became apparent that all the curtains were drawn. A large mahogany dining table was positioned centrally, complete with twelve chairs, while dressers on one side carried enough china and silverware to host a small army.

"So this is where it happened." Margot looked up at the ceiling as she wandered in. It must have been close to four metres high, and lined with exposed timbers from the floor above.

Didier moved between the table and the fireplace and

pointed at the huge central beam that carried the joists. "See that hook?"

Margot moved around the table to get a better view but it would have been difficult to miss: a chunky piece of black ironwork hammered into the timber.

"He tied a rope to that and put a noose around his neck."

"Has no one ever thought to remove it?"

"Amélie had the lock fitted shortly after his death. I imagine the entire room became a no-go zone."

It must have been a constant reminder, though, walking past that door every day. If that had happened in her house, Margot doubted she'd have been able to stay a single day longer. It wasn't surprising Amélie had ultimately decided to move back to Paris.

"Where was Amélie when it happened?"

"Upstairs, with a migraine. They'd just got back from church so she went straight to bed. A couple of hours later she woke up, apparently with a feeling that something was wrong. She went downstairs to find Roselyn sitting on the floor in that doorway, playing with one of her toys. Pascal was just inside, standing on the very spot you're standing now."

Margot felt a shiver pass through her. She looked down at the floorboards and involuntarily stepped aside.

"According to Gaston he was mesmerised. They virtually had to carry him from the room."

Margot let her eyes travel around the space, trying to picture the scene. Two wide-eyed children staring up at their father, hanging there by the neck. How could anyone even begin to understand the effect it must have had upon them?

"I understand he left no note."

"No. Louis's history of depression was well known, but his death still came as a shock. He was a solitary soul at heart. When you talked with him you could tell something more was going on in his head, like he had thoughts he had no intention of sharing. Those kinds of thoughts have a way of eating you up. That's my feeling, anyway."

It was all beginning to feel a little bit morbid so Margot went back to the hall. She wandered down to the far end where a tall sash window looked out onto the veranda. The ironwork wrapped around two sides of the house and gave an elevated view of the parterre they'd walked through earlier. On the wooden deck was a swing seat, a table with an integrated chess board, a couple of lounge chairs. If she'd got her bearings correct, the return leg faced west, making it the perfect place for a sundowner. It would be nice to think the family had enjoyed at least some of their time there. Margot turned as Alia and Didier came to re-join her.

"How do we get into the chamber?"

"We have to go around the back and up across the meadow," Didier said. "It's a bit of a trek."

"You mean there's no way of accessing it from the house?"

Didier shook his head. "The surveyors searched for another way in, but the chamber's entirely independent."

"Can you show me?"

"Of course. Follow me."

The three of them trooped out through the front door. On the way, Didier collected a flashlight from the boot of the car and then set off along the footpath that ran around the villa's east wing. Passing a gap in a yew hedge, Margot spotted the perfect blue rectangle of the swimming pool. It was criminal to think it never got used. Steps led up to a terrace from where they accessed the meadow which turned out to be much steeper than it had looked from the bottom. They were only halfway up when Didier had to pause for a breather.

"It didn't look like this when the bodies were found," he said, wiping the sweat from his brow with a handkerchief. "This whole area had become completely overgrown."

"Was Gaston still working here at the time?"

"Oh yes, but it was too much for him on his own. When Amélie started getting into debt she had to cut back on their hours. A lot of jobs never got done."

While they were waiting for Didier to recover, Margot took a wider look around. At the top of the meadow, a post and rail fence ran along the edge of the woods. Perhaps fifty metres from where they stood a field gate led to a track that disappeared into the trees. "What's through there?"

"Beyond the gate?"

Margot nodded.

"That's the smugglers' trail. It goes up into the mountains and then over the border into Spain."

"It's part of a long-distance trail," Alia said. "It's mainly hikers and cyclists who use it nowadays."

"The entrance to the passage is just inside the gate," Didier said, readying himself for the final stretch. "I told you it was a bit of a trek."

Puffing and panting, they carried on up to the gate. It was secured with a padlock and chain, but again Didier had a key. A few metres to one side, a post and wire fence ringed a depression in the ground, overgrown with grass and tangled with briar. There was nothing to indicate a tunnel.

"They sealed it with a steel sheet when the investigation concluded," Didier said, scratching the back of his head. "No one's been down there in years. It may take some getting in to."

They climbed over the fence and set to work. A pair of shears or a machete would have come in handy, but they made do with their hands and feet. Margot hacked at the vines with her heels until a stinging nettle caught her bare ankle. She winced, beginning to see why Didier had advised on a change of clothes.

It didn't take long to uncover a sheet of rusty chequer-plate steel. Bolts had been fitted through holes on all four sides, but it seemed to have been a half-hearted job since, at least on the section Margot could see, there was nothing for the shafts to screw in to.

"Let me do the lifting." Didier spread his legs and bent his back. Fingertips tucked under one edge, he heaved, but the sheet barely moved, still held by the vegetation. Alia and Margot got down to help, and after two or three strong pulls the three of them managed to get it upright.

A snake wriggled into the long grass. They let the steel sheet fall, stepping back from the whoosh of stale air. A hole, around two metres deep, lay before them. A brick archway formed the entrance to the tunnel, and on the side closest to them, a short aluminium ladder provided an easy way of getting into the hole. Didier climbed down, and since there wasn't much space Margot and Alia remained at the top. He switched on the flashlight and shone it into the tunnel. Margot hunkered down to try and see in, but the space beyond was a featureless void.

"Are you sure you want to go in?" Didier asked, looking up.

"Is it that narrow all the way down?"

"From what I recall it widens out at the bottom. The chamber itself is bigger."

"Are you claustrophobic?" Alia asked, picking up on her hesitation.

Margot straightened. "A little. I used to have nightmares about being trapped inside a coffin."

Alia smiled with sympathy. "I was okay when I went down and I'm not usually good with confined spaces."

"There's no danger of collapse," Didier said, giving the brickwork a firm pat. "They had an engineer check it all out. It's been here for well over a century. I doubt it's going to fall down any time soon."

Margot drew in a breath. The desire to see what was down there was too strong to resist and there was no question of her backing out. "All right," she nodded. "Let's go."

Margot waited for Didier to go in and then climbed down the ladder. Alia brought up the rear.

"Mind your head on the roof timbers," Didier called back. He'd not gone far but already he'd disappeared, his disembodied voice deadened by the mass of earth. "They're quite low in places."

Margot stooped as she went in. The first thing that surprised her was the gradient. Steps had been cut into the floor to make it easier to get down, but the tops of the risers had worn so smooth it was effectively a slope. She imagined all the heavy boots trampling in and out during the course of the investigation. Growing conscious of the increasing mass of soil around them, Margot worked on keeping her fears at bay. To make matters worse, Didier was moving at a snail's pace – looking back every few seconds to check she was okay – meaning she kept getting sandwiched as Alia closed in from behind. She pressed a hand to his back. "You can go a little faster if you like." Thankfully he got the message.

A few minutes later the cone of light from his flashlight expanded to reveal a wider space. "Not far now," he said. The ground levelled out and finally they were there. Relieved, Margot quickly moved past him.

She found herself in a stone-walled chamber, perhaps three metres by five, the ceiling a full metre clear of their heads. The stonework was in good condition with evidence of smooth plaster having once covered its surface. The ground stepped up to a raised level where the floor was covered in smooth stone slabs.

Margot activated the torch on her phone. She carefully traced the light around the walls, picking out every detail. She'd seen the photographs taken by the crime scene technicians – clear bright images taken under the glare of powerful lights – but actually being down here, with the clammy air on her face, only a small flashlight to see by, was a whole different experience.

"The bodies were heaped over there." Didier stepped up onto the platform and shone his light into the farthest corner. "Just piled one on top of the other."

A small amount of dirt had collected there now, brought in by the tree root that had grown through.

"The smell must have been terrible."

"It was their faces that haunted me most. One of them looked like he'd died screaming."

Margot briefly caught sight of Didier's face as her light shone past him. He seemed lost in his thoughts, re-living the horrible event. Alia moved to his side and rubbed his arm, bringing him back.

"The killer had extracted all of their teeth," Didier went on. "Some of them were found down there on the floor, slipped between the cracks."

"And there were no clothes?"

"No. Either he undressed them before bringing them down or he took their clothes away."

Margot continued her inspection of the walls. Candle-nooks had been incorporated into the stonework in several places, along with two big steel rings – one fixed to the floor at the opposite end to where the bodies had been found, the other in the ceiling. Lengths of barbed wire had originally been attached to them, presumably as part of the tortuous bindings. Nearby, some marks had been carved into the stone. Margot squatted for a closer look. They appeared to be a random collection of letters and symbols, some of them quite distinct but making no sense. How long each victim had remained alive down here remained unknown, but at some point each of them would have opened their eyes onto the scene from a nightmare. Given the timeline, it was likely that four of them had woken to find their unfortunate predecessors already lying dead in the corner. The screams, when they came, would have gone unheard.

"Where are we in relation to the villa?"

Didier traced his light along the longest wall. "According to the survey, this wall forms part of the foundation of the rear elevation. The nearest room above us is the kitchen."

"And how deep?"

"There's three and a half metres of soil over our heads right now."

"So it must have been built at the same time as the villa?"

"This stone is from the same region as they used in the house, but whether the original owners knew of its existence is impossible to say. One theory is the builders were in league with smugglers. Its proximity to the smugglers' trail suggests it was used for some clandestine purpose. But then, it might just have been a folly. Or built for some other purpose. I doubt we'll ever find out."

Margot scanned the ceiling and studied the remainder of the space but there was nothing to indicate any means of access other than through the tunnel. It was probably one of the worst places imaginable to meet one's end.

She'd seen enough. A word to Didier and they were on their way out.

It was a relief to emerge into the light. Margot climbed the ladder as quickly as she could and walked down through the gate to escape the shadow of the trees. Basking in the sunshine helped drive the chill from her bones. Hell would have to freeze over before she went down there again.

After they'd finished securing the steel plate, Didier and Alia came over. The mood remained subdued as Margot lit a cigarette. At least with some nicotine inside her she began to feel human again.

"What do you think?" Didier asked, dusting off his hands.

Margot ground the burnt-out match into her portable silver ashtray. "It's hard to believe no one from the house knew it was there." Clearly, it had been dug in that location so that it couldn't be seen from the villa, but Amélie and her family had lived there for over thirty years. One of them must surely have stumbled across it at some point. "Are you sure Gaston wasn't aware of it?"

"That was what he said and I've no reason to disbelieve him. The estate only extends as far as this fence. The woods belong to someone else. It was only because the contractors were clearing out the fence line that they discovered it when they did."

"And Pascal? Do you believe he never came exploring up here?"

Didier shrugged. "I honestly have no idea. What happened down there was the work of a psychopath. Pascal may be many things but I'm not sure I would say he's insane."

"Hmm," Margot said. The thing with psychopaths was that they often maintained a perfectly normal exterior whilst concealing the darkest of thoughts within. "Hopefully I'll get to judge for myself."

Didier frowned. "You're meeting him?"

"Célia was hoping to set up a meeting."

There was a pause before he replied. "Well, be careful, Madame. Insane or not, he's not someone to be trifled with."

There was no mobile phone coverage at the villa so Margot had to wait until they got back to the village before checking her messages. One notification popped up: a voicemail from Florian. She called him back as she and Didier were on their way into the house.

"Célia's spoken with Pascal Deveraux," Florian explained. "He's agreed to meet you at eleven o'clock tomorrow. Will that be okay?"

Margot stepped back out into the yard. "Where does he live?

"Saint Cyprien. I'll text you the address."

Her phone pinged immediately. Margot pulled it away from her ear and glanced at the message. She was familiar with Saint Cyprien but didn't recognise the address. "Thank you, Florian. I'll be there."

Didier, putting away his flashlight in a cupboard, had evidently overheard. "Pascal?"

Margot nodded as she came back in. She gave him a brave little smile. "There's no backing out now. I'm meeting him tomorrow at eleven."

5

The apartment block in Saint-Cyprien was a far cry from the villa Belle Époque. It stood close to the sea, in a complex of five, and although its landscaped grounds and communal swimming pool might once have made it an attractive place to live, neglect had turned it into a rather sad-looking blot on the landscape.

Margot arrived at ten-forty, feeling slightly unwell. She'd had a poor night's sleep. Her room at the auberge had been hot and airless, the window jammed shut, an odour of dog exuding from the lumpy mattress at each toss and turn. She'd woken at five with a stiff neck and a pain behind the eyes.

Being early, and feeling a little apprehensive, she took her time climbing the stairs. With windows on every landing the view improved the higher she got. By the time she reached the fourth floor an expanse of bright blue sea was revealed to her, though the view was somewhat spoiled by the orange plastic slides and fake green grass of the nearby waterpark.

Pascal's apartment was at the front of the building. The door began to open as Margot approached and an eyeball appeared in the gap. For a moment she thought she was being stared at by a small child, but he must have been stooping because when he opened it fully the man who materialised stood at a height of six feet or more. His mop of blond hair was thinning on top, but his film-star looks hadn't entirely deserted him: a pair of crystal blue eyes looked her up and down with an air of appreciation. Hairs stood up on the back of Margot's neck.

"Monsieur Deveraux?"

"Margot Renard?"

An amused glint remained in his eye as they lightly shook hands. "How nice to meet you. Do come in."

"Thank you."

The apartment was larger than Margot had anticipated. Pascal withdrew to the end of the hall and then stood aside as if eager she take it all in. The salon was big enough to accommodate three large sofas and numerous other pieces of furniture. An elegant Baroque mirror hung above the mock fireplace while an Eames-style lounger and ottoman were positioned in front of the TV. Despite his reduced circumstances, he clearly hadn't lost his expensive tastes. The walls were covered with works of art, the floor with an Indian rug. Everything was spick and span. According to Célia he'd never married, and at forty-five years of age he was childless. One look at his apartment suggested that was just the way he liked it.

"Thank you for agreeing to see me."

"Cousin Célia was most insistent."

"I hope I haven't put you to any trouble."

"On the contrary. I've been looking forward to it."

Margot gave him a closer inspection: his shoes were polished, his shirt-cuffs pressed. It was almost like he'd dressed for the occasion. She waited, hoping he might say more, but his lips remained sealed. Finally he succumbed and produced a small laugh.

"Here we are, standing around like a couple of lemons. I haven't even offered you a drink." He crossed the room and opened the doors on a mirror-lined drinks cabinet. "What will you have?"

It was well stocked with brandies and liqueurs but Margot wanted to keep a clear head. "Just an orange juice, please."

"Really?" He paused with his hand on a bottle of Beluga Gold Line, seeming disappointed.

"It's a little too early for me," Margot lied. "But don't let me stop you."

He wavered, clearly no stranger to drinking vodka at this time of the morning, but then thought better of it. Closing the cabinet, he excused himself to go into the kitchen.

While he was gone, Margot viewed the art on his walls. He had an eclectic mix: sketches and paintings, drawings and prints – a trio of impressionist oils probably the most striking thing to catch her eye. One was quite remarkable in its use of colour. Hearing Pascal come back, Margot turned to accept the glass from him. She couldn't help noticing his hands. For a man who appeared to have never done a day's labour in his life his fingers were strong and cord-like.

"You have some wonderful pieces."

"Thank you."

They stood side by side to regard them. "Which one do you like best?"

"Oh, it's impossible to single one out," Margot said. "But this one is pretty amazing." She indicated a size 30 canvas saturated with blues and greens – a cypress tree beneath a hot blue sky. "On the one hand it lacks definition, but the colours are so evocative. You instantly know you're in the Mediterranean."

He seemed impressed. "Is this your kind of thing, then?"

"Very much," Margot said, sipping her juice. "I'd be happy to produce something a tenth as good as this."

"You paint?"

"A little."

"My sister produced this."

"Roselyn?" Margot felt a tightening in her throat. She hadn't intended to get onto the subject of his sister so soon but now that he'd mentioned it.

Pascal smiled, but the smile faded as he returned his eyes to the painting. "It's her way of exorcising the demons, I suppose."

"And what about you?"

"Me?" He regarded her with curiosity.

What did he do to exorcise his demons – was that how he'd interpreted her question? She certainly hadn't meant it that way. "Do you paint?" Margot quickly clarified.

He seemed amused to have caught her on the hop. "I exorcised my demons long ago. I assume Célia's been giving you the lowdown on me."

"Just the bare facts." Margot found herself looking into his eyes. The thought she might be standing there, chatting so casually with the man who'd gone down into that chamber and killed those men in such a horrible way thrust itself into the forefront of her mind. You would think you could tell. That there would be some giveaway, some lasting trace of the terrible images that had been captured by his retinas; an indication that this was a person unlike the rest of us. But there was nothing. Either he was innocent, or the killings weighed not a jot on his conscience. She turned back to the painting.

"She's very talented."

"I'll be sure to tell her."

"Does she exhibit?"

"Roselyn? No, she loathes attention."

"That's a pity. I'd love to meet her."

She didn't live very far away. According to Célia, Roselyn had married a wealthy industrialist ten years ago and then divorced him eighteen months later. Part of the settlement had been a large house in the centre of Perpignan, though despite several attempts to make contact, Célia had heard nothing back. Pascal spent a few moments considering her suggestion but then shook his head. "I really don't think that would be a good idea."

His tone suggested it wasn't up for debate.

He turned abruptly and went back to the sofas. When Margot followed, he made a vague gesture with his hand to suggest she sit down, though he remained standing and moved to the window at the rear. There wasn't much of a view: just the back of another concrete block. Perhaps he just wanted her to see him in profile: one foot up on the radiator, one hand tucked casually into the pocket on his trousers. Whatever he was doing he seemed to need to affect a pose.

"So, you're reinvestigating the case? The notorious villa Belle Époque murders." He leaned in closer to the glass. Something out there had captured his attention though when Margot looked there was nothing, just pigeons pecking in a gutter. It could have been his own reflection he was admiring – she imagined he spent a large portion of his day standing in front of a mirror. She chose the cream leather sofa and sat down in the centre.

"Célia just wants to make sure everything was handled properly."

"Dotted all the i's and crossed all the t's?"

"Something like that."

"I'm surprised. You're not her normal type."

"I beg your pardon?"

He pulled away slightly from the glass, appearing to catch her reaction via the reflection. He smiled again, but whatever the joke was he had no intention of sharing it. He took his foot off the radiator and turned. "Dear old cousin C. How is the old boot?"

Margot remained confused. "She's fine."

"She's dying, you know."

"What?"

"Didn't she tell you?"

"I had no idea."

"Uterine cancer. They operated, went through all the treatments, but you can guarantee it will come back. Cancer's an insidious thing."

Margot took a moment to gather her thoughts. No one in the office had said anything. Perhaps she should have realised – all those coughing fits she'd witnessed over the past few months. The smile was still lurking on Pascal's lips.

"I hope I'm not being too abrupt."

"It was just a surprise, that's all. She looks so fit."

"She always has, but I doubt she'll see seventy."

Margot felt decidedly at sea. She seemed unable to tune in to whatever wavelength he was on and her intended line of questioning had gone completely out of her head. Noticing an ashtray, she reached into her bag. "Mind if I smoke?"

He raised an eyebrow. Margot paused, packet of *Gitanes* in her hand. "I noticed the ashtray," she explained.

His eyes flicked between the cigarettes and her face, the first time he'd seemed uncertain. "I've been trying to give up my bad habits."

"And here I am tempting you."

His eyes illuminated, like she'd suddenly gone up in his estimation. Margot stood, and shook the packet to tease one out. He hesitated before taking it, but then slid it out and placed it between his lips. Margot reached for her matches, but a familiar metallic *click* made her turn back and see the flaming lighter already in his hand.

"Old habits die hard," he said. He lit his own first, then hers.

Margot resumed her seat and this time Pascal sat across from her, on the tan leather sofa, stretching his arms over the tops of the cushions and crossing his legs. Every movement he made seemed rehearsed. She imagined, even when he was sat here alone, he would play out a similar series of moves, try out his poses, an imaginary audience watching from somewhere unseen.

"Perhaps I should let you ask me some questions. Since that's why you came." He inhaled, and held the smoke in his lungs for several long seconds before leaking it out through his nostrils like a slumbering dragon.

Margot took a drag from hers. With some nicotine inside her she began to feel a little more settled.

"Did you have any theories on who killed those men?"

"In order to have a theory one would need to establish a motive. Means, motive and opportunity – isn't that what the police look for?"

"Sometimes the motive exists only inside the killer's mind. It's impossible for anyone else to deduce."

He smiled. "In that case, no – I had no theories."

"What was it like growing up there?"

"The Belle Époque?"

She nodded.

He leaned forward to tap his cigarette over the ashtray despite the fact he'd barely had time to generate any ash.

"Have you been?"

"I was there yesterday?"

"And what did you think?"

"I thought I was asking the questions?"

He smiled. "To be honest I found it rather dull. All those trees ..."

"You had no idea the chamber was there?"

"None whatsoever."

"You never went exploring?"

"Mooching around in the woods – why on earth would I want to do that? Besides, the woods were off-limits."

"All the more reason to go up there, I'd have thought." Margot raised an eyebrow prompting a mirrored response.

"Really? You like going off-limits, do you?"

Margot didn't respond. After a pause, he got up and returned to the window, the non-existent view calling to him again. "No. To answer your question, I never did go exploring. I'm more of an indoor bod: books, chess, the odd game of cards."

And then some, Margot thought, given the size of his gambling debts.

"Did you ever have friends over?"

"Hardly."

"Why's that?"

"Mother would never have allowed it."

"Oh, why not?"

He didn't turn around but Margot could see the slightly pained look on his face. For a few moments he seemed lost in thought.

"I never liked my parents. My mother was cruel; my father barely acknowledged me."

"In what way was she cruel?"

"She used to lock us in our rooms, Roselyn and I." He smiled wryly. "It's not as harsh as it sounds. She thought she was protecting us."

"From whom?"

"Whoever she believed was out to get us."

He was painting a very different picture to the one Margot had got from Célia. "And yet you had a lot of parties."

He refocussed, looking at her via the reflection. "I thought you were talking about when we were children. The parties came later." He opened the window and tapped ash from his cigarette. "Mother preferred living in Paris so Roselyn and I would often go down on our own. Invite a few friends. Occasionally things got out of hand. You know how it is."

"Is that what happened when that man almost drowned in your swimming pool? Things got out of hand?"

Now he turned. A smile was lurking, though this time he managed to contain it. Had she finally struck a nerve?

"You *have* been doing your homework."

"It's my job."

"That was an accident."

"He stumbled and fell?"

"Yes."

"What was the nature of your relationship?"

"With whom?"

"The man who nearly drowned?"

Pascal turned back to the window, looking bored now. Margot persisted:

"I heard he was trying to get friendly with Roselyn. How did that make you feel?"

He didn't respond at all this time. As much as half a minute must have gone by while he stood there, his face a blank canvas, seemingly oblivious to her existence. Margot began to fear she'd pushed him too far and was trying to think of a way to row back when he said,

"Is Gaston still around?"

Now it was her turn to look surprised. "The caretaker? Yes, I met him yesterday."

He tapped another lump of ash from his cigarette. "I'm not one for telling others how to do their jobs, but if I were the one investigating this case, I'd ask myself: who had the best knowledge of the grounds and the outbuildings? Do you really think it's likely he never came across the entrance to that passage?"

"You're saying he's lying?"

"He was always up in those woods, ferreting around. His sort usually are."

Margot frowned. "His sort?"

"I'm surprised the new owners kept him on, given his history."

Margot was at a loss. "I've no idea what you're talking about."

"Really?" His eyes shone provocatively. "All those years living on his own. What do you suppose he got up to in that cottage of his, hmm? In the dark and lonely nights of winter."

His nostrils were flared, his lips slightly parted. For the first time Margot felt a chill run through her, fearing the genii had finally been let out of the bottle. But she sustained his gaze. A moment later he'd bottled himself back up.

"There. I've said too much."

He had a final pull on his cigarette and then flicked the still-lit stub down onto the street. Then he turned again, hands in his pockets, all smiles once more.

"Was I of any help?"

6

It was lunchtime when Margot got back to Saint-Clair-de-l'Ouillat and the place was so quiet she would have heard a pin drop. Even the church bell failed to strike when the hour turned to one. Margot stood outside the auberge, watching with a sense of abandonment as the taxi drove away.

The front desk was unmanned. The key to her room was hanging on the rack behind the counter – she could easily have reached it – but with little desire to go back up to that stuffy bedroom she left it where it was. To her left, a thin door connected to a small bar, and finding it similarly deserted, Margot bought a bottle of water from the vending machine.

She stepped back outside, into the blazing sun. With time on her hands she went for a stroll. There wasn't a great deal to see: one through road; a couple of lanes; a small shady square. A dozen or more houses lined the main street but there was no sign of any people. Apart from the auberge and the boulangerie, the only other establishment was a café in the square and opposite that was a rather grand Mairie, set back behind a black iron railing, both the tricolour and the flag of Catalonia dangling from its pristine flagpole. Margot sat down on a bench next to an ornamental fountain and gazed around. It was so quiet that in half an hour the only sign of life was the *whoosh, whoosh, whoosh* of three Lycra-clad cyclists racing by, heads down like they were on a mission to catch up with *Le Tour*.

A partially concealed door between the café and the Mairie caught her eye. A rustic timber pergola covered a short blind alley at the end of which an open door offered a glimpse into a dimly-lit room. The signboard was too far away to read so she went for a closer look. *Musée d'Archéologie et d'Histoire*. Intrigued, Margot went inside.

It appeared to be just one large room. All four walls were lined with display cabinets featuring archaeological finds from the area while the main feature was a free-standing diorama set up on a long table that ran down the centre of the room. It depicted a scene from the Battle of Truillas, part of the War of the Pyrenees, which had, according to the information plaque, been fought in the 1790s. Margot leaned in for a closer look. It was an incredible piece of craftwork: miniature figures set in a sculptured landscape of *papier-mâché* mountains and dense pine forests. There were figures on horseback; men firing canons; flag-waving soldiers leading the charge into battle. A series of framed cards explained that the project had been a collaboration between several local schools, the whole thing funded by the museum's benefactor, Louis Deveraux. A notice on the wall explained that Louis had had a passion for archaeology and went on to detail several other projects he'd helped fund. There was a headshot of the man himself: a face that could have been Pascal ten years from now. Margot very much doubted the boy would be following in his father's philanthropic footsteps, however.

She returned to the square, thinking she might walk down to the police house, but the café was rolling up its shutters so she bought a coffee instead. The sound of raised voices drew her attention. Scanning round, Margot spotted Didier standing in the road down by the turn-off to the police house. He was arguing with a woman, stoutly-built, aged sixty or more. They were too far away for her to hear what was being said, but Didier was being quite forceful. The woman, evidently made of stern stuff, was giving as good as she got. The disagreement quickly burned out and they parted ways: Didier marched towards the auberge while the woman set off up the hill. He hadn't noticed Margot sitting there. She could easily have called out, but instead she waited, watching what he would do. After ducking into the auberge, he came back out and scanned around, looking rather shifty. He hesitated when he spotted her, perhaps realising she'd been watching, but then smiled jovially as he crossed the street.

"There you are. I was just coming to look for you." He sat down beside her.

"Problem?" Margot queried.

He faked a baffled look so she sent a glance back down the road. Cottoning on, Didier tried to laugh it off. "That was Madame Baudet, the housekeeper up at the villa."

Margot looked again but the housekeeper had gone. Didier quickly continued,

"How did it go with Pascal?"

Margot took her cigarettes from her bag and struck a match. "Weirdly."

"He's an odd fish, that's for sure."

"I got the impression he was rather enjoying it. Like it was a game."

"The *brigade criminelle* never managed to get anything out of him so I wouldn't be too hard on yourself."

"Hmm." Margot wasn't convinced. He was intelligent and narcissistic, and that was usually a dangerous combination. "How well do you know Gaston?"

"Gaston? He's been a fixture of the village longer than I have. Why?"

Margot drew on her cigarette. "Something Pascal said."

"Oh, and what was that?" He seemed keen to know.

"He said he was surprised the new owners had kept him on, given his history."

"His *history*?"

Margot nodded.

Didier smiled wryly. "I get it. Well, they've never got on, that's for sure. I'll tell you why. Once, when Pascal was a young boy, he threw his mother's pet cat from the top of the turret."

Margot gaped at him.

"Yes. Terrible, I know. The poor thing survived, but Gaston had seen him do it. He told Amélie, and despite the boy's denials she believed him. So sometime later, Pascal told his mother that Gaston had been spying on Roselyn at the swimming pool, watching her get changed and so forth. He said he'd been doing it for years, ever since Roselyn was a little girl."

"You mean—"

"It wasn't true. It was pure vindictiveness. But rumours spread, and you know what they say: mud sticks. Gaston's never been married; he likes to keep himself to himself, but is that any justification to brand him a paedophile?"

"Are you sure there was no truth to it?"

"None whatsoever. The problem is some people can't resist spreading malicious gossip."

"That was a horrible lie to spread."

"He's been a pariah in the village ever since."

A car drove by. The driver waved and Didier waved back. Living in a village as sleepy as this clearly had its charms, but Margot knew she would come to loathe it. Gossip and rumours; everyone knowing each other's business. She'd loved the anonymity of Paris, being able to lose herself in a crowd of thousands.

"Was Madame Baudet the housekeeper when the Deverauxs lived in the villa?"

"Yes. She's been there for years. She and Gaston were taken on at pretty much the same time."

"It was good of the new owners to keep them on."

"It makes sense, I suppose, if you've got the money."

"Will she be there this afternoon?"

"Madame Baudet? No. She was just heading into town."

"What about tomorrow?"

He looked at her with curiosity. "Probably, why?"

"I wouldn't mind speaking to her. I might go over there in the morning."

"Okay. I'll drive you."

She'd meant alone but didn't protest. She sipped her coffee, and then changed the subject.

"I was wondering: how do you get onto the smugglers' trail?"

"Well, there are several ways. The nearest access is a lay-by up on the old forest road."

"And you can walk to the back of the villa from there?"

"Oh yes. The trail brings you to that field gate we saw yesterday, though we always keep it locked."

"In that case, could you drive me to the lay-by and then let me walk the rest of the way?"

"On your own?"

She nodded. "I'd like to get the lie of the land."

He breathed in. "Very well. We'll go first thing in the morning."

"Thank you."

A yawn crept up on her. Margot covered her mouth. "Sorry. I didn't get much sleep last night."

Didier chuckled. "You didn't like the auberge?"

"It wasn't the best of beds."

He leaned in conspiratorially. "Don't let on I said this, but you're not the first to complain."

"I did wonder."

"Don't worry. I have the perfect solution." He got to his feet. "Come and stay with us."

"No, honestly I—"

"I insist. We always keep the spare room made up. And Alia would love to have company."

"Are you sure?"

"Of course I'm sure. Come on. We'll collect your bags on the way."

———

The front door was wide open but it didn't seem anyone was home. When Didier called Alia's name all that came back was silence.

Up a rickety staircase, a low-ceilinged corridor gave access to the three bedrooms: Alia's at the front, Didier's in the centre; and then another short corridor went off at an oblique angle to connect with the third. Didier opened the door to a light and airy bedroom, complete with a cast-iron fireplace. The entire room, including the sloping rafters, had been painted a soft shade of cream. The floorboards were freshly waxed, the bed linen looked brand new. A shaped window next to the chimney had a picture-perfect view of the garden, and through it came the sound of the river.

"Alia did all the decoration."

"It's beautiful."

"Will this be suitable?"

Margot smiled. "Suitable? It's perfect." It was a vast improvement on the room at the auberge, that was for sure.

He set down her bag at the foot of the bed. "In that case I'll leave you to settle in. I have an errand to run."

"No problem. Will Alia be back soon?" She trailed him back down the stairs.

"Possibly, although she's often out all day. Help yourself to anything in the kitchen." Just inside the door, he reached round to unhook a set of keys from an overburdened rack. "And call me if you need anything."

"I will."

Half a minute later, Margot was alone in the police station, feeling slightly bemused. The front door was still wide open, held in place with a cast-iron wedge. It was hard to believe that places like this still existed in the 21st Century. She wandered through to the hall, and explored behind the counter. Alia's office was just as untidy as the kitchen, with books and papers piled here, there and everywhere. Margot was baffled by how anyone could work in such a cluttered space. Less was definitely more where she was concerned. A shelf next to the window was laden with a collection of books: medical texts, a selection of sci-fi and fantasy novels, along with bundles of old paper maps. Realising she was snooping, Margot took herself upstairs to unpack.

With no idea when Alia would be back she changed her clothes and went for a walk. From the kitchen door, she followed the path through the garden then out onto the dirt track via the gate. Thinking she might get to the river that way, Margot continued down to the garage, but the vegetation was so dense it was impossible to get past. The doors to the garage had been locked with a heavy chain and padlock, she noticed.

She backtracked, and honing in on the sound of the river found an alternative route via a gap in a screen of tall grasses. The river was small and fast-flowing, perhaps three metres wide, and littered with rocks. Upstream, boulders broke up the flow, creating whirls and eddies and small pockets of frothy white foam. A grass bank sloped down to a narrow beach of pebbles so she took off her sandals and stepped in up to her ankles. Some small brown fish swam by, the water so clear she could see every detail. It reminded Margot of her boarding school days. Despite its beautiful setting, however, she'd not been happy there. When you're ten years old and your parents tell you they're sending you away, it's hard not to wonder what you did to upset them.

She got back out and sat down on the grass, soaking up the sunshine. Tiredness caught up on her and she could have happily fallen asleep, but just as she was thinking about lying down, she was startled by what sounded like a chicken gone berserk. Curious, Margot grabbed her sandals and hurried back to the garden.

Pushing through the screen of tall grasses she found no sign of a deranged chicken, just Alia, picking vegetables.

"Salut," Margot called out, puzzled.

Alia looked round in surprise, then waved cheerfully. "Salut."

"I heard someone cry out," Margot explained as she approached.

"Oh." Alia lowered her eyes, embarrassed. "One of the hens keeps getting out. I was trying to put her away. Sorry."

Margot's smile broadened as she deduced the identity of the deranged chicken impersonator. Alia carried on picking some haricot verts, a wicker basket hooked over one arm. Margot went to help.

"It's me who should be apologising. I didn't mean to overhear."

"Were you down by the river?"

"Yes. It's beautiful down there, isn't it?"

"It is. Papa phoned me. He said he'd asked you to stay."

"I hope that's okay?"

"Of course. How did it go with Pascal?"

"Hmm," Margot said, and Alia immediately caught her drift. "Have you ever met him?"

"Once or twice, though I've never actually spoken to him."

The bushes were loaded with beans; Margot had soon picked a large handful. She transferred them to Alia's basket and then moved on to the next bush.

"You must have been what, nineteen when the bodies were found?"

"Just under nineteen, yes."

"So, sixteen or seventeen when the killings took place?"

"That's right. It's pretty scary when you think about it. The villa's only three kilometres from here, if you go across the fields. We were sleeping in our beds while all that was going on."

"I know what you mean. I used to live in one of the big old apartment buildings in Paris. We had neighbours on both sides, and apartments above and below. I often used to wonder what people were getting up to on the other sides of those walls."

"You never know, do you? There are some strawberries around here."

Margot followed as Alia ducked under the low branches of an apricot tree. Basking in a pocket of golden sunlight was a table laden with troughs. Big juicy red strawberries hung over the sides, just begging to be plucked and eaten. The first one Margot picked went straight into her mouth.

"Do you see much of Gaston?"

"Not really. I don't have much cause to go up to the villa." Alia paused, and waited for Margot to catch her eye. "Has someone been talking?"

"Just something Pascal said."

Alia went back to picking the fruit. "I'm sure there's no truth to those rumours. Papa would have said."

Spotting another fine example, Margot couldn't resist

devouring it. God had clearly been having a good day when he'd designed the strawberry.

Alia weighed the basket in her hand. "That should be enough. Shall we go in?"

Mouth full, Margot could only nod.

They took the fruits of their labour into the kitchen. Alia dumped the beans on the worktop and started trimming them while Margot washed the strawberries in a colander in the sink.

"How long have Gaston and your father been friends?"

"Oh, ages. Ever since I've been here."

"And Madame Baudet?"

"What about her?"

"Are they friends, too? I only ask because I just saw them arguing just now."

"Really?" Alia seemed surprised. "Papa and Madame Baudet?"

"Yes."

Alia shook her head. "I've no idea what that was about. They're usually quite pally."

Through the open door they heard a vehicle pull up. "That'll be Papa with the shopping. I'd better give him a hand."

"I'll come too." Margot quickly wiped her hands on a tea towel and followed her out.

A tatty old van was parked by the gate. Didier unloaded the shopping bags from the passenger seat while Margot and Alia carried them into the kitchen.

"You will be dining with us, won't you?" Didier asked as he unloaded packets of meat, spirals of sausage, wrapped-up cheese, and several bottles of wine onto the counter. "I'm making a kefta tagine."

Margot grinned excitedly at the sight of so much lovely food. "How could I resist?" She hadn't felt so at home in ages.

Margot had a bath, and at six o'clock came downstairs to help with the meal. Didier and Alia were both already at work in the kitchen – Alia hardly recognisable out of her uniform. Margot clasped her hands.

"Right then – give me a job."

Didier came out from behind the worktop, shirt sleeves already rolled up. "You're our guest. The only thing we need you to do is sit down and relax."

"I'd rather help."

"I completely forbid it."

"At least let me pour some wine."

He didn't take much persuading on that score. He pointed to the cupboard.

There were plenty of bottles though not a particularly wide selection: a Sauvignon, a couple of Pinot Gris, a nice old Rioja. Margot chose the Rioja and took three glasses down from a shelf.

"I used to cook this dish all the time for Alia, didn't I, my sweet?" Didier said, unwrapping a parcel of minced beef.

"My mother was from Morocco," Alia explained.

"My wife, Sylvie and I adopted her when she was a baby."

Alia chopped up a small onion, then added it to the bowl into which Didier had put the beef. He sprinkled the mixture with chopped parsley, paprika and cumin, and finally some chopped coriander.

"This is the secret ingredient," Didier said, dusting it with something from a jar.

"Mmm, cinnamon." Margot inhaled deeply. "It smells wonderful already."

Didier kneaded the mixture for a couple of minutes and then formed it into meatballs. When they were done, he covered them with a tea towel and put them to one side while they made the sauce. Alia cut the tomatoes in half, removed the seeds, and then grated the flesh to a pulp; meanwhile, Didier sautéd some onion in the tagine. After adding some garlic, Alia poured in the grated tomatoes. They finished it off with some paprika, cumin, salt and pepper and, for good measure, a little more chopped parsley and coriander. Didier left it to simmer.

"Bravo!" Margot said and handed them their glasses. They moved across to the table.

"Sylvie and I divorced when Alia was eighteen," Didier said. "In case you were wondering."

"I still see *Maman*," Alia said.

"It was all very amicable. You go over there most weekends, don't you my dear?"

"Mm-hmm."

Margot raised her glass. "Well, cheers to the both of you. You make a wonderful team."

"Yes, we do," Didier said. He gave his daughter a hug and machine-gun-kissed the side of her head, making Alia giggle and pull away. "I don't know what I would do without her."

The meal tasted every bit as good as it smelt and afterwards Margot insisted upon helping with dessert. Didier had previously soaked some dates in cardamom and coffee so Margot whipped up some mascarpone with egg yolk and sugar. Outside, it was growing dark but the air was still warm so they took their dishes and another bottle of wine into the yard. Alia and Margot squeezed together on a small wooden bench while Didier sank into an old wicker chair. Bats swooped back and forth over their heads, feasting on insects swarming over the river.

"So, Margot," Didier said. "What are your thoughts on the case?"

"I think it's strange that none of the victims have been identified," she said. "After all this time. Someone must be missing them."

"The police called in all the missing person's reports for the area," Didier said. "But of course, we no longer investigate missing persons unless there's suspicion of a crime. I'm sure many slipped through the net."

"Did anything unusual happen in the village during that time?"

Didier thought about it, then shook his head. "There's not a great deal goes on in Saint-Clair-de-l'Ouillat."

"There was that one incident, though," Alia said.

Margot turned to find Alia with a thoughtful look on her face. "What was that?"

She looked at her father. "Remember that man I saw in the village that time?"

Didier nodded.

"I was coming back from uni with some friends," Alia went on. "We were driving past the square when this man stepped out in front of us. He looked like he was drunk, or on drugs. We pulled over and I got out. I told him my father was a policeman and said we could help, but he ran off."

"You've no idea who he was?"

"No. But I've always remembered his face; it was very distinctive – lots of freckles and a small mouth. We didn't think anything more of it at the time, and of course this was a few years before the bodies were found."

"So why do you think there might be a connection?"

"Well, when I took over the station, I went through our old records and found a missing person's file. I recognised his face straight away. It turned out he'd been reported missing the day after I'd seen him, but there was no connection with the village so we didn't get notified. Not until later, when the file turned up with a load of other papers."

"How long had he been missing by then?"

"It must have been four or five years."

Margot gave that some thought. It was unfortunate that France had no national database of missing persons. It surely would have helped. "What did you do?"

"I told the police in Toulouse, saying I'd seen him that night."

"And what did they say?"

Alia shrugged. "I don't know. No one ever came back to me."

One of the bats flew so low over their heads that Margot instinctively ducked. "Do you remember his name?"

Alia shook her head. "I assumed it wasn't important and forgot all about it."

Margot drank some wine. "Let me look into that. I'll see if anyone checked."

"We may have kept a copy on file." She turned to her father. "Papa, can you remember if—"

But Didier was fast asleep.

Margot and Alia shared a tender-hearted smile. Alia quietly got up and took the empty glass from his hand. "Papa," she said gently into his ear. "Why don't you go to bed?"

He stirred grumpily, eyelids fluttering like he was seeing the world for the very first time. "What? I was just resting my eyes, that's all."

"Margot said your snoring was the loudest thing she's ever heard."

Didier looked horrified, but Margot came to his rescue.

"Your daughter has a very wicked sense of humour. Please don't stay up on my account."

"Are you sure?"

"Of course."

"In that case I think I'll head up."

He got up out of his chair and Margot rose, too. "Thank you for a lovely meal." She kissed him on both cheeks.

After he'd gone, they cleared up and stacked the dirty crockery in the sink. There was another bottle of Rioja in the cupboard and somehow it ended up in Margot's right hand. "Look what I found?"

Alia narrowed her eyes. "Where on earth did that come from?"

Margot faked innocence. "I've no idea."

"I'm not much of a drinker."

"Really?" Her note of sarcasm was clear. The poor girl had only drunk two small glasses and was already quite giggly. "Don't drink, don't smoke ... you're a smart girl," Margot said, but one more wouldn't do any harm. She pulled the cork.

They took their glasses and the bottle through to the office. Alia opened an inner door and switched on the light. Inside was a walk-in cupboard, two walls of which were lined with metal filing cabinets. Alia set her glass down on the top.

"If we did take a copy it should be in here," she said. "My father likes to keep every scrap of paper that comes in."

Alia located the drawer for the relevant year and extracted a handful of bulging files. Margot lightened the load and together they went back to the office. Seating themselves on the floor, they were soon surrounded by papers, and Alia hadn't been joking. After a quick flick through, Margot found masses of documents, from parking fines to till receipts, some of them dating back twenty years.

"Can you remember which police station took the report?"

"No. It was in amongst a whole pile of other files."

"Never mind. If it's here we'll find it."

But after an hour of searching neither of them managed to

locate anything relating to a missing person's report. Margot was getting pins and needles in her leg and had to stand up. She retrieved her glass of wine from the counter and tried to walk it off. The only sound was the ticking of an old clock.

She glanced at some of the books. "*Crash Course Pathology, Pathology Illustrated* ... Someone enjoys a bit of light bedtime reading."

Alia left the papers and went to sit on the window sill. "Those are mine. I was thinking about becoming a forensic pathologist."

Margot regarded her in surprise. "Really?"

"But it would mean going back to uni and doing a medical degree."

"What did you study at Toulouse?"

"Sociology and Linguistics. I started a law course, as well, but then Papa fell ill and I had to come back. We decided it was time for him to retire so I took over the station. I always said I would."

"I studied law. In London and then Paris."

"That must have been interesting."

"Not really. I worked as a defence *avocat* for a while, but it wasn't what I'd hoped it would be. Although, in a roundabout way it's brought me to where I am now so I can't complain. Have you ever thought about joining the *Police Nationale*?"

Alia nodded. "I'm not really sure what I want to do. And Papa needs me here, so ..."

"I'm sure he doesn't expect you to sacrifice your career."

"No, but he's been very good to me. When I was little I got meningitis. *Maman* couldn't get time off work so Papa stayed home to look after me."

"That was nice of him."

"And *Maman* couldn't conceive so I'm like their only child."

Alia went back to the paperwork so Margot took her place at the vacated window sill. She moved her face right up to the glass. A swamp of blackness reigned outside, not a single light in view.

"What do you do for entertainment around here?"

"Papa usually goes to bed around nine. I stay up and read."

Margot turned to look at her. "No boyfriend?"

Alia shook her head. "The village is full of old men."

"*Girl*friend?"

The poor girl blushed. "No."

Margot laughed. "You're only young once, you know. Don't let life pass you by." She knelt down beside her and picked up another file. "Your father's lucky to have you. And don't you ever let him forget it."

7

The next morning Didier said he would take Margot up to the lay-by in his van. It was a Citroën model H, a true classic, he claimed, though when he opened the doors to his garage and revealed that his pride and joy was actually the same old rust bucket she'd seen him bring home the shopping in yesterday, Margot had difficulty feigning excitement. Judging by the amount of mould growing on its snub-nosed grille it certainly had not been cherished.

"Don't be mistaken by its appearance," Didier said, picking up on her hesitation. He had her wait outside while he clambered in. "There's plenty of life in the old girl yet."

A puff of smoke belched from the exhaust when he started it up. He pulled forward to let Margot get in and then quickly went back to lock the garage doors. Margot searched for a seatbelt, but there didn't appear to be one; not that it mattered – she doubted the van was capable of getting up to a speed where safety might be a concern. In the door mirror, she watched Didier lock the garage doors with a chain and a padlock.

He turned left at the end of the track and took the same road they'd used to get to the villa, only this time when they reached the turn-off he carried straight on. In places, the road was barely wider than the van itself and there were numerous blind bends. According to a road sign, the Spanish border was only 6 km away.

The lay-by was on a bend. Didier steered through an opening in a row of small trees and pulled up on dusty expanse of pot-holed tarmac. When he turned off the ignition, silence reigned.

Margot got out. Trees surrounded them in every direction apart from on the inside edge of the lay-by where a steep barren slope led up the side of a hill. Despite the altitude, it was baking hot. She took off the thin jacket she was wearing and left it on the seat.

"See that goat track?"

Didier moved round to her side of the van and pointed to a zig-zagging line that ascended the barren slope. Margot screened her eyes from the dazzling sun.

"I see it."

"Follow that up to the top. When you get to the main track, turn left, so you're heading downhill. After half a kilometre you'll come to a fork. Go left again, to stay in the woods, and that will bring you to the field gate we went through yesterday."

Margot allowed her gaze to drift upwards. A small flock of vultures was circling overhead. In the few minutes they'd been there not a single vehicle had passed by.

"It's awfully quiet out here."

"This road's a dead end. There's nothing beyond this point other than a few empty farm buildings." He gave her an inquisitive look. "Are you sure you don't want me to come with you?"

"I'll be fine."

"Have you got plenty of water?"

Margot patted her bag.

"Ask Gaston to give me a call when you're ready to come

back." He turned to go. "But don't let him see you climb over the gate," he chuckled. "Otherwise he'll be out with his shotgun."

"Thank you. I'll bear that in mind."

The van drove off, leaving behind a cloud of dust. Margot waited for it to settle and then spent a few moments taking in the isolation. She tried to imagine what it would be like out here in the dead of night, not a single soul around. The perfect place, you would think, for disposing of bodies, though hardly the most practical route for getting them down into the chamber. Carrying a body up that goat track would certainly not have been easy.

Margot tied up her hair. Keen to work off some of the calories of last night's meal she set off at a lively pace. The goat track was barely wide enough to put one foot in front of the other, and with the sun bearing down on the top of her head it proved quite an ordeal. In places the ground was crawling with ants. She didn't pause until she'd got right to the top, and finding some welcome shade beneath the branches of a fir tree, she took a drink from her water bottle.

The main track was wider than she'd imagined. Ruts in the ground suggested it had once been used by vehicles, though judging by the length of the grass she doubted anyone had driven it in years. No doubt in days gone by smugglers would have brought in their bounty on horse and cart.

She put away her water bottle and then, ignoring Didier's advice, turned right. The track climbed up through the trees and took her to a place where the ground was rockier. An incline studded with boulders rose to her left, and as they looked easy to climb Margot went to explore. She scaled them with ease, though was sweating by the time she got to the top. From a small plateau, a short scramble up a patch of scree brought her to the summit of a low peak. Enlivened by the exercise, she spent a few minutes taking in the view. In the direction she'd been heading, the smugglers' trail continued down the side of next valley before rising to a gap in a ridge. Beyond that rose a range of higher mountains on the other side of which had to be Spain. It was invigorating to think that if she carried on walking she could be in there in less than an hour.

But that would have to wait for another day – she was meant to be looking at the villa. After another drink of water, Margot descended the incline and retraced her route to the top of the barren slope.

Twenty minutes later she reached the fork Didier had spoken of. The right-hand route looked the most well-used, the softer earth revealing traces of tyre tracks. The trees prevented her from seeing where it went, but the lie of the land suggested it skirted the back of the villa.

Margot went left as Didier had instructed and soon found herself approaching the field gate. The entrance to the tunnel was situated just a few metres to her right. Without knowing it was there she was unlikely to have spotted it. Leaning on the top rail of the gate, she gazed down upon the rear of the villa Belle Époque. There was no sign of any activity. She could easily climb over, but not wanting to risk the wrath of Gaston she returned to the fork and went to explore the righthand route instead.

Patches of tarmac appeared between the tufts of grass, suggesting it had once been paved, and it soon became apparent the track was running parallel with the villa's west wing. There was the veranda she'd admired from inside, and with the track being elevated a good view was to be gained into that side of the garden. A wall screened the lower windows, but a little farther Margot discovered another locked gate, this one constructed of boarded timber. Peering through gaps, she saw what must once have been a stable-yard. Out of curiosity, she walked the remaining length of the track, and a minute later came to the road. She recognised the bend to her left, meaning the main entrance was little more than half a kilometre away. She wondered why Didier hadn't mentioned this way in.

Backtracking to the stable-yard, she checked to make sure Gaston wasn't out patrolling and then climbed over the wall. One of the outbuildings had windows, but peeking through them revealed nothing other than some rusty old farm machinery.

A door in an archway led to the terrace at the rear of the villa and Margot emerged into sunshine. A window was open on the farthest corner. Someone was moving around inside, but the window was so high up she couldn't see in.

"Bonjour," Margot called out hopefully.

Whoever was there suddenly fell silent. A short pause followed before a face appeared. The woman Didier had been arguing with looked out from the window, scowling as her eyes took Margot in.

"Madame Baudet?"

"Who's asking?"

"My name's Margot Renard. I work for Judge Deveraux."

The housekeeper didn't seem surprised. "Aye, Didier said you'd be coming."

Did he now? Who needed a telephone with Didier around? Margot concealed her irritation. "Do you mind if I ask you a few questions?"

Madame Baudet took a moment to think about it, but then gestured to her left. "You can come in through the back. The door's not locked."

Margot stepped over a wide stone threshold into a cool dark boot room. A door led through to the kitchen where Madame Baudet stood waiting, radiating suspicion. The room was every bit as grand as the other rooms Margot had seen, although it clearly hadn't been updated for some time. A huge cast iron range dominated the outer wall, a welcome sight in the depths of winter, no doubt. Copper-bottomed pans hung from a rack suspended from the ceiling. Dozens of pieces of majolica were spread across the old pine table, and gaps on the shelves of the dresser suggested Madame Baudet had been cleaning the crockery. Margot smiled to try and lighten the mood.

"You must have lost count of the number of times you've cleaned all that."

Madame Baudet remained on the opposite side of the table, looking rather nervous, having hardly altered her position since Margot had come in. The only thing that moved were her eyes which studiously followed Margot's every movement.

"It's my job. I don't mind."

"A shame no one uses it."

The housekeeper twitched her shoulders. Margot picked up one of the pieces – a beautiful green and yellow scalloped plate. Turning it over, she saw the stamp of Sarreguemines. She carefully set it back down. "I suppose Didier told you why I'm here?"

She nodded.

"I understand you worked here at the time of the murders."

"I've worked here for over forty years. Started when I was twenty."

"You must have got to know the Deverauxs well in all that time."

She made no comment. Margot moved a little further around the table.

"Did you like working for them?"

For the first time the housekeeper's eyes shifted. "It wasn't so bad when Louis was alive. He was a good man."

"And Amélie?"

She sniffed. "We usually managed to avoid each other."

"Oh, why was that?"

"Louis always made it clear he didn't see us as staff. He often asked me to sit up at the table with them. But Amélie, she was the opposite."

Margot continued to move around the table, casting her eyes over the pieces of crockery. Whether she was aware of it or not, Madame Baudet moved in tandem, always keeping the same distance between them. Margot paused and turned when she drew level with the open window. She could see the meadow from there, and the field gate up at the top. She returned her gaze to the housekeeper.

"I met Pascal yesterday."

"Oh yes."

"He said something that's stuck with me. That Amélie used to lock them in their rooms."

Madame Baudet didn't bat an eyelid. "She had some funny ways, all right."

"So was it true?"

"I imagine so."

"Was she ever violent towards them?"

The housekeeper shook her head. "Not that I saw. I don't think she meant to be cruel. Being a mother didn't come naturally to her. And the children were no angels."

Margot nodded in understanding. A child throwing a pet cat from the top of the turret was hardly symptomatic of a happy household. But then, how could she even begin to imagine what life must have been like in the aftermath of Louis's suicide? Going in and out of these rooms with the scene of that tragic event so close by.

"Do you still live in the villa?"

"I have an apartment over there." Madame Baudet indicated a door across the passage.

"Mind if I take a look?"

"Help yourself."

Margot went in. It was a small, two-room apartment, plainly

furnished. A single bed and a sofa in one room, a blue enamel bath and sanitaryware in the other. The window had the same aspect as the one in the kitchen and she could just about see the field gate, though it would have been entirely possible for someone to access the tunnel without being seen from the house, particularly at the time of the killings when the vegetation was overgrown.

"Were you here the night the boy nearly drowned in the swimming pool?"

"I was never here when they had parties. I used to spend the night with my sister in Prades. But Gaston told me what happened. It took a lot of cleaning up, I know that. They had to drain the pool because of all the blood and the broken glass."

There was nothing else to see in the room so Margot strolled back to the kitchen, the housekeeper trailing in her wake.

"Were you surprised when Amélie decided to sell?"

"Not really. She was never happy here."

"Even though it was her ancestral home?"

"That meant nothing to her. She was more at home in Paris."

"So she didn't resent Pascal, then? Given it was his debts that forced her to sell?"

"Not that I knew of. Though she didn't like him gambling. She made that clear."

Margot had run out of questions and was thinking about leaving but promptly remembered something. "What were you arguing about?"

"Eh?"

"Yesterday. You and Didier. I saw you in the village."

Her eyes narrowed. "Nothing that's anyone's business."

Margot smiled politely. She would get it out of them one way or another. "I'll let you get back to your crockery."

"It's always the same with the rich."

"Pardon?"

Now that Margot had decided to leave, Madame Baudet seemed keen to get something off her chest.

"They act like they've not got a penny, yet there's Madame, living in her fancy apartment in Paris. Worth millions, no doubt. And they expect us to keep working for peanuts."

"When was this?"

"When Pascal got into debt. She said she couldn't afford to keep paying us. The fact we had a roof over our heads should have been payment enough, she said. And they expected us to keep working same as before."

"Did they pay you when the villa was sold?"

"She promised to, but nothing's ever materialised. They owe us thousands."

"Perhaps I could mention it to Célia."

Madame Baudet steadfastly shook her head. "Won't do no good. The likes of us is to be used by the likes of them, that's how she sees it."

"Have the new owners being paying you?"

"Oh yes. They pay, all right. But the Deverauxs ..." Her face wound itself up so tightly it looked like she might spit. "They're a different breed altogether."

Margot thanked her for her time and left.

8

Alia stared through the windscreen with unfocussed eyes, her thoughts gone walkabout. Somewhere in the dark recesses of her mind lurked the name – the boy with the freckles, the one she'd seen wandering around the village that night. Because now she came to think about it, yes, she had read his name on the file – she'd mentioned it when she'd called the police in Toulouse: *Hello. I've just come across a missing person's report. I'm sure I saw this man in my village five years ago. His name? Yes, his name is ...*

Enrique?

No, that wasn't it.

Alia went back into her memory and tried to recover more detail. A friend had been driving them home for the weekend; she and her other friend Gégé had been in the back. As they'd driven into the village, a young man had stumbled into the road acting like a reject from a zombie movie. He'd been wearing ... black jeans, a black tee-shirt, black trainers ... or had it all just looked black because it had been dark? Hmm.

A cyclist came zooming towards her, reminding Alia she was supposed to be zapping motorists.

She was parked in a pull-in at the bottom of the hill, just before the *Bienvenue* sign, the radar gun in her lap. Speeding had become the mayor's current pet peeve after descending this very hill on his own bicycle two weeks ago. A speeding tourist had raced by, overtaking so closely that the turbulence had almost sucked him off his pedals (no mean feat given what a sizeable man the mayor was). So the next day he'd dug out the old radar gun and insisted she sit out here at every available opportunity. When a second cyclist approached, Alia stuck her arm out of the window and zapped him – *pow*! She checked the reading – 52 km/h – and nodded her head, impressed. Exceeding the speed limit by 2 km/h. Did the mayor want her to ticket cyclists, too?

She gave him a friendly wave instead and continued the interrogation of her mind.

Margot had contacted the police in Toulouse and asked them to look into Alia's report. They'd promised to get back to her, but in all probability nothing had been done. Why should they have taken it seriously? She was only a village officer, and a novice one at that. Investigating crime was not her job. Speeding cyclists, yes – a *policière municipale* was fully qualified to operate a radar gun. Stray dogs on the loose, absolutely. It was well within her remit to round up an errant mutt and return it to the owner together with a lecture on what codes had been violated. Carry out an arrest? ... Now that was a tricky one, verging on the limit of her powers. Yes, she could carry out an arrest, but the offender had to be delivered to an officer of the *Police Nationale* or the *Gendarmerie* at the earliest opportunity. Heaven forbid the village officer should attempt to think for themselves.

Estoban – was that the name she'd seen on the file?

No, it wasn't Estoban. She was fast running out of mental lightbulbs.

There had been something about his name that was familiar,

though; that much she could remember. Like he shared it with someone famous. Memories were strange and wonderful things. They were not like photographs, stored in some giant album at the back of your brain. No, she'd read it in a book. Memories were reconstructed every time you recalled them, replicating the original event with a duplicate pattern of firing neurons, just like the mind was experiencing it all over again. Only, the replication was never perfect: anomalies often crept in. Which was why eyewitness testimony was inherently unreliable, the fact that six different people could have six different recollections of exactly the same event and each of them would essentially be correct.

Alia sighed, bored. She looked at her watch. Nine-thirty. Twenty minutes she'd been sitting here, and apart from the two cyclists and the *boulanger*'s van had seen nothing but crickets. She imagined Lemeiux being chased down the hill by an angry bear. She would zap him with her radar gun before pulling him into the safety of the car. His relief at being rescued would rapidly turn to anger when Alia issued him with a speeding ticket.

But I was running to get away from the bear! he would protest.

Yes, Monsieur Lémieux, but you were going so fast you exceeded the speed limit!

Maybe she was wasted here. Maybe she should take Margot's advice and set her sights higher. She tossed the radar gun onto the back seat and started the car.

And then it came to her like a bomb going off in her head: Erec!

That was his name. Erec. But Erec what?

It wasn't a lot to go on but it was a start. Alia drove back to the police house without further ado.

In the office, she switched on her computer and drummed her fingers on the desk while she waited for it to boot. How was she going to find a man named Erec who'd gone missing seven years ago? Hmm. It was not going to be easy. She tried social media and did a search on groups for missing persons. There were plenty of them; some of them charities helping to reunite lost loved ones; others set up by anxious relatives. The format was fairly standard: people posted a photo and brief details of whoever had gone missing and potential sightings would be added in the comments.

The second one she tried looked the most promising. It had thousands of members, and lots of recent activity. There were hundreds of posts, many of them dating back years. In some, the picture of the missing person had been replaced by an image of a party popper, declaring the person had subsequently been found. Many others were still listed as missing without trace.

Some of the stories were heart-breaking: a boy aged twelve, gone missing on the outskirts of Paris. Last seen wearing a blue and white duffel coat his grandma had bought him.

She scrolled down.

A man aged fifty with learning difficulties. Diabetic, gone missing on Christmas Eve. Someone in the comments had said they'd seen a man matching his description walking next to a river in the early hours.

She scrolled down.

A mother and her small child, evicted from her apartment in Lyon for not paying the rent. A charity worker was pleading for help. The post had been shared one hundred and seventy-two times. Two hundred and twelve comments had been left. Volunteer search parties had been organised; frustration expressed that the case had gone ignored by the media, despite a small child being involved. Some speculated it was because a football tournament had been going on at the time; others that it was down to the fact the woman and her child were Syrian refugees.

Alia slumped back in her seat. What a cruel, cruel world. When she'd turned eighteen, she'd asked the adoption authorities for all the information they had on her biological family, and they'd not had much. Little baby Alia had been found on the steps of a *notaire*'s office in Toulouse, her name the only thing that had been written on the note pinned to the basket. An eagle-eyed neighbour had seen a distressed woman leaving the scene. By some small miracle, the authorities had tracked the woman down and found her to be a Moroccan national of no fixed abode, but the moment they'd turned their backs the mystery woman had disappeared. Alia's questions had remained unanswered ever since: had she been an only child? Was her mother still alive? Had her biological father even known she'd existed? How desperate must those first few months of her mother's life have been in order for her to give up her own flesh and blood? She would probably never know. One thing was for sure: if Didier and Sylvie hadn't come along when they had, little baby Alia's life could have turned out very differently. Perhaps the job of a *policière municipale* wasn't so bad after all.

The words on the screen came back into focus and Alia slapped herself on the forehead. Why was she being so dumb? Why didn't she just do a page search for the word 'Erec'? Lady Luck must have been smiling on her because when she did that very thing only three posts were highlighted. The subject of the first had since been found; the second referred to a small boy. She scrolled down to the third and found herself looking at a photo of a young man with freckles, and clapped her hands in delight.

Erec Dubois. She'd found her missing man!

9

Smoke was rising from the direction of Gaston's cottage, tainting the air with the odour of burning wood. Margot took the shortcut through the walled garden and found him pushing an overloaded wheelbarrow towards a smouldering bonfire. Since she'd come upon him from behind, Margot paused, having an idea. She unscrewed the lid of her water bottle and emptied the contents into a flower bed.

"Bonjour," she called out.

Gaston looked round. He wore the same unwelcoming expression as on the previous day. Margot attempted to disarm him with a smile.

"It's a never-ending job at this time of year."

"Uh?"

"Pulling up weeds," she elaborated. "That was my job when I was little. My parents used to pay me fifty pence for every bucketful I collected, though I think half the ones I uprooted were flowers."

Gaston lowered his wheelbarrow and wiped his hands on a rag. As Margot drew near, she began to get a different sense of him: less unfriendly; more perhaps that he didn't quite know what to make of her. He probably wasn't in the habit of receiving visitors.

"You're here with Didier?"

"No. I came alone. I wanted to walk along the smugglers' trail. It's lovely up there, isn't it?"

He glanced in the direction of the meadow though it was too far away to see. The radiant heat from the bonfire was adding to the already high temperature and it must have been well over forty degrees, though Gaston appeared unperturbed. Margot fanned herself with her hand. "Phew! I don't suppose you could top me up, could you?" She held out her empty water bottle.

Gaston regarded it without moving. It seemed for a moment that he wasn't going to oblige, but then he took the bottle. Margot followed as he plodded along the concrete path that led to his front door.

"You do a wonderful job looking after the gardens."

"It's not just me. Two or three others come in."

"It must have been difficult for you when the Deverauxs got into debt. I heard the grounds got into quite a state."

"I wasn't being paid so why should I work?"

"Absolutely. I would have done the same in your position. Did you help with the restoration?"

"No."

They reached the front door and Gaston halted so sharply that Margot almost bumped into him. "Sorry."

"Wait there."

He went inside, pushing the door shut behind him.

Margot waited a moment and then moved quickly around the side of the house. At the rear was a lean-to extension with a window looking into a sitting room. A quick glance revealed nothing unusual. Beyond that was a frosted glass window, presumably to the bathroom. She had no idea what she was expecting to find – a kidnapped child? A torture chamber? Some ideas, when they get planted in your head, are hard to uproot. Returning to the front of the cottage, Margot found a window on the other side of the kitchen. Gaston stood at the sink, his back to her. The shotgun leaning in the corner caught her eye – so Didier hadn't been entirely joking. She was back at the front door just as the caretaker returned with her water bottle.

"Thank you."

Margot took a sip. Smoke from the bonfire began wafting in their direction so she took a step back. At one point during the investigation the police had discovered a fragment of clothing on a bonfire, speculating it had once belonged to one of the victims. But the fragment had been little more than a zipper and no useful forensics had been obtained.

They were distracted by the sound of a car approaching. The walled garden prevented them from seeing it, but there was no mistaking the throaty rumble of a big V12 coming up the drive. Margot looked at Gaston. "Are you expecting someone?"

He seemed puzzled. "The gate should be locked." He strode off in the direction of the villa.

Margot went after him. They reached the lawn just in time to see the car pull up in front of the house – a classic Alfa Romeo spider. Clutch in, the driver revved his engine as if heralding his arrival.

Gaston's pace slowed when he saw it. Margot caught up, wondering why he'd hesitated, but when the driver got out of the car the penny dropped. Standing before them was the unmistakeable figure of Pascal Deveraux.

He waved, though it was obvious they'd seen him. He stood there, hands in his pockets, waiting for them to go to him. Master and servant. Some things never changed. Gaston cast an uncertain glance at Margot, and they crossed the lawn together.

"Fancy meeting you here," he said when they reached the gravel.

"What are the odds?" Margot replied flatly. She looked him up and down. She hated to admit it but he looked rather stylish in a pair of white cotton slacks and a polo shirt.

"I was in the area. Thought I'd drop by."

"And let yourself in?"

He smiled. "It's lucky I still had this." He removed his right hand from his trouser pocket and held up a big iron key very much like the one she'd seen Didier use. "I'm surprised they haven't changed the locks. You must get all-sorts mooching around up here."

His eyes dimmed as he shifted his gaze to the caretaker. Gaston mumbled something in response before tipping his head and retreating. Pascal moved to Margot's side and together they watched him head back to his bonfire.

"Wasn't interrupting, was I?"

"I was just looking around."

"And did you find anything of interest?"

There he was again – tempting. "I was talking to Madame Baudet."

"That old battle-axe. What's she got to say for herself?"

"Not much."

"Oh, come now. Do tell. What's she been saying about me?"

Despite his cavalier attitude he seemed keen to know. Didn't all narcissists have that hunger to find out what other people thought of them? Instead of giving him the answer he wanted, however, Margot turned to look at the house, her eyes travelling to the top of the turret. She was tempted to ask him about the incident with the cat – it was easily a fifteen-metre drop; small miracle the poor thing had survived – but decided against it.

"How long's it been since you've been back?"

Realising he wasn't going to get an answer, Pascal turned

with her. "Six years. To be honest, I was hoping to find it a relic. Places like this deserve to be confined to the dustbin of history, don't you agree?"

"Were you really just passing?"

"Am I that transparent?"

Hardly, Margot thought.

"Actually, I came to see you."

"Did you now?" She turned to face him. His eyes twinkled impishly.

"I called in at the police house. Didier said I might find you here."

"And why were you looking?"

"I'm visiting my sister this afternoon. I wondered if you might like to tag along."

"I thought you said that wouldn't be a good idea."

"I changed my mind."

She hesitated. The chances of meeting either of the Deveraux women had seemed slim up till now, but Margot wasn't in the habit of getting into cars with men she hardly knew. "Are you sure she'll be okay with that?"

"She'll be fine, as long as you're with me."

He moved to the passenger side and opened the door, then stood waiting

Margot stayed put. She got the feeling the only way she was going to be allowed to speak to Roselyn would be on his terms, but she reminded herself who she was dealing with here. She took out her phone. "I'd better just give the station a call." Then instantly realised her mistake.

"There's no signal out here," Pascal said. "This place is a notorious dead zone."

Margot wasted a few extra moments staring at her screen. She quickly tapped out a message with her thumbs, assuming it would send automatically once they were within range, and left it sitting in her outbox.

"Besides," Pascal went on, "there's no time. Roselyn will have a fit if we're late. Come on – hop in." He clapped his hands twice, like he was summoning the dog.

10

Alia devoured the screen with hungry eyes. According to the online group, Erec Dubois was aged 26, 1.75m tall, weighed approximately 75kg. Last reported sighting was Banyuls-sur-Mer where he'd left his mother's apartment dressed in a black Scorpions T-shirt, dark blue jeans, a pair of new Nike trainers. Alia clicked on the profile of the user who'd set up the post but their timeline hadn't been active for several years. No matter. She knew just the person to help. She sent an email to her friend, Gégé:

How's life in the records office? Can you do me a favour?

A reply came straight back:

For you, anything.

In person, Gégé was an archetypal geek who spent every waking moment with his eyes glued to one screen or another, but in the world of online communication he fancied himself as the world's greatest lover.

Can you try and locate a missing person's report? A white male. Erec Dubious. Last seen in Banyuls.

When was he reported missing?

Seven years ago. I think he was the guy we saw in my village that night, remember?

No.

You were in the car. It was a Friday night. We were driving home for the weekend.

If it was a Friday I was probably wasted.

Gégé, you've never been wasted in your life.

A delay, before he came back with: *Leave it with me.*

Her father came home a few minutes later. He leaned on the counter, eyebrows knitted. "What's the matter with you? You look like you've had an epiphany."

Alia realised she'd been staring into space. She came to.

"Come and have a look at this." She waved him round to her side of the desk and quickly explained what she'd found. Didier took a few moments to process it.

"You mean this is the man you saw that night?"

"I think so. His name's Erec Dubois."

"What else do you know about him?"

Right on cue, a reply came back from Gégé. Alia opened the email, together with the attached file. She read out loud: "This is the missing person's report. Mother's name is Janine Dubois. She last saw him when he left the apartment that Friday evening. There were no suspicious circumstances so the police didn't investigate."

A second email quickly followed. "It's Gégé again."

"What's he got to say now?"

Alia continued reading out loud: "That's not all. Your super friend Gégé … *tut* … *blah, blah blah* … The search on his name flagged up another file. A report of criminal damage. Erec Dubois claimed that someone tried to drive a car into him outside the casino in Sète. The driver's version was that Erec had attacked his vehicle without provocation. No witnesses. No action taken."

Alia sat back in her seat while her father continued to frown at her.

"When did this happen?" he asked.

Instead of emailing, she took out her phone and messaged him: *when was this?*

Six months before he was reported missing

She showed the screen to her father and then quickly typed back: *who was driving the car*

There was another short delay before a reply came back: *a guy named pascal deveraux*

Alia and her father stared at each other in silent disbelief. Didier was the first to come to his senses.

"Ask him to check what address he gave."

Alia typed back: *what address did pascal deveraux give*

Your neck of the woods. The villa Belle Époque. Is that what you were expecting?

Alia almost dropped her phone as she read the text. Her mind started tying itself in knots. "So what does this mean?"

"It means," said her father, thinking out loud. "That six months before this man went missing he had an altercation with Pascal Deveraux."

"And the day he went missing I saw him in our village."

"And this was what, seven years ago?"

Alia nodded. "During the same period the killings took place."

The idea had surely come to them both at the same time, but it was Alia who got out of her seat and went into the filing room. She snatched out the file on the Belle Époque murders and pulled out the summary of the mortuary reports. Victim number one: 1.75m tall, weighed an estimated 75 kg, aged between twenty and thirty. Alia's mouth fell open.

"What is it?" her father asked, coming to her side.

Alia placed the sheet on the desk next to the printout of Erec

Dubois's missing person's report. She sat down while her father caught up.

"Their vital statistics match," he said.

She nodded. "Erec Dubois was the first victim." It felt strange to hear those words come out of her mouth but it had to be true. Once again, the two of them locked eyes as the gravity of what she'd uncovered rapidly sank in. Alia came back to her senses.

"Where's Margot?"

"I presume she's still up at the villa. Although ...." Her father looked worried.

"What?"

"Pascal came looking for her."

"When?"

He consulted his watch. "About an hour ago. I told him she was up there."

Alia grabbed her phone, but when she tapped Margot's number it cut straight to voicemail.

"I'll call Gaston." Didier headed for the phone in the kitchen, but Alia was already on her feet and hurrying out the door.

———

The wheels squealed as Alia turned sharply into the entrance of the villa Belle Époque. Finding the gates wide open, she accelerated on up the drive. She pulled up on an empty expanse of gravel and quickly got out of the car.

"Madame Renard. Margot!"

The villa looked down on her, serene and indifferent.

She set off around the back, but spotting Gaston by the walled garden promptly changed course. He'd paused at the gate, looking surprised.

"Have you seen Margot Renard?"

He jutted his chin. "She's just gone."

"Gone where?"

"Went off with him. Pascal."

Alia lowered her voice as she drew near. "Did she say where they were going?"

Gaston shrugged. "He was driving some fancy car. I've no idea what he was up to." He shrugged again and went back to his garden.

11

The Alfa sped through the gates, fishtailing as the wheels spun on the gravel. Pascal continued to accelerate down the lane, the pull from the big V12 so potent that Margot could feel her body being pushed deep into the thick leather upholstery. He dropped into third as they approached a bend, fed it neatly through a chicane, and then floored it again as the road opened up. The surge of power was so exhilarating that Margot couldn't help smiling, though she turned away when Pascal flicked her a glance. Soon they came to another village and he dutifully slowed down. The blurry thing the world had just become quickly came back into focus.

"Nice car."

"Thank you."

"Is it yours?"

Pulling up at a junction, Pascal cast her another sideways glance. Posing again: sunglasses on, left arm casually leaning out the window. He seemed to read something more into her words than what she'd intended.

"How can a man in my financial position afford a car like this – is that what you meant?"

It hadn't been, but Margot left a pause to give him a chance to elaborate. He mulled it over for a moment or two.

"I borrowed it from a friend."

"It must be nice having friends like that."

That seemed to amuse him. "It's not, trust me."

What kind of friends did a man like him have? It would be interesting to find out. Margot checked her phone while they were waiting for a car to go by. Annoyingly, the text still hadn't sent.

Once they were free of the village he gunned it again. Lungs filling with warm fresh air, it really was invigorating. You would think that as you grew older you would yearn for life at a more sedate pace, be conservative, not take risks, but right now Margot couldn't give two hoots for that. That need for speed was alive and well and kicking inside. As the landscape opened up, the road became a perfect black ribbon meandering along the valley floor. They made swift progress, swatting away lesser traffic on the straights, the Alfa gripping the bends like its wheels were in tracks. But the route soon tightened up, the bends became less predictable, cyclists got in their way. The euphoria ended abruptly when a planned overtake of a dump truck was thwarted by an oncoming bus.

Teeth gritted, Pascal crunched it all the way down into second. He made a poor job concealing his annoyance. Margot could feel the frustration coming off him as he looked for another opportunity to overtake: thrusting his head out, nudging the car over, swerving out of the way at the very last moment. She gripped the sides of her seat with unease.

They came to an incline with solid white lines and had to slow even more. The truck must have been fully loaded because it struggled immediately, thick black diesel fumes belching into their faces. A stray stone escaped from its rear flap and pinged off their windscreen. Taking a chance on the shortest of straights, Pascal hauled the wheel, dropped a gear, and then buried his foot in the floor. A car appeared; for one electrifying moment it looked like they were certain to crash; but the V12 catapulted them to freedom in a blistering display of power.

Pascal kept up the pace as they ascended the hill, but a bend at the top took him by surprise. He got the apex all wrong; had to brake sharply and wrestle with the wheel to keep them on track. The rear end slid, and there was a horrible jolt as one of the wheels dropped off the edge of the road. They made it through to the next stretch in one piece but the car began to weave alarmingly. Pascal thumped the steering wheel in frustration.

"Damn it!"

"What it is?"

He glared into his mirrors. "Flat tyre."

They limped along for a hundred metres or more, and when a lay-by appeared, pulled in. The injured Alfa sat purring away, listing to one side like an injured animal. Pascal didn't move for a whole twenty seconds, and when Margot looked at him he seemed embarrassed. To add insult to injury, the truck they'd overtaken rumbled by, wafting another cloud of diesel fumes in their faces.

"Shall I call a tow truck?" Margot offered.

Pascal firmly shook his head. "I'll change it."

"You sure?"

He turned off the ignition. Throwing open his door, he got out and went to the rear. After giving the blown-out tyre a small kick, he opened the boot.

Margot got out of the car. Thinking it wise to stay out of the way, she walked a little further down the lay-by. From a break in the trees, she could see all the way down the hill to the village they'd just driven through. She checked her phone – her message was still in the outbox, but there was a voicemail from

Alia. She tapped the button to call back, and then gripped the phone between ear and shoulder while she took a cigarette from her bag. "You called?"

"Where are you?"

"On the way to Perpignan. We've just had a blow-out."

"You're with Pascal?"

Margot had just placed a cigarette between her lips and was searching her bag for a matchbook. "Mm-hm."

"Are you okay?"

She took the unlit cigarette from her mouth. "Yes. Why?"

"Can you talk?"

Pascal had moved out of sight, either hidden behind the open boot or crouched on the far side of the car. Margot transferred the phone to her right hand. "What is it?"

"I've got something on that boy I saw in our village that night."

"You found the file?"

"No. But I remembered his name and then searched in an online group for missing persons. His name's Erec Dubois, from Banyuls-sur-Mer. His mother reported him missing the day after I saw him."

"And he's not been seen since?"

"Not alive, no."

Margot listened in amazement as Alia explained the link with the Belle Époque murders. "You're quite sure about this?"

"Yes. It all checks out. And I looked at the photo of his body from the chamber. I know it's not scientific, but from what I could see it was a pretty close match."

"That's excellent work, Alia."

"Thank you. But that's not all."

"Go on."

"Erec claimed he was the victim of a hit and run outside a nightclub in Sète. And you'll never guess who the driver was."

"Who?"

"Pascal Deveraux."

An MPV had just pulled into the lay-by so Margot turned her back on the noise. It came to a halt twenty metres down the tarmac.

"Margot? Are you still there?"

"I'm here." Margot's brain took a moment to catch up. "Have you told anyone else about this?"

"No. I was thinking of going to Banyuls to see his mother."

"Okay."

"But what about you? Where exactly are you?"

"Parked in a lay-by. Pascal's taking me to meet his sister."

A family of four had emerged from the MPV, stretching their limbs like they'd been cooped up too long. Margot glanced over her shoulder. Pascal had finished fitting the new wheel and was stowing the damaged one in the boot. He was looking pleased with himself.

"Will you be all right?" Alia said.

Pascal came over, wiping his hands on a handkerchief. Margot turned away. "I have to go. I'll call you when we get there." She quickly hung up.

"Problem?" Pascal gave her an inquisitive look.

If someone tells you not to look at the birthmark on the man's forehead and the man then walks into the room, what's the first thing you do? Sometimes you can't help blurting things out, like the brain short-circuits.

"Does the name Erec Dubois mean anything to you?"

"Who?"

"Erec Dubois."

Margot studied his face, looking for the slightest tick, the tiniest giveaway that she'd struck a nerve. But he calmly shook his head, seemingly unperturbed.

"Can't say it does. Why?"

Margot continued to regard him. If he was guilty, hearing his victim's name would surely have had some effect. Perhaps Alia had read too much into it. Or he was a better actor than she'd given him credit for.

"No reason." Margot put away her unlit cigarette and smiled. "We'd best get going. We don't want to keep Roselyn waiting."

Although the tyre change had gone well, the incident seemed to have dented his confidence because when they got going again Pascal drove with a little more consideration. Either that or something else was preying on his mind. They didn't speak. When they came to a junction and had to wait for a coach to go by, at least ten minutes must have passed without either of them uttering a word. But when the coach moved on, his eyes snapped back to life.

"Let's take the scenic route."

He put on his sunglasses and hauled the wheel hard to the left. Across the road, Margot noticed the sign for Perpignan, clearly pointing to the right.

"Are you sure there's time?"

"Trust me. This is a shortcut." The new rubber on the freshly-changed tyre squealed as he pulled away from the junction.

The road he'd chosen turned out to be much less busy. They didn't encounter a single vehicle as they drove up through a tract of fir trees, climbing all the way. The bends got tighter, the air thinner.

"I've been doing a little detective work of my own," Pascal said. Behind the sunglasses, Margot imaged that amused glint in his eye.

"Oh yes?"

"The other day, when I met you, I was intrigued. So I did a little digging."

She shifted uncomfortably in her seat, wondering where he was going with this. "And did you find out anything interesting?"

"Your father was a High Court judge."

It wouldn't have taken Sherlock Holmes to discover that. "Is that all?"

"You used to dive competitively."

Margot blushed. Who had he been talking to? "That was a lifetime ago." And it had only lasted a year. A shoulder injury had put paid to any thoughts of taking it further. "Anything else?"

"Your husband worked in the Paris police."

Her mood darkened. "And?"

"He was an outstanding detective, by all accounts."

"He was murdered while on duty."

"And awarded a medal for his bravery."

"It was the proudest day of my life."

There was a pause while he negotiated a particularly challenging bend, tight against sheer rock. On the opposite side there was no barrier; just a drop down into nothingness.

"Was it worth it, though?"

Margot turned sharply to face him. "Was what worth it?"

"Giving his life for a job."

She straightened her spine. "My husband believed in justice. As do I."

He laughed. Perhaps that had sounded a touch pompous but if it did he could shove it. If people didn't get their just desserts then what was the point? When the road straightened up, his gaze strayed back to her side.

"Is it really that simple?" he said. "Innocence or guilt. Black or white. Who has the right to decide?"

"Anyone with a decent moral code."

"You think I lack one?"

Margot said nothing.

He drove on for a while, his mood growing subdued. The road was climbing high up into the mountains now and it didn't look like they would be coming to a main road any time soon.

"Let's be honest: do you really think I killed all those men?"

Margot remained silent.

"They investigated for fourteen months. God knows how many times they interrogated me, asking the same questions, over and over. They wanted me to confess. Even offered me a plea bargain, would you believe. There were times when I was tempted to give in, just to put an end to it. And after all that time they didn't come up with a single piece of evidence to implicate me. Not one scrap."

Absence of evidence was not evidence of absence, she was tempted to remind him.

"And yet, even now, people still give me that look; wondering if it's true or not. I saw it in your eyes when you first came to my apartment. So, tell me, daughter of a High Court judge, widow of a Paris policeman – where's the justice in that?"

Margot continued looking at him, refusing to be drawn. "Are you sure this is a shortcut?"

He sighed, and then smiled, before accelerating up another steep incline.

Another series of switchbacks brought them to the top of the pass. The road cut through a ridge, and as they emerged on the other side the landscape appeared to double in size. Craggy peaks circled them in, bare slabs of rock catching the bright yellow rays of the morning sun. As they started the descent, the road looped round and hugged the edge of a ravine. Pascal slowed as they came to a marked viewpoint, but since the pull-in was occupied he drove on a little further and pulled up on the verge. Margot peered out of her window. Beyond the metre-wide strip the ground fell away sharply.

"This is one of my favourite spots." Pascal flung open his door. "Come on. I'll show you." Full of beans, he walked a little way back up the road.

Margot remained in her seat. Glancing across, she saw that he'd left the keys in the ignition. All she had to do was slide over.

"Margot. Are you coming?" he called out. "There's an incredible view from over here."

Margot turned her head. He was standing around twenty metres away, looking out over the ravine from the edge of the road.

"I thought we were pressed for time," she called back. It was twelve o'clock. At best, they must have been half an hour from Perpignan. "What time did you tell Roselyn we'd be there?"

"I didn't. In any case, I told you – this is a shortcut."

He stepped down off the edge and disappeared.

Curious, Margot got out. She walked up to the spot where she'd last seen him and found he'd gone down a short steep path to a promontory where a huge piece of rock jutted out over the chasm. He was standing right on the edge, lost in the enormity of it all. His head slowly turned as if sensing she was there.

"Come on down," he smiled. "It'll take your breath away. I promise."

Margot had no fear of heights, but there was no knowing what might be going on inside his head. Up at the marked viewpoint, the other car had gone. In the five minutes they'd been there no other vehicles had passed by. Pascal turned back to the ravine, seeming happy to wait. With scant few options, Margot descended the path. She stepped onto the slab of rock, though kept her distance, from both Pascal and the edge.

"I love the mountain air, don't you?" he said softly.

Margot took a step closer. "I prefer the sea air. The smell of the ozone."

"You're not afraid of heights, are you?"

"No."

"Then come out to the edge. It's a wonderful feeling."

He waited. Margot's limbs seemed to move of their own accord, taking her right out to the lip of the overhang. Her left foot caught a pebble, sending it plummeting into the ravine. It was several seconds before they heard it hit the bottom.

"Exhilarating, isn't it?" he said. "Just one more step and your life could be over."

Margot peered over the edge. She tried to imagine what it would feel like to fall from such a great height. All that empty space, and then the unimaginable pain of hitting hard rock. Cooler air was draughting up from the chasm, turning her arms to gooseflesh. The tiny blonde hairs on the tops of her forearms were like a miniature marching army.

"You feel it, too, don't you?"

"What?" Margot frowned.

"*L'appel du vide.*"

The call of the void.

The urge to jump.

She couldn't deny it. It had nothing to do with suicide. More of an impulse. A desire to hurl yourself into the unknown, let the fates decide.

"I wonder what holds you back," she muttered, more to herself. The impulsive thought versus the instinct for survival.

"Don't they say your whole life flashes before you?" Pascal said.

Maybe it did, but since no one had ever survived to tell the tale how would one know?

Margot blinked. Realising what she was doing, she pulled

herself out of the trance. Pascal had taken off his sunglasses, and when Margot turned she was surprised to find his eyes had gone a little bit glassy.

"That man you mentioned."

"Erec Dubois?"

He nodded. "I do remember him now."

"Oh?"

"We were in the casino in Sète. He was with this girl. I remember her saying she'd seen one of my films. She asked for an autograph. She seemed rather nice. But I could tell he was jealous. So later, he followed me out and started attacking my car. Even threw a traffic cone at the windscreen, would you believe."

"He claimed you tried to run into him."

Pascal slowly shook his head. He turned, and came away from the edge.

"He panicked when the police came. Tried to run off. When they caught him, he made up some story about me trying to run him over. He'd clearly been drinking."

It seemed a plausible explanation. But then why had Erec turned up in Saint-Clair-de-l'Ouillat six months later? Margot left that question unasked for now.

12

At the very stroke of noon, like a man whose stomach was driven by clockwork, Papa came in from the garden.

"Do you fancy some tomatoes for lunch?" He held up a couple of the Marmande beef tomatoes he'd been growing. "I was going to make a salad with some capers and olives."

It did sound tempting but Alia had plans. She logged out of her computer and passed him on her way through to the kitchen. "Actually, I was about to go out."

"Have you heard from Margot?"

"She said she would call when she gets to Perpignan."

"So where are you off to?"

"Banyuls. I'm going to speak to Erec Dubois's mother."

"What for?"

"Just to ask a few questions." She grabbed her car keys and notebook from the table. "If I'm not back by two o'clock could you cover for me?"

"Of course. But what about your lunch?"

Alia stepped back in and grabbed a peach from the fruit bowl, smiling brightly.

Banyuls was heaving. From the jam-packed seafront the

satnav took her into a maze of little streets on the north side of town. She missed the address at first and then, with nowhere to park, was forced to leave the car at the top of the hill and walk down.

The apartment was above a tattoo parlour; the name 'Dubois' around halfway down the list of door buzzers. A lengthy pause followed after Alia pushed the button.

"Yes?"

"Janine Dubois?"

"What do you want?"

"My name's Alia Leon. I'm with the police."

Silence. Alia recalled the one and only time she'd had to break bad news. Someone's dog had got run over, and when she'd traced down the owner, a tearful six-year-old girl had come to the door. Every second had been torture. She continued, "It's about your son, Erec."

"You've found him?" Even through the tinny speaker she could sense a mother's desperation.

"Could we talk inside, please?"

Another short pause before the lock clicked.

Two flights of concrete stairs led up to a single door, motion sensors flicking on lights as she ascended. She knocked; a voice told her to come in. Alia entered a small salon where she found Janine Dubois looking up anxiously from a wheelchair.

"Oh, sorry," Alia said quickly. Sorry for what? Sorry you're in a wheelchair? "For getting your hopes up just now, I mean," she clarified.

"So you haven't found him?"

"No."

Her face dropped.

According to the records, Erec's mother was fifty-six but either grief or illness had made her look at least ten years older.

She wheeled herself around the coffee table and stretched to remove a towel from the sofa. "You can sit down."

Alia would have preferred to remain standing, but not wanting to appear rude she perched on the edge of the seat. She took out her pencil and notebook.

"It's the not knowing that's so bad," Janine went on. "If someone could just tell me where he was then perhaps I could get some peace."

Alia lowered her eyes. If her suspicions were proved correct and Erec was confirmed as one of the victims then someday, not far from now, a police officer would have to sit here and do just that. She chose her tenses carefully: "Is Erec your only child?"

She nodded. "It was his birthday last month. I baked him a cake. Set up the table and everything." She dabbed her nose with a tissue.

"What sort of cake?"

"A raspberry Charlotte."

"Ooh, that sounds nice."

The memory brought a sheen to the proud mother's eye. "I used to bake one every Sunday. He'd eat it when he came home from football."

Alia's eyes moved to the mantelpiece where a framed photograph of a boy in school uniform took pride of place. She pointed. "Is that Erec?"

Janine nodded. Reaching up from her wheelchair, she took it down and passed it over. "That was his first year at the lycée. They grow up so quickly, don't they?"

He would had been sixteen in the photo – ten years before Alia had seen him in the village. Not quite so many freckles but the resemblance was clear. She returned the photo to the mantelpiece.

"I know you've probably been asked this question a dozen

times before, but could you tell me what happened the last day you saw him?"

Janine sighed. "He came home from work at the usual time, around six. He said he was going to a party with some friends so he didn't eat much. He left around seven. I sat here and watched him walk through that door. I told him not to be late, much good that was ever going to do."

"Did he often stay out late?"

"He was no angel."

"Who's party was he going to?"

"I've no idea."

"And the friends you mentioned – can you remember any of their names?"

She inhaled deeply through her mouth. "He didn't talk much about his friends. He never brought anyone back. I don't know if he was ashamed of me, being stuck in this thing."

"What about a girlfriend?"

"None that I knew of."

Alia drew a squiggly line in her notebook, putting off asking her next question.

"Do you know if Erec had any connection with Saint-Clair-de-l'Ouillat?"

"Where?"

She repeated it. Janine shook her head.

"What's so important about there?"

"It's possible Erec was seen in the village the night he went missing."

She seemed curious. "I never knew that."

Alia lowered her eyes. "It's only just come to light." Most of the pages of her notebook were covered in doodles but she leafed through them for effect. Still with her eyes lowered, she said, "Does the name Pascal Deveraux mean anything to you?"

"Who?"

Now Alia looked up. "Pascal Deveraux."

She waited. Janine gave it some thought. Would she put two and two together, make the connection? 'Movie-star's house of horrors.' But Janine shook her head. "I've not heard of him."

"He never mentioned someone trying to run him into him? Outside the casino in Sète."

She seemed surprised. "When was this?"

"Six months before he went missing."

"That's news to me."

Clearly there was no shortage of secrets in this family.

"Like I said, Erec was no angel. He liked to wind people up. Sometimes that got him into trouble. But he was a good boy at heart. He would never have harmed a fly."

Alia nodded. "Did he have a job?"

"He worked at the winery."

"Which one?"

"Domaine du Roc. Up on the hill."

Alia wrote that down. "How long had he worked there?"

"Five or six years."

"Did he enjoy it?"

She shrugged. "It was the only job he ever stuck with so yes. And, wait a minute. He had a friend there as well." She sank her forehead in her hand while she strained to think. "Now, what was his name, Jean ... Jacques ... No – Jorge! That's it."

"Jorge who?"

"I never knew his family name."

"Does he still work there?"

"I wouldn't know."

Alia breathed in. Realising she'd run out of questions she smiled. She put away her notebook and got to her feet, but Janine began looking at her in an odd way.

"Wait a minute."

"Yes."

"Deveraux – something about that name does sound familiar."

Alia moved her eyes. Fearing the bomb was finally about to go off she had a sudden urge to leave. "If you do remember anything could you please give me a call?" She wrote her number on a page of her notebook and tore it off. When she attempted to hand it over, Janine was still deep in thought so Alia left it on the table.

At the door she turned back, feeling guilty about leaving her in the dark. Her son was almost certainly dead and his remains already disposed of, some paperwork in an anonymous office all there was to mark his passing. She deserved to know.

"I'll do everything I can to find out what happened to your son, Madame Dubois. I promise."

Domaine du Roc was located a few kilometres inland, on a network of hillsides facing the sea. Alia drove past rows and rows of vines as she followed the road up to the visitors' centre. She parked in the car park, in the shade of a palm tree, and remained in her seat while she checked her phone. A message from Margot:

Stuck in traffic on the outskirts of Perpignan.

Alia typed back: *I'm checking out Erec's place of work. I'll let you know how I get on.*

The winery buildings were grouped on a terrace cut into the slope. From the car park, a neat gravel path took her through a display of antique wine-making equipment and then to a fancy glass atrium that housed the visitors' centre. Peering into the smoked glass windows revealed nothing apart from her own reflection, but assuming it was going to be smart inside Alia straightened her tie and adjusted her trousers.

The interior was every bit as swanky as she'd imagined. A series of huge black and white prints covered one wall, illustrating various stages of the wine-making process, while a line of oak barrels ran along another, each one laden with bottles of wine. A tour group were being shown round by a guide who fancied himself as the next Maurice Chevalier so Alia waited for them to shuffle off back into the sunshine before approaching a freeform glass desk where a young blonde woman sat posing in front of an Apple computer.

"Bonjour."

"Can I help?"

Alia dug into her pocket for the copy of the photo she'd taken from Erec's file. She unfolded it on the desk. "I'm looking for information on this man – Erec Dubois. I was told he used to work here."

"When was this?"

"Seven years ago."

The receptionist shook her head. "I've only been here six months. Sorry." She handed it back.

"Is there a manager I could speak to?"

It seemed an effort for her to lift up her phone but she just about managed it. For some reason she felt the need to drag her fake red fingernails through her bleached blonde hair as she did so. After two short words she carefully replaced the receiver as if it too were made of glass. "He'll be out in a moment."

Alia stepped away from the desk. While she was waiting, she strolled to some shelves and looked at the bottles of wine they had for sale, blanching when she took note of the price tags. Several minutes went by. She studied her watch. Bored of pacing, Alia stood still and stared at the receptionist. Wouldn't it be funny if some freak of static electricity caused her hair to spontaneously catch fire? Alia would be forced to snatch up the fire extinguisher from over there, jump up onto the desk, and drench those perfect blonde strands with extinguisher fluid while the poor little darling shrieked in horror. Would she still look so chic when forced to greet her next visitor with her hair all frazzled and burned? The receptionist looked up. They exchanged a polite smile. Finally, after what must have been ten minutes, a man came out. He sent a glance in Alia's direction, but then ignored her completely and leaned over the desk to speak to the receptionist. Another thirty seconds passed before he deigned to approach.

"Yes?"

He was a tall man with a beard and bad breath. The minty-tinged sewage gas that emerged from his mouth was potent enough to floor a camel from ten paces, but somehow Alia held her composure.

"I'm looking for information on this man." She showed him the picture. "Erec Dubois."

The manager gave it a split-second glance. "What about him?"

"Do you remember him?"

"Wasn't he the one who went missing?"

"Yes."

"What do you need to know?"

"Anything you can tell me about him."

The manager sunk his hands into his pockets and breathed in deeply. Those poor, poor lungs. "At any one time we employ over twenty people here at Domaine du Roc, double that at harvest time. You expect me to remember a man who worked here seven years ago?"

"No, but—"

"Where are you from?"

"I beg your pardon?" Alia suddenly felt hot inside her uniform.

He sniffed. "You're wearing the uniform of a *policière municipale*. You're not from around here."

"I'm from Saint-Clair-de-l'Ouillat."

"Hmph." He gave her a look of mild disgust. "Is that it? I'm a busy man."

Alia felt about two centimetres tall but she held her ground. "His mother said he used to work with someone named Jorge."

"And?"

"Does Jorge still work here?"

"Jorge is still here," the receptionist said, taking a sudden interest. "He'll be working out in the fields."

"Can I speak to him?"

"Not while he's working," the manager put in.

"He finishes at four," the receptionist added gleefully.

Alia glanced at her watch. It was only two-thirty. She mumbled her thanks and quietly left the building.

She hung around the car park for a while, debating whether or not to go home. *Where are you from?* He'd just been asking which police station, hadn't he? Sometimes, when you're surrounded by a wall of white faces, it wasn't easy to tell.

She called her father and asked him to look after the station for another couple of hours and then, curious to see where Erec would have worked, walked up the empty road to the vineyards. Once past the buildings of the winery, nothing but open countryside surrounded her and almost every hillside in sight was stacked with vines laid out in neat green rows. Alia paused at the nearest field. Shielding her eyes from the sun, she spotted six or seven figures working out there, pruning and tying in by hand. At the end of the valley lay a perfect triangle of deep blue sea. Despite the manager, it seemed a pretty nice place to work.

A small gate provided pedestrian access onto the fields. It was far enough away from the winery buildings not to be seen and Alia was tempted to go in, but reluctant to risk another encounter with the malodorous manager she went back to the car instead. It was far too hot inside the vehicle so she sat on a kerb, reading her book.

Alia was back at the gate dead on four. The field workers were heading in so she turned around and started to go back down the hill to intercept them. But then one of the men separated himself from the others and headed up towards the gate via a dusty path at the edge of the field. Alia watched with widening eyes as a bronzed, bare-chested man drew near.

"Salut," he smiled, waving a friendly hand.

Alia looked over her shoulder, thinking he might be addressing someone else, but no one was there.

"Bonjour," she called back, awkwardly returning the wave. They met on opposite sides of the gate, and when he paused to swig from his bottle of water, Alia couldn't prevent her eyes from drifting over his torso. His arms were tattooed, his chest muscular. He must have had at least half a dozen friendship bracelets on each wrist. Her gaze strayed down to the exposed waistband of his boxer shorts. He was very good-looking.

"Are you looking for me?"

Alia blushed. "Sorry. No. I'm looking for Jorge Moreau."

He grinned at the same time he swallowed, forcing him to cough to clear water from his lungs. "I'm Jorge."

"Really?"

"What can I do for you?"

Her mind briefly went blank. "I ... wanted to ask you some questions."

"Questions about what?"

"Erec Dubois."

His face grew a little more serious. "Erec? Has he turned up?"

"We're just following a new lead. We think he was seen in Saint-Clair-de-l'Ouillat on the night he went missing."

"Where?"

"Saint-Clair-de-l'Ouillat. It's a small village, around an hour from here. You've not heard of it?"

He gave it some thought but then shook his head. "Sorry."

Alia felt she ought to be writing something down but feared her hands would get tied up in knots if she tried to take her notebook out of her pocket. She clasped them behind her back instead. "Did you see him the day he went missing?"

"Yeah. He was here, at work. All day from what I recall."

"And that night – his mother said he was going to a party."

"I don't know anything about that."

"So you didn't go with him?"

"No. We were good friends, but we didn't go everywhere together. Look – do you mind if I get something to eat while we talk?"

"Er ... Okay."

"I'm just up here." He pointed to a gap in the hedge on the opposite side of the road.

There was no sign of any houses but Alia went with him. He put on his tee-shirt as they walked.

"Why didn't you come down?"

"Sorry?"

"Earlier. I saw you watching from the road."

"Oh, your boss said I had to wait until you'd finished."

Jorge tutted. "He's a surly old bastard when he wants to be."

The gap in the hedge led to a meadow, the grass parched and brown but resplendent with wildflowers. A field of vines lay to the left while a small olive grove extended over the ground to the right. There was still no sign of a dwelling, however, and Alia slowed. "Are you sure this is where you live?"

He smiled. "Of course. I'm just down here." He pointed to the nearest corner where a white Mercedes Sprinter was parked beneath an olive tree. Alia regarded him in surprise.

"You live in a van?"

"Yeah."

"All by yourself?"

"Mostly. Nothing wrong with that, is there?"

Her smile widened. "No, I suppose not."

They continued on down. It was a recent model and in good condition with a wind-out canopy on one side. To the rear was a barbecue pit fashioned out of rocks, along with a large log which he must have dragged in from somewhere to use as a bench. Alia kept her distance as he opened the sliding door in the side of the van, imagining the state it would be in, but the interior, when she saw it, made her blink in surprise. It was a perfect little home on wheels: a raised platform at the back accommodated a double bed complete with soft furnishings; the floor and the ceiling were lined in strip-wood; a tinted glass panel in the roof let in loads of light. He'd got all the creature comforts: a little gas hob, an inset copper sink, a fancy kitchen tap, a mosaic tiled splashback. In every nook and cranny were dinky cupboards – he'd even got a bookcase built into the space behind the driver's seat and the shelves were stuffed with old paperbacks, many of them classics.

"Where do you buy a van like this?" Alia marvelled.

He'd just taken a couple of fold-up chair from the space at the back and was setting them up in the shade of the canopy.

"I built it."

"*Built* it? How?"

"I bought the van, fitted it all out."

"How long did that take?"

He shrugged. "Dunno. I didn't really keep track."

She would have loved to climb in and have a proper look around, see what he'd got in all those cupboards. The table was decorated with a sprig of lavender in an empty cola bottle.

"You live here all the time?"

"I usually come up in the spring. Then after the harvest I go down to Spain. Work my way around the coast."

"Cool," Alia said. Put that way she could see the attractions of van life.

She continued to watch as he went on setting up. He opened a door to a compartment under the bed and extracted a cool box which he then set down between the two chairs. A rustic chopping board laid on an upturned quarter-barrel made a perfect low table. Finally, he took a bottle of white wine from the fridge and held it up. "Care to join me?"

Alia shook her head.

"Maybe next time, then." He winked.

Alia felt heat rise to her cheeks. She still wasn't sure what to do with her hands so she left them linked behind her back. Catching a glimpse of herself in the door mirror, she was reminded of how ridiculous she looked in her oversized uniform. The first thing she was going to do when she got home was have another word with the mayor.

"You can sit down."

He'd made himself comfortable on one of the deckchairs. Alia eyed the chair beside him, but knew she wouldn't feel comfortable in it so sat on the log instead. She watched him pour the wine.

"Don't you get fed up of wine, after working in a vineyard all day?"

"Not really. It's in my blood. My family own a vineyard in Bordeaux."

"Oh, wow."

"That's where I grew up."

One by one he pulled things out of the cooler and arranged them on his makeshift table. He'd got a selection of cheeses, some sundried tomatoes, a jar of olives, some pickled artichoke hearts. Together with a baguette he retrieved from the passenger door pocket he'd soon constructed quite a feast. Alia's stomach rumbled at the sight of it all.

"So how come you work here if your family own a vineyard?"

"My dad died a few years back. I've got two older brothers, and we didn't see eye to eye. They wanted to modernise; I prefer the traditional methods."

"So you let them take over?"

He nodded, having just filled his mouth with wine. "I've not got much of a business brain anyway."

He peeled back the wrapper on a round of brie and cut into it with a small knife. The aroma that came off it was so ripe Alia instantly regretted skipping her lunch. She leaned forward, crossing her arms. A small, unhappy creature seemed to have taken up residence in her belly.

"So what did you want to know about Erec?"

Alia refocussed. She took out her notebook and pen. "What kind of person was he?"

Jorge gave it some thought. "Fun-loving, easy-going. A bit cheeky. He used to like winding people up, and it got him into trouble sometimes."

"What kind of trouble?"

He tore off a chunk of bread with his teeth. "Nothing serious; just fooling around." He didn't seem to like talking with his mouth full so there was a pause while he chewed. "He had an eye for the ladies, and it didn't matter to him if they were attached or not. He got into a few bust-ups with jealous boyfriends over the years."

"You mean he got into fights?"

"It never got that far. Erec usually found a way of talking himself out of it. He had a way with words."

"Did he tell you that someone once tried to run him over?"

Jorge looked puzzled. "When was that?"

"About six months before he went missing."

He shook his head. "He never said anything to me."

A cricket jumped onto her boot. Alia briefly contemplated swatting it and slipping it into her mouth.

"What job did he have here?"

"He worked on the fields, same as me."

"Did anything unusual happen the day he went missing?"

Jorge had just forked a big lump of artichoke heart into his mouth and there was a pause while he munched on it. Alia became conscious of the solitary peach she'd eaten on the way over sitting in the pit of her stomach. All she wanted to do was fill her mouth with bread and cheese.

"Sorry," he said, washing down his mouthful with a gulp of wine. "I didn't eat much at lunch."

"That's okay."

"It was September time, wasn't it?"

Alia nodded. "A Friday."

"I can't remember anything unusual happening."

"There was nothing odd about his behaviour in the days before?"

"Not that I noticed."

"And he never said anything to you about the party he'd been invited to?"

"Like I said, we weren't joined at the hip."

Realising she hadn't even opened her notebook, Alia put it away. Jorge had taken a salami out of the cool box and the smell of smoky sausage was making her mouth water. Would it really be so unprofessional of her to join him? Ask for a few slices of that ham; finish off that piece of brie he'd left sitting on the edge of the breadboard; spear the last gherkin floating in the jar and shove it, wholesale, into her mouth ...

"Can I ask you something?"

Alia blinked. She instinctively moved her hand to her mouth, fearing she might have been drooling. "Yes?"

Taking a respite from stuffing his belly, Jorge leaned back in his seat. "Why are you asking all these questions now? It's been seven years."

"Like I said, new information."

"You mean that village you mentioned?"

Alia nodded. "Saint-Clair-de-l'Ouillat. It's where I'm from. Actually, I was the one who saw him."

His eyes widened. "No kidding?"

"I thought he was drunk. But, if you knew my village, you'd know how unlikely that is."

"So what do you think he was doing out there?"

Alia looked into his eyes. It would be so easy to tell him the full story, let him know the manner in which his friend had most likely met his end. But at some point the *Police Nationale* would have to be involved and she wouldn't want them thinking she'd been stepping on anyone's toes. She shrugged. "Was he much of a drinker?"

"Same as anyone that age, I guess."

"What about drugs?"

"A bit of hash now and again."

"Nothing stronger?"

He shook his head.

Alia nodded, and was thinking of another question to ask when his face lit up.

"Have you checked his locker?"

"Which locker?"

"Down in the winery. He used to come to work on his scooter and store his gear in there."

"Okay. Thanks, I'll check that out." Though given the manager's attitude earlier there didn't seem much chance of them seeing it without a search warrant.

Alia was almost ready to give in and take up his offer of some food when her phone rang. Margot's name appeared on the screen. That last piece of brie would have to remain unloved.

13

Slowed by traffic on the outskirts of Perpignan they didn't arrive until after three. Pascal drove into the heart of the town and pulled up outside a Bourgeois townhouse close to the Palace of the Kings of Mallorca.

"Best let me do the talking," he said as he bounded up the front steps. He paused at the door. "There's no knowing what mood she'll be in."

No one came to answer so Pascal unlocked the door with a key that was attached to his keychain. They stepped into a large hallway, the air heavy with the scent of polished wood and citrus fruits.

"Roselyn?" he called out. "Are you decent?"

No response.

He ushered Margot inside with a smile. "I imagine she's out in the garden. She loves being outdoors."

Margot followed him through a grand salon, a crystal chandelier one of the many fine items to catch her eye. The marriage may not have lasted long but clearly Roselyn had not done badly out of it. They went through a pair of open doors into an orangery where another set of bi-folds drew them onto a terrace.

Steps led down into a lush green paradise of a garden, but Pascal paused on the top step, turning to Margot with an abashed look. Curious, Margot looked past him: down by a stone fountain a woman stood painting at an easel, stark naked.

"I do apologise," he said.

Behind his apparent embarrassment, however, Pascal appeared to be smirking. Margot got the impression he was pleased they'd caught his sister like this.

Have I shocked you? his eyes appeared to be saying.

He turned, and skipped down the steps. "Roselyn, dear, do cover up. You have a visitor."

Roselyn looked round. She made no attempt to cover herself, and even when they'd joined her at the fountain she remained naked before them, totally unabashed. With her voluptuous white curves and copper-tinted hair she could have been a character from a painting by Reubens. Pascal reached for the chiffon gown that was draped over a stone bench and hooked it onto her shoulders, kissing the top of her arm as he did so.

"You know you're supposed to stay out of the sun. Skin as delicate as yours will sear in this heat."

When Roselyn turned, he greeted her with a kiss on the lips. After a deliberate pause, his eyes flicked back to Margot's.

What about now?

"Who's this?" Roselyn said.

"You remember Cousin Célia?"

"Yes."

"Well, this lady works for her. Her name's Margot Renard."

Margot stepped forward. "How very nice to meet you."

She extended a hand but Roselyn regarded it as if a handshake were a novelty. The pictures Alia had shown her may have been ten years old, but in the flesh – and there was still plenty of it on show – Roselyn had barely aged: her skin was still taut, her cheekbones very much pronounced. A happy little smile seemed etched on her face, and her pupils were dilated. Amongst the items on the stone table, Margot noticed a tell-tale bottle of pills.

Roselyn finally reached out and gently shook Margot's hand. The pause turned awkward so Margot gazed around. "You have a lovely garden."

It was hard to believe they were in the middle of a busy town. Dense planting did much to insulate them from the hustle and bustle of their surroundings, and a liberal use of semi-tropical species gave it the feeling of being somewhere far away. The splash and babble of the fountain, together with the heat, was soporific.

"Why are you here?" The question was child-like in its innocence.

Pascal emitted a small laugh. He wrapped his arms around his sister from behind. "Come now, dear. Let's not be rude. Margot's a very nice lady. She's promised not to say anything that might upset you. Isn't that right, Margot?"

His eyes flashed back to Margot's as he nestled his chin in the crook of his sister's shoulder.

How about now?

When Margot didn't give him the reaction he'd no doubt been hoping for, he changed tack. Releasing Roselyn from his embrace he went to the stone table. "Why don't I get us some drinks?" A jug of gloopy red liquid sat on a tray in the centre. "Ooh, pomegranate juice. My favourite." He held it up to his nose and inhaled deeply. "Margot – can I tempt you?"

Margot conceded a slight nod of her head. Glad of the distraction, she took his place at Roselyn's side. "I hope we're not disturbing you. Do you mind if I take a look?" She indicated the easel.

Roselyn hesitated for a moment but then stepped aside.

Margot's eyes widened as she took in the painting. It was an abstract view of the garden, a riot of colour applied in broad bold strokes, a true feast for the eyes. "This is incredible."

"Margot paints."

"Do you?" Roselyn seemed intrigued.

Margot took a step back. "Oh, nothing of this calibre. It's just a hobby."

"Oh, come now. Don't be modest," Pascal said as he handed out the drinks: a highball glass for himself and Margot; a plastic beaker for Roselyn. "Tell Roselyn all about it. I'm sure she would love to hear."

"What do you paint?" Roselyn enquired.

Margot felt a little more confident with a glass in her hand. "Well, I like painting the sea. There's a nice little harbour where I live, although I can never seem to find the right shade of blue."

"That's easy," Roselyn said. "Use Prussian blue for the deeper sea." She located the relevant tube in her paint box and squeezed a small pea onto her palette. "Mix it with cerulean if you want it lighter. Then use cobalt higher up." She squeezed out another two peas and then combined them expertly on a corner of her palette to create a simple but effective seascape. "See?"

"That's amazing." Margot's heart rose. Talent, when experienced in the raw, was a joyful thing to behold. "I have been taking lessons but I think I'm a little too impatient."

"Perhaps Roselyn could give you some lessons," Pascal commented. Posing again, one hand in his pocket, glass in the other, he looked her up and down with lascivious eyes. "I'd love to see the two of you together sometime."

Now? asked his face.

Margot regarded him in consternation. Was this the reason he'd brought her here – to play perverse games? She cleared her throat, and pointedly angled away.

"How much garden do you have here, Roselyn?"
"Oh, rather a lot, I should think."
"It really is very beautiful."
"Would you like to walk round?"
"I'd love to."

Anything to escape the leering look Pascal was still giving her.

They strolled along the footpath, carrying their drinks with them. Pascal took his sister's arm, and as the path was only wide enough for two, Margot followed at a discreet distance. From the fountain, they went down some steps into a sunken area where an abundance of ferns and small palms created the effect of a grotto. Water was running down the exposed rocks, collecting in a series of linked ponds. On one side, Margot's eyes were drawn to a rather fine collection of Hawaiian Ti.

"Is this a Bromeliad?" She halted next to a star-shaped plant with the most remarkable pink flowers. Roselyn unhooked herself from her brother's arm in order to see better.

"That's the pineapple Bromeliad. Do you like it?"

"I think it's beautiful." The reason for the name was obvious given the flower resembled a miniature pink pineapple. "I'm sure I used to have one as an indoor plant, though it wasn't nearly as big as this."

Roselyn regarded her as if she'd just discovered something freshly intriguing. When they continued, it was Margot Roselyn chose to walk beside, forcing Pascal to take up the rear. They returned to the higher level via a different set of steps, these ones narrow and rocky, and as the ground was slippery Roselyn held tightly onto her arm. If anything, she was being a little too clingy. It was like being a teenager again, arm-in-arm with her best friend, though to Margot nothing about it felt normal. When they got to the top, Roselyn continued to cling on.

"Who's your favourite artist?" She gave Margot's arm another tight squeeze.

"Oh, that's a tricky one."

"Go on, tell me."

Margot sipped from her glass while she gave it some thought. "Monet for his garden, Degas for his ballet dancers."

Roselyn squealed. "I like Monet as well."

"Did you know his father wanted him to be a grocer? He never believed he would make it as an artist and thought he should join the family firm instead. Who's your favourite?"

"Ummm – Dali."

"Dali? Now he was a strange one." And, given the history of this family, a potential minefield in the area of 'fun facts'. Margot had to think for a few moments. "I read somewhere that he used to pay his restaurant bills by drawing on his cheques, thinking no one would cash them because of the value of the art. If I tried that I doubt I'd get away with two cups of tea."

They laughed. As they turned a corner, Margot glanced over her shoulder. Pascal was trailing behind, looking a little put out. They'd circled the lower part of the garden and were heading back towards the fountain. Fearing this unexpected intimacy with Roselyn was about to come to an end, Margot went out on a limb.

"I suppose you're used to beautiful gardens, having been brought up at the villa Belle Époque."

"The Belle Époque?"

"Yes. The gardens there are beautiful."

"You've been?"

"I have."

They slowed when they reached the fountain. As Pascal caught up, Roselyn cast him a glance – seeking his approval, perhaps. Pascal said nothing, seemingly happy to let her continue.

"It must have been wonderful having all that space to run around in," Margot prompted.

"I don't remember much about it."

"Of course."

They sat down on the stone bench. Margot had a sip of her pomegranate juice. "The mind can be a funny thing. Sometimes I can't even remember what happened yesterday, yet many of my childhood memories are still vivid. And sometimes, if something very bad happens to us, the mind can protect us. Hide the memories away."

Roselyn seemed intrigued. Pascal was standing right beside her now but he continued to stay silent. Margot pushed on,

"Is there anything in particular you do remember about the villa?"

Her face lit up. "Gaston."

"Gaston? Yes." Margot smiled. "He's still there. What do you remember about him?"

"Gaston the smelly old gardener. He lived in that silly little house. With his smelly bonfires."

"Oh yes. He was having a bonfire yesterday. Did you like Gaston?"

Roselyn firmly shook her head.

"Oh, why not?"

She shyly lowered her eyes. Margot continued:

"What about the swimming pool – do you remember that?"

Roselyn nodded.

"I love swimming," Margot went on. "Especially in the sea. I love that feeling of being immersed in water, don't you?"

Roselyn appeared to agree.

"Do you remember the parties you and your brother used to have?"

In her peripheral vision Margot noticed Pascal move to the table. His arm reached for the jug of pomegranate juice, but midway there he let go of his glass. Hitting the ground, it shattered into a dozen pieces, sending pomegranate juice running across the slabs. As the puddle neared her feet, Roselyn shrieked, and pulled her legs up to her chest. Margot flashed him a look of astonishment. He'd dropped it intentionally. She was certain of it.

Roselyn became a dithering mess. Pushing between them, Pascal took her place.

"There, there, my sweet." He wrapped his arms around her, edging Margot out. "I'm sure Margot didn't mean to upset you."

Margot stood up, heat rising to her cheeks. Damn him and his blasted games.

"Clean that up, would you?" Pascal said, trailing her a glance as he helped his sister get to her feet. He ushered her away, leaving Margot staring angrily at the back of his head.

Margot marched into the house. She'd been intending to find a dustpan and brush, but when she crossed the hall on her way to the kitchen her eyes were drawn to the front door instead. Investigation or not, she was sorely tempted to walk straight out.

Roselyn had calmed down by the time she went back out. They were sitting on the soft chairs in the orangery, Pascal stroking her hair. Margot walked by, dustpan and brush in hand, but Pascal called her back.

"Leave that."

She paused.

"I'll sort it out later."

Margot put the dustpan and brush down on the floor. Watching him untangle from his sister's embrace made her feel sick. Whatever was going on in his head she'd lost all interest in finding out. He joined her at the bi-fold doors before drawing her to one side.

"I'm afraid I won't be able to drive you back. I have an appointment in an hour."

Margot stiffened her spine. "That's perfectly all right." She wouldn't have accepted a lift from him anyway. "I'll just go and say goodbye to Roselyn."

She tried to move past him but he caught her arm. "Best not," he said.

His cord-like fingers dug into her tricep, sending pain through to the bone. The genii flashed in his eyes before he smiled and let go. "Allow me to show you out."

He followed her all the way to the front door. Margot paused, itching to tell him exactly what she thought of him, but all she could get out was a terse, "Goodbye." She reached for the handle.

"She wasn't always like this, you know," Pascal said. "Once, she was magnificent."

Margot looked at him. "So why did you drop the glass?"

His mouth formed an expression that was ostensibly a smile but which conveyed something altogether different. He leaned past her to turn the latch. "Give Célia my best."

14

Thirty minutes later Margot was sitting in Alia's police car, being driven back to Saint-Clair-de-l'Ouillat. Recounting the events of the afternoon had succeeded in working a little of the frustration out of her system, but she was still annoyed.

"I sincerely hope I never see that man again," Margot said, snatching her cigarettes from her bag while they were stuck in traffic. She lowered the window and lit up. "Twisted is hardly the word."

"That bad?" Alia said.

"I think I'm going to need a bath when we get home."

"So what do we do now?"

"Good question. You've done an inspired job, Alia, you really have, but all the evidence we have so far is circumstantial. There's nothing to prove he was actually involved in any of the murders."

"What about the incident in Sète?"

"Pascal's explanation seemed plausible. In the end it's just one person's word against another. And how sure are you that it was Erec you saw that night?"

"Not one hundred per cent but pretty sure."

"We would need to prove Erec was the first victim. I'm not quite sure how we would go about that."

"There's his mother. We could get a DNA sample from her."

"True. But we would need to be certain of our facts before we ask her."

"So are you still treating Pascal as a suspect?"

Alia seemed a little crestfallen. Margot reached over and squeezed her hand.

"We're on the right track, I'm sure of it, but part of me thinks he's just playing games. He likes the attention. Or maybe he's protecting someone. I don't know." She sighed. The few hours she'd spent in his company had been exhausting. "Did you get anything useful from Erec's mother?"

"Not much. Erec told her he was going to a party that night but she didn't know where. And she knew nothing about the incident in Sète. But—" She paused while she negotiated the traffic on a particularly busy roundabout. "I found out he used to work in a winery. His friend asked if I'd looked in his locker."

"Did you?"

"No. The manager wasn't very cooperative. To be honest he was quite rude. He asked me where I was from."

Margot turned to her with a frown. "How do you mean?"

Alia shifted in her seat. "He might just have meant which police station was I from."

They drove on for a while without speaking. Margot drew on her cigarette. Whatever the man's intention had been, it was obvious Alia had been upset by it. "I'll give Célia a call when we get back. See if we have grounds for a search warrant."

The turning to the highway came up so she stubbed out her half-smoked cigarette and raised the window. Half an hour later they arrived in Saint-Clair-de-l'Ouillat.

Down at the end of the track, Didier was locking his garage. Margot got out by the gate while Alia parked the car.

"Good to see you safely back," Didier called out, strolling over. "I hear you've had an eventful day."

"You could say that. Actually, do you mind if I just grab my coat? I left it on the seat of your van." She moved to walk past.

But Didier stayed put. "I've just locked up."

"Let me have the key, then. I won't be a second." Margot held out her hand.

He continued to look nonplussed. Alia came to join them, bringing him back to life. "It's okay," he said. "You two go on; I'll get your coat. You look like you could do with a drink."

Didier was being rather shifty again, but Margot was too tired to think about it, and she was certainly in need of a drink. She followed Alia up to the house.

———

They ate dinner, and at nine o'clock Margot went up to her room, drained and unsettled. She sat at the open window and watched the bats swoop over the river. It helped settle her nerves, aerial marvels that they were.

Going to bed so early proved a mistake, however, and after tossing and turning for what seemed like hours she had to get up. Looking at her watch, she was stunned to see it was still only twenty past ten. She put on her robe and went downstairs.

A soft light drew her to the kitchen. Making no sound, Margot looked in from the door. The interior light from the open fridge revealed Didier in his pyjamas, sneakily eating a chunk of cheese. He hadn't seen her so Margot coughed politely. Turning, he guiltily put down the knife he'd been holding.

"Sorry," Margot smiled. "I didn't mean to sneak up on you."

Didier swallowed his mouthful and brushed the crumbs from his pyjama top. "Alia keeps nagging me to lose weight." He patted his belly. "But cheese is a hard thing to resist."

"Tell me about it."

He closed the fridge door and flicked on the ceiling light. "Is everything okay?"

"Yes. I just came down for a glass of water."

"Help yourself."

He stepped aside. Margot went to the sink to fill a tumbler. She gulped down two mouthfuls and afterwards turned to face him.

"I had a little heart trouble last year," Didier explained, taking a seat at the table.

"Nothing serious, I hope?"

"They had to put in a stent. I've had no problems since, but Alia likes to fuss."

"That's because she cares about you."

"I know. But there's life in this old dog yet."

Margot moved around the counter and joined him at the table. "She's a smart girl."

"I know. At school, she was always coming top in her class."

"She could go a long way in the *police judiciare.*"

He folded his arms. "No doubt she could but she's never said anything about joining."

"Maybe she feels obligated."

"To whom?"

"To you."

Didier chuckled. "You think she's wasted here?"

"Don't you?"

He looked her in the eye. "There's more to life than having a career. If Alia said she wanted to join the *Police Nationale*, I assure you I would do everything possible to support her. But I'm not going to push. She's old enough to make up her own mind."

Margot conceded a small nod. Perhaps he was right. And in any case, she had no right to interfere. She took another gulp of water. "I meant to say, I found another way into the back of the villa. There's a second driveway a little further along."

Didier slowly nodded his head. Obviously, he already knew. "You spoke to Madame Baudet."

Margot gave him a closer look, not sure if that had been a question or a statement. Were all her movements being relayed back and forth between the two of them? "We had an interesting chat."

He nodded again. No doubt he'd already been briefed on what had been said. Margot continued to look him in the eye, but it didn't seem she would be getting anything more out of him. He raised himself from his seat.

"Anyway. It's time I was in bed. Goodnight, Margot."

"Goodnight, Didier."

She watched him go to the door and then whispered: "Don't worry. I'll keep schtum."

He turned, looking caught out. "Pardon?"

"About the cheese," Margot explained. "I won't let on to Alia."

"Ah. Yes, of course." He had to manufacture a small laugh. "Thank you."

He made a strange gesture of touching his forehead, and then went up.

The next morning, Margot didn't wake until seven and she went downstairs to find Alia already outside, collecting eggs from the henhouse. The sun had not long come up and the sky was clear and electric blue, the air an agreeable twenty degrees.

"Salut." Alia smiled brightly as she came in, passing Margot on the doorstep. Margot had just lit a cigarette and felt guilty for polluting the morning air.

"Sorry. Technically, I've given up."

"Technically?" Alia queried, seemingly bemused. "So how does that work?"

"It only counts if someone sees me," Margot grinned and buried the packet in the bottom of her bag.

She had a couple more puffs and then stubbed it out. She was just about to go in when a vehicle drove by on the track. Scanning round, she was surprised to see Didier's van heading towards the garage. "Your father's out early."

"Oh, he's been to fetch the bread. He fell out with the local boulangerie so he drives all the way to Céret."

"Does he need a hand?"

"No, leave him. He'll be fine. How do you like your eggs?"

Margot joined her in the kitchen. Alia was filling a pan with water so Margot took some plates out of the cupboard. "Soft boiled, please."

"Toast or bread?"

She had a sudden craving for boiled egg and soldiers, plenty of salt – how she'd loved that as a child. She made her request and then fetched the butter from the fridge. While they were waiting for the water to boil, they dried and put away the washing up.

"Your father told me about his heart condition."

"He's been all right since the operation, touch wood." Alia rapped her knuckles on the breadboard.

"Has he never thought of retiring properly? He always seems busy."

"It's best he stays active, I think. He'd be a nightmare cooped up here all day, believe me."

"What does he get up to in that garage of his?"

"I don't like to ask. You know what they're like – men and their sheds."

Not particularly. Hugo had never had a shed. He'd once

come up with the idea of building a model railway in their second bedroom and had drawn up all the plans. But not a single piece of track had ever been laid. Work always came first.

When Didier came in, they put on a hearty breakfast: homemade apricot jam on crusty white bread, pastries and cakes. Alia ate so much it was hard to imagine how she concealed it inside that tiny frame of hers. As soon as they'd finished, Didier went out again, saying he needed to help a friend with some fencing.

By nine o'clock, the front door was open and Alia was at her desk. Margot made the coffee and took two cups through to the office. She waited until nine-thirty before calling Florian; he told her to call back in fifteen minutes and at five to ten Margot finally got to speak to Célia.

"How are you getting on?"

Margot was missing the nicotine hit from her morning cigarette and paced between the office and the kitchen while she spoke.

"Pretty good, actually. They've got a wonderful *policière municipale* here." She made sure she was standing right next to Alia when she said that. The poor girl grinned bashfully. Margot brought Célia up to speed on all that had happened.

"I wondered if you might contact the police in Toulouse. See if they ever followed up on Alia's report."

"Of course."

"And we need to think about getting a formal identification. We may have to approach Erec's mother for a DNA sample."

"I'll speak to the *procureur* about that."

"I'd also like to have a proper look around the winery where Erec worked. The manager wasn't very cooperative."

"Very well. I'll contact the *gendarmerie* in Banyuls. See if they can have someone meet you there."

"Thank you."

It seemed the conversation had come to an end, and as Célia

was clearly busy Margot was reluctant to keep her any longer, but what Pascal had said about her health continued to trouble her.

"There was one other thing."

"Yes."

On the spot, Margot quickly changed her mind. Was it really any of her business? "It doesn't matter. I'll speak to you when I get back."

Margot stared at the photo of Erec Dubois. Twenty-six years old, his whole life ahead of him. Then one day he crosses swords with the wrong person and his life comes to a brutal end. Was that what had happened? Maybe. Margot wasn't convinced.

"Have you got the mortuary reports handy?"

Alia sifted through the papers on her desk and, locating the relevant folder, handed it over. Margot sat on the window sill while she leafed through.

Despite having been down there the longest, the extent of skeletonization in the first victim was less pronounced than in most of the others. The cause of death had not been conclusively determined but there were several likely candidates: a broken parietal bone indicative of a severe blow to the head; a nick in the C2 vertebra consistent with a deep knife wound; similar marks on three of the ribs suggesting he'd been stabbed at least once in the neck and several times in the chest. And, if that wasn't enough, all his teeth had been removed – the pattern of corrosion on the jaw bones leading the pathologist to conclude that acid had been used at some point during the extraction process. Whether this had been done pre- or post-mortem had been impossible to determine.

"If Erec was the first victim," Margot said, "I don't envy the person who has to tell his mother. The killer certainly went to town on him."

Alia turned her chair. "I think the fourth victim was the worst. His whole body had been bound in barbed wire. And he'd been stabbed in the face and had all his fingers amputated."

Margot shook her head in dismay. "Do you think there's any significance to the fact all the victims were men?"

"The police ruled out a sexual motive."

"I know. But a motive based on gender might still have played a part. A man-hating man? A man-hating woman?"

Alia shrugged with her eyebrows.

Another of the crime scene photos captured Margot's attention – this one a blow-up of the writing that had been carved into the walls of the chamber. In the opinion of a linguistics expert, the marks were nothing more than a random sequence of letters, but there was something familiar to Margot's eyes. She looked closer, focussing on one letter in particular.

"Have you got a magnifying glass?"

Alia searched and then took one out of her desk drawer.

Margot set the images down on the desk and stooped to peer through. "I'm sure I've seen this before."

"What?"

Margot pointed at the capital 'R': the stem had been extended upwards and an elaborate swash added to the leg. "That's how Roselyn signs her paintings."

Alia took a turn looking through the magnifying glass. "Are you sure?"

"I'm positive. Pascal had several of her works in his apartment."

"So what does that mean?"

An image of Roselyn pouring acid into Erec Dubois's mouth flashed through Margot's head. It would have been interesting to find out her views on men. "It means Roselyn must have been down in that chamber at some point."

"But when? She could have done that as a child."

"True, but it proves one thing."

"What's that?"

Margot dropped the file on the desk. "They've both been lying to us since the beginning."

Florian called back at three to say that a lieutenant from the *gendarmerie* in Banyuls had agreed to meet them at the winery the next morning. Alia rearranged her schedule to make sure she could go.

Didier didn't come home until ten. According to Alia, he often stayed out all day, helping farmers or friends with one thing or another. Standing alone on the kitchen doorstep, smoking her final cigarette of the day, Margot watched as the lights from his van pierced the darkness on the other side of the hedge.

An idea popped into her head. Alia was upstairs, having a bath, so Margot carefully stubbed out her cigarette and then, making as little noise as possible, went out into the garden. She crept along the footpath, and when she reached the gate leaned out. The van's headlights were pointing towards her, meaning he'd turned it around and reversed up to the garage. The engine was off and she could hear voices, two men speaking in low tones.

Remaining on the garden side of the hedge, Margot worked her way parallel with the track. When the lawn came to an end, she picked a way through the long grass until she was all but level with the garage. Above the hedgerow, the halo from the van's headlights extended all the way up to the house. The men were still talking, and now that she was closer Margot recognised the voices of Didier and Gaston.

She still couldn't quite make out what they were saying, however. If she could only get closer ... Margot extended her stride, working her way carefully between the trees, seeing more detail now that her eyes had adapted to the dark. But she'd only taken two steps when a panicked flapping of wings stopped her in her tracks – an equally spooked duck burst from the undergrowth and took to the air before gliding down to the river.

Margot froze. She strained her hearing, but on the other side of the hedge the voices had gone quiet.

Without further ado, she made her way stealthily back to the house.

15

It was nine o'clock and the winery had only just opened its doors when Margot and Alia crossed the car park to join the lieutenant waiting outside. He greeted them with a friendly nod.

"I'm surprised you've had problems," he said as they entered the fancy glass atrium. "I know the owners. I'm sure they'll be keen to cooperate."

"Let's hope their manager's singing from the same hymn sheet," Margot said and led the way to the reception desk.

It seemed the lieutenant was going to be proved right because Margot had barely made the introductions when the manager came out. He shook the lieutenant's hand, smiled warmly at Margot, nodded at Alia. Despite the air conditioning, the pits of his shirt were stained with sweat.

As he and the lieutenant got talking the manager put on a display of helpfulness that was sickening in its obsequiousness: *Would you like this? Would you like that?* If they'd asked him to bend over and drop his trousers he probably would have obliged.

"I understand you wanted to see the lockers," he said, turning his attention to Margot.

"We would like to see every bit of information you have on Erec Dubois, if you don't mind."

"Of course. Please follow me," he grinned idiotically.

He led the way to a door marked PRIVATE, the lieutenant taking up the rear.

"He wasn't this helpful yesterday," Alia muttered as they followed a short way behind.

Margot gave her a sympathetic look. "When men try to belittle women it's usually because they're compensating for something."

How much of that he overheard Margot couldn't be sure but the manager's bonhomie appeared to dim a fraction.

He took them down a windowless corridor. Turning left at the end, he opened the door to a canteen. An opening in the longest wall led to an L-shaped space where the walls were lined with lockers.

"According to our records..." the manager consulted a scrap of paper in his hand, "Erec Dubois rented 12A." He pointed it out; the four of them grouped in front of it. "When an employee uses a locker we make a small deduction from their wages, so our records are accurate."

How very generous. Margot tried the door but it was locked. "I presume someone else uses it now?"

"Yes. But I'm told we still have the contents. They were cleared out three months after Erec went missing."

"Could we see them?"

"Assuming our warehouse manager has managed to locate them. Let's check with him now."

They crossed a room full of huge oak barrels and passed the entrance to the room where the wine was made: a clinical space full of stainless-steel tanks and coils of plastic tubing. Technology was a wonderful thing. Margot smiled as she recalled the time she'd had a go at the old-fashioned method – stomping grapes at a wine festival. Some world-class bore had tried to make out that only by treading the grapes could the wine's true flavour profile be properly evoked. Margot had laughed in his face.

In the yard, a forklift was manoeuvring so they had to wait. Finally, they went in through an unmarked door to an older part of the building where the space was crowded with racking. When a workman in overalls appeared, the manager called him over.

"Any luck?"

"We've found it."

"Excellent." The manager silently clapped his hands.

The workman briefly disappeared between two rows of racking before returning with a battered archive box which he set down on a table. Margot, Alia and the lieutenant gathered round.

"So everything that was in Erec's locker went in here?" Margot asked.

"That's correct."

She removed the lid. There wasn't a great deal to see: a black hoodie, a tin with some roll-ups, a pair of old beach sandals still with some sand in them. There was no motorcycle gear, so given that he'd come to work that day he must have left the premises at the end of his shift. At the bottom was a collection of old motorcycle magazines. Margot turned back to the manager.

"Has no one ever asked to see these before?"

"You're the first."

"Didn't you inform his mother?"

The manager shuffled his feet, looking embarrassed. "I'm not sure. I would have to check."

Margot turned away with a dismissive shake of her head.

She waited while Alia looked through. It didn't seem they were going to find anything that might give them a clue as to where Erec had gone and Margot began to feel a little embarrassed herself, but then, as Alia leafed through one of the motorcycle magazines, a card fell out. Margot stooped to pick it up. It was a business card: the name 'Naxos' spelled out in a jazzy, multicoloured font. A telephone number below it. No address. She showed it to the others. "Any idea what this is?"

There were blank looks all round.

"Could we hold onto it?"

"Of course," the manager said. "I doubt he'll be needing it now." He chuckled, but realising he was the only one amused promptly shut up. Margot fixed him with a cold stare.

"Thank you for being so cooperative."

The lieutenant accompanied them back to the car. He seemed in a thoughtful mood and had said little while they'd been inside, but once they'd crossed the road he paused.

"May I see that again?" He held out his hand.

Margot passed him the card. They waited while he studied it.

"I'm pretty sure this telephone number is for Barcelona," he said. "I recognise the code. And going by these jazzy graphics my guess is the Naxos is a cannabis club."

Margot frowned. "A *cannabis* club?"

The lieutenant nodded. "You're not aware of them?"

"No."

"They're quite common in some parts of Spain. They operate as social clubs: members are allowed to go there to smoke for personal use."

"You mean they're legal?"

"Yes. As long as the owners follow a few basic rules."

"Who checks up on them?"

He shrugged. "I would imagine the local police keep an eye on them. It's not unheard of for them to be used as a front for organised crime, but generally they're not considered a problem. Catalonia's drug laws are rather more liberal than here in France." He handed her back the card. "If there's nothing else?"

"Did you have any clue what might have happened to Erec?"

He shook his head. "I checked our records. A gendarme visited the mother's apartment the day after he went missing. One of the neighbours said they often heard arguing. The officer assumed Erec had grown tired of living there and moved on."

"And not made contact in seven years?"

"It was a reasonable assumption at the time. It's unfortunate, but we don't have the resources to follow up every case."

Margot nodded. "Of course. Thanks for your help."

The lieutenant touched the peak of his kepi and went on his way.

The morning sun was fiercely hot so once they'd got back to the car park they retreated to the shade of a palm tree. Margot lit a cigarette while she considered what to do. "So what was Erec doing going to a cannabis club?" she wondered out loud.

"We could ask Jorge."

Margot gave Alia a closer look. "The man in the van?"

"He said they used to go out together."

Margot smiled. Why was that perky young face looking so eager?

"All right. Where can we find him?"

A short walk up the road brought them to a small plateau from where a panoramic view over the fields could be gained. Margot leaned against the post and rail fence. A few people were out working on the vines, though from a distance they all looked the same with their wide-brimmed sun hats on.

"He was down here yesterday," Alia said and led the way through a small gate.

A dirt path ran down the edge of the field and they paused at the end of each row, checking to see if he was there. The valley was a perfect suntrap and Margot took her time, soaking up the heat. Alia was a little quicker on her feet and had soon gone down to the bottom where she halted and called out:

"Over here!"

When Margot caught up, she found her pointing at a blue and white hut, nestling at the point where several of the fields met. The door was on the far side so he wouldn't have seen them. They reached it and peered round, only to be greeted by a man bending over, searching for something on the undershelf of a table, cotton shorts stretched tight over his rear. Margot folded her arms. Several moments may have passed while the two of them stood staring, not making a sound, reluctant to spoil the view. Finally, sensing their presence, the man straightened. His smile widened as he recognised Alia.

"Hello again. Two visits in two days – to what do I owe this pleasure?"

His hazel eyes soaked up each of them in turn, and now Margot got it. She waited for Alia to respond, but the poor girl had gone shy. Rolling her eyes, Margot unfolded her arms.

"You're Jorge, I presume?"

"That's what it says on my passport."

"My colleague here tells me you were friends with Erec Dubois."

"I was. Or am, if he's still alive."

She dug into her pocket and took out the card. "Have you heard of this place?"

He came out of the shed and into the sunlight, running a hand through his mop of black hair. "The Naxos. Yeah, I know it."

"You've been there?"

"A few times. I've got some cousins in Barcelona."

"What kind of place is it?"

His eyes flicked back and forth between them, perhaps sensing a trap. "It's a cannabis club. But it's all legit. They follow the rules and everything."

"So you admit to being a member?"

"They don't let you in if you're not," he grinned. "Why are you asking?"

"We found the card in Erec's locker."

"Okay."

"Was Erec a member?"

He nodded. "I was the one who introduced him."

"Did you go down there together?"

"We usually went down for the whole weekend. Hit the beach on the Sunday. Chillax."

Chillax? He was so laidback Margot got the impression every weekend was a chillaxing weekend in his world. She was still holding the card in her hand.

"Could you write down the address for us please?"

"Sure." He took the card and stepped back into the tool shed. Pulling the lid off a marker pen with his teeth, he wrote down the address on the back. "You don't think the club had anything to do with Erec's disappearance, do you?" He stepped out, handing her back the card.

"We're just following up a lead."

"When did you last go down there?" Alia asked.

"With Erec?"

She nodded.

He gave it some thought. "It must have been … I dunno, a few months before he went missing. Can't really remember."

"Are you still a member?" Margot asked.

"Oh yeah. I still go down every once in a while."

Margot tucked the card away in her pocket. At least they had something to go on now.

She scanned around, her eyes settling on the little piece of blue sea at the end of the valley. If her mental geography was correct, Argents was only a short walk up the coast. "Nice place to work."

"I'm sure there are worse places."

"Did Erec like it here?"

"I guess so."

"So he had no enemies you knew of?"

Jorge shook his head.

Bunches of big fat grapes hung from the vines, plump and juicy. "Are these Grenache?"

"This is Grenache noir. Over there we grow gris and blanc. We'll probably start harvesting at the end of the month."

"You still do it by hand?"

"Oh yeah. It's one of the best times of the year. Lots of people come in to help."

The steepness of the terrain would have made it difficult getting in a mechanical harvester, Margot guessed. "I shall have to try a bottle." Or two.

He smiled. "You should come round for a tasting some time. I can give you both the full tour."

A rather naughty thought occurred to her but Margot said nothing. She turned her head to Alia to see if there was anything she wanted to add but it seemed not. They thanked him for his time.

They were perhaps halfway along the row when he called out:

"Come back again, if you like. If you think of any more questions."

They paused. "Don't worry," Margot called back. "We will."

She and Alia shared a girlish grin as they turned to go on. It was ridiculous, but for a few moments she was sixteen again.

16

Papa was manning the reception desk when they got back to the police house, although 'manning' was rather a loose interpretation of what her father was actually doing: slumped in the chair with his chin on his chest, breathing verging on snoring. Alia shared a soft-hearted look with Margot as they went in through the front door, then crept playfully behind the counter.

"Papa," she said, leaning to his ear. "The village has been invaded by the Swiss and they've stolen all our cheese."

His head jerked up so abruptly Alia admonished herself. Startling a man with a heart condition was probably not the wisest of moves.

"What? When? Where?" He looked around in bleary-eyed confusion.

Alia hugged him from the side and kissed the top of his head. "Don't worry. The cheese is safe. Thank you for looking after the desk for me." She swivelled the chair to usher him out. "But I think I'd better take over now."

On the drive back from Banyuls they'd come up with a plan: Alia would find out everything she could about the Naxos while Margot showed Erec's photo around the village in case anyone else had seen him that night. So as soon as Margot went out, Alia got busy on the computer.

She noted down the address Jorge had written on the card and then typed it into Maps. The Naxos was located in the Gothic Quarter, right in the heart of Barcelona. She did a virtual walkthrough, navigating some dark and dingy streets, but when she got to the address all it showed was an anonymous pair of black doors.

"I'm just popping out," her father called from the kitchen. "I've made lunch for you and Margot."

"Thank you, Papa."

Next, Alia checked company records. Nothing came up. Perhaps social clubs didn't operate as businesses in which case there would be little available online. She spent a fruitless half-hour on more general searches, and then gave up and messaged Gégé: *Do you have anything on cannabis clubs? Specifically, the Naxos in Barcelona?*

A reply pinged straight back: *Gégé will be out of the office until 9:00 tomorrow. Don't lose hope.*

Alia sighed. She drummed her fingers on the desk. Out of ideas, her mind wandered. Jorge Moreau ... curiosity getting the better of her, she did a quick search on 'vineyards in Bordeaux'. Maison du Moreau came up on the first page. She clicked on the link and found herself perusing a sleek and fancy website. The winery was a sizeable operation: seventeen hectares of land producing one hundred thousand bottles of wine a year. One hundred thousand – that was an awful lot of corks. They also rented out accommodation: fancy rooms in a converted stone barn, luxury pods in a glamp-site next to a river. According to the 'Meet the Team' page, it was owned and run by Jorge's two brothers. One small, irrational part of Alia's brain was pleased to see they were not nearly as handsome as their younger sibling.

She leaned back in her chair while she sipped her coffee. Yet he'd given up all that to live in a van? Hmmm. She could see the appeal of travelling – just think of all the places you could go – but what about practicalities? Where did he wash? And shower? He looked quite well turned out, even in his work clothes. Maybe he had an outdoor shower hooked up to the water system in the van. Hands wrapped around her mug, Alia played a movie in her mind: Jorge showering in the shade of the olive tree on a hot summer night, lathering himself up with a big floppy sponge. Soapy water was running down the cleft of his back and onto his shaven thighs. She'd returned to ask him a few more questions, caught him unawares.

Hey, Jorge – I need to ask you some more questions.

Sure, he would say. *But can you give me a hand with this first?* And then he would toss her his big soapy sponge …

Realising she was grinning like a nutcase, Alia snapped out of it. She put down her mug and went back to the computer.

———

The auberge was the only place in the village that sold cigarettes and so, despite the risk of awkwardness – *you didn't like our accommodation, Madame? Our beds are not good enough for you, is that it?* – Margot stepped into the lobby. Fortunately, the desk was unmanned so she nipped through to the adjoining bar and waited at the tobacco counter. Then her luck ran out as the woman who'd previously checked her in came to serve. Margot purchased twenty *Gitanes* and left with a terse exchange of smiles.

Several white vans were parked in the square and it looked a flea market was being set up. Margot took Erec's photo out of her bag and went to ask around.

No one recognised him. Apart from one old gent who claimed he saw him delivering vegetables from the back of a van every Friday morning, wore a patch over one eye, and went by the name 'Jacques Cousteau'. Margot smiled politely. Every village had one.

She switched her attention to the stalls. Amongst the many items of bric-a-brac for sale was a table full of pewter and silverware. An ornate silver centrepiece caught her eye; specifically, the crest – two gold swans behind a decorative shield. Margot frowned.

"Could I take a look at that, please?" She said to the middle-aged woman behind the table.

The woman carefully picked up the centrepiece and handed it over. "That's solid silver. Nineteenth Century."

Closer up, Margot was certain it was the same crest she'd seen on a silver platter at the villa Belle Époque. If it was genuine it would be worth thousands, yet they had it priced at just two hundred euros.

Margot continued to hold onto it. "Do you mind if I ask where you got this?"

The woman called to a man stood next to a white van who promptly came over. He seemed quite affable at first, but when the woman relayed Margot's question his manner turned less friendly. "Not sure. I would have to check."

He reached out and took it from her, then stared until Margot got the message.

Oh yes – she got the message, all right. Margot went straight back to the police house.

Entering via the front gate, she approached the door though didn't go in. Listening from the threshold, she could hear Alia in the office, tapping at her keyboard. Margot silently turned around, went back to the track, and hastened down to the garage. She didn't like going behind their backs like this but Didier was up to something and she was determined to find out what.

The doors to the garage were secured with the chain and padlock. Exploring around the left-hand side, Margot discovered a personnel door, also locked. Next to it was a small window, but the glass had been covered with black-out film and it was impossible to see in.

She quickly returned to the house and this time snuck into the kitchen. Margot's fingers traced the key-rack for anything that resembled a padlock key. Finding three likely candidates, she carefully unhooked them.

But back at the garage, none of them opened the padlock on the chain. Cursing her bad luck, she tried the personnel door instead, and flinched when the first key she tried turned through a full 360. Nerves tingling, she carefully removed the padlock. How would she explain herself if Alia or Didier caught her right now? All the trust she'd established would be gone in an instant. Reaching inside, she flicked on the light.

A pair of fluorescent tubes flickered into life. Margot stepped into a space that was warm but damp. The garage was rudimentary in construction: a dirt floor, a corrugated iron roof, a patchwork of timber and concrete panels for the walls. A smell of either oil or mould seemed to emanate from every surface.

After standing still and surveying the space for several moments, Margot moved towards the rear where a tarpaulin covered a lumpy pile of objects. Firewood logs had been placed on top to hold it down, and it took her a while to free a corner. Her eyes widened as she peeled it back. Stacked on edge were a number of paintings in fancy gold frames. They were too tightly wedged to extract one, but if the frames were anything to go by they were quality items. Margot removed another log and pulled the tarpaulin back a further metre or so. Three packing crates were revealed. Two were fully nailed down but the lid on the third was loose. She moved the lid to one side, and began pulling out the straw packaging until something metallic caught the light. Lifting out a silver candlestick, she observed the same swan and shield crest as she'd seen on the centrepiece. She dug down further and uncovered a piece of majolica. Checking the underside, she saw they bore the same Sarreguemines stamp she'd observed on the crockery Madame Baudet had been cleaning. Margot's jaw dropped. What on earth had he been up to?

She was so engrossed in what she'd been doing she didn't hear the footsteps until it was too late. By the time she did turn around, Didier was already looking in from the door.

17

The expression on Didier's face went through a series of changes: first surprise; then anger; and finally what appeared to be relief. For many moments he and Margot stared at each other, locked in a moment of time. Margot was the first to come to her senses and she grabbed one of the candlesticks.

"These are from the Belle Époque." She held it in the air between them like the object itself were his accuser. "I saw one just like it in the dining room."

Didier didn't move, seemingly struck dumb.

"Well?" Margot snapped, fighting a rising tide of anger. If he wasn't going to be mad about this then she sure as hell was. "Are you going to tell me what they're doing here?"

He shook his head. "It's not what it looks like."

"Isn't it? I've just been to the market. Someone was selling a matching silver centrepiece."

"Please, Margot. I'll explain, I promise. But don't tell Alia."

"What on earth have you been up to?"

"It's a long story."

"Then you'd better start talking."

"Just promise me you won't tell Alia."

"You should have thought of that before."

"I know. You're right. But before you do anything just listen to what I have to say."

The candlestick was growing heavy in Margot's hand so she put it down. She waited, but Didier had suddenly turned mute again. "Well? I'm listening."

"It wasn't stealing."

"Erm, taking something that doesn't belong to you – I think most people would call that stealing."

"Then call it retribution."

"For whom?"

"Gaston and Madame Baudet. After the way the Deverauxs treated them it was the least they deserved."

The wind was suddenly taken out of Margot's sails. Now it began to make sense. "The unpaid wages?"

He nodded. "Amélie Deveraux owes them thousands. You really think she and Pascal should get away with it?"

"It's still theft."

"So is taking someone's time without paying them for it. Have you any idea what Madame Baudet went through? She has a sister with MS. The care home charge a small fortune. When the Deverauxs stopped paying what was she meant to do – just leave her to suffer?"

With all that furniture lying around the villa, unused and unwanted, who could blame her for giving in to temptation? Margot sat down on the edge of the packing crate and sighed.

"And the lies they told about Gaston," Didier went on, coming to her side. "They knew what damage they'd done yet none of them ever tried to make amends. That's pure wickedness."

"So what's your role in all of this?"

"Madame Baudet chooses which items to take. She's always moving things around so it's not like anyone's going to notice.

She stores them in one of the old stables, or if it's heavy, Gaston and I help move it. Then every so often I do a collection in the van."

"How long has it been going on?"

"Three or four years."

Margot tutted. "And you, a policeman."

"Everything we took belonged to the Deverauxs," Didier protested.

"Technically, it belongs to the new owners. In the eyes of the law you were stealing from them."

"And they have so much money they can let a place like that sit empty for years." He jutted his chin angrily. "There's no way you can tell me that's right."

Margot sympathised. When the deck was stacked so heavily against some people who could blame them for breaking the rules?

"I took nothing for myself," Didier stressed. "Every centime we made went straight to Gaston and Madame Baudet."

"Where did you sell it?"

"There's a trader I know in Toulouse. No questions asked."

"And the piece I saw in the market?"

Didier shook his head, annoyed. He turned around and sat down on the lip of the crate. "That was Madame Baudet's doing. She got impatient. Started selling things without going through me."

"So that was why you were arguing the other day?"

He nodded.

"And Alia?"

His eyes snapped back to hers. "She knows nothing about any of this. I assure you, it's entirely my doing."

Margot let her eyes wander around the space, not sure what to do. She sighed again. "You can't carry on."

"I know."

"Everything that's here will need to be returned."

He nodded. "I'll start taking it back first thing in the morning. But first give me your word you won't tell Alia."

"Won't tell Alia what?"

They both looked up sharply. Alia stood in the doorway, a confused look growing on her face.

"Papa. What's going on?"

Margot and Didier rose to their feet as one. Neither of them said a word as Alia walked towards them, questioning them with her eyes. Margot automatically moved aside, letting Alia's gaze fall upon the open crate. When they still didn't react, Alia reached in and picked up the candlestick.

"What's this?" She faced her father in disbelief.

For a moment it looked like Didier might stand his ground and face up to what he'd done, but it all got too much for him. He turned on his heel and rushed out the door. Alia was all for going after him, but Margot grabbed her arm.

"Let him go."

Alia's eyes shone wildly so Margot released her, then sighed gloomily. Now she was the one with some explaining to do.

18

The clock on Alia's bedside table was showing 23:21 when her father eventually came home. Lying on her back in the dark, she listened to familiar sounds come in through her open window: the bump of the suspension as his van trundled along the track, the rattle of the chain as he unlocked the garage doors. As a little girl, she would often stand at that window, her chin barely higher than the sill, waiting for him to come home. Her father, the policeman. She would imagine he'd been out catching criminals, bundling them into the back of his van, driving them down to the cells. Now here he was: her father, the thief.

Ten minutes passed before she heard him open the kitchen door. He tried to be quiet as he ascended the stairs, avoiding the treads that creaked the most. Alia turned her head to the side and stared at the slit of light at the bottom of her door, watching the shadows of feet move outside. They'd rarely argued. She could count on the fingers of one hand the number of times she'd truly been mad at him, even as a teenager. But this was different. Her father had committed a crime and it was her duty to uphold the law.

But doesn't the child we once were still linger within us?

Doesn't it still exist somewhere in those dark recesses of our minds? She knew her father was standing there, debating whether to knock and come in. And that little girl was alive and well and calling from somewhere deep within, willing him to do so. He would sit on the edge of her bed, stroke her hair, apologise for what he'd done, and tell her that everything was going to be all right.

But little girls don't always get what they want. Alia rolled over, turning her back on the door.

Alia rose before dawn. She completed her chores and ate breakfast alone at the kitchen table, toasting some of yesterday's bread. She was busy doing the washing up when her father appeared at the door. Alia kept her back turned as he muttered a greeting. When he went out to buy bread, she migrated to her office even though it was only seven-thirty.

Margot came down a few minutes later. Alia watched her glance into the kitchen before changing course and approaching the counter. She looked in with a frown. "I thought I heard your father get up?"

"He's gone to the boulangerie."

"Have you said anything to him yet?"

Alia shook her head. After pausing a moment, Margot came closer.

"I know it's no consolation but he's promised to take everything back."

Alia clenched her jaw. She wanted to open up, was keen to tell someone how she felt, but the words wouldn't come. How could she even begin to explain how disappointed she was?

"There's no excusing what he's done, Alia, but at least his

motives were honourable. He was trying to help Gaston and Madame Baudet."

"He's been handling stolen goods! Right here, at the police house."

"I know." Margot nodded with sympathy. "It's put you in a very difficult position."

Whether or not to arrest her own father – was that what Margot meant? The very idea seemed preposterous, after everything he'd done for her. But she was a police officer. It was her duty. How could she continue in her job if she didn't act?

"Would it help if I spoke to him?"

Alia shook her head. "I'll do it. But not yet." She leaned forward on the desk, still too angry to discuss it.

Fortunately, Margot sensed she wasn't in the mood for talking and left her alone. Alia was glad to throw herself back into work.

Gégé hadn't got back to her yet so she took out her phone and sent him a text: *Did you get that email I sent yesterday?*

It was still only eight o'clock but Gégé, as ever, had his eyes on a screen. He messaged straight back: *You mean the one where you were asking me out on a date?*

Alia rolled her eyes. *No. That one ended up in my bin, oddly. I'm talking about cannabis clubs.*

Is this a side to you I've not seen before?

Alia was in no mood for playing games. *It's to do with that missing person I asked you about.*

Oh. Okay. I'm on the bus right now. I'll check when I get in.

Margot popped her head around the door to say she was going out to show Erec's photo around the village, having got distracted yesterday, so Alia went back to her own research. The Naxos had its own website. The photos of the interior showed a funky environment with brightly-coloured sofas, a pool table, and what appeared to be a tyre swing. They were perfectly upfront about what went on, even had a 'menu' of all the different reefers they had available. According to another website, there were over three hundred such clubs in Barcelona alone, rapidly establishing it as the Amsterdam of southern Europe. Alia concluded she'd lived a sheltered life because she'd never even heard of them before. The website had little in the way of detail, however, so she made herself a fresh cup of coffee and waited for Gégé to email back.

An hour later her phone pinged.

You're in luck.

Why?

Check your inbox.

Alia immediately switched to her computer and opened Mail.

The Naxos is on our records. Europol ran a big operation three years ago and our drugs brigade worked with them. They visited the Naxos and gave it a clean bill of health. What's your interest?

She emailed back: *The missing man I asked you about used to be a member. Do you know who owns the club?*

A man named Farooq Al-Said. Born in Egypt. Aged 42. He emigrated to France twenty-two years ago. As far as I can see he has no criminal record, but he was once brought in for questioning by the police in Marseilles. Suspicion of illegal money lending.

Have you got his home address?

It's the same as the Naxos.

Alia thought for a moment and then typed back: *So for these clubs to be legal everyone who goes there has to be a member? Correct?*

Correct.

Is there any way of finding a list of members?

She stared at the screen while she waited for a reply. It was 9:30. She was meant to be out with the radar gun but what the heck. The little red bubble appeared on Mail:

Your luck continues. The Barcelona police shared information with us, including a full list of members which they took from the club's computer. It's four years old but given the date of disappearance it might be useful.

Is Erec Dubious on it?

He is.

"Wow!" said Alia out loud, before realising there was no one there to hear. She was genuinely amazed by how quickly this was coming together.

Can you email me the list?

Here.

An Excel file came attached to his email. Alia immediately set it to print and then typed back: *Thanks Gégé.*

There was a tonne of information: names, telephone numbers, addresses. This would keep her busy for a while. Her phone pinged while she was busy looking through: *So when are we going on that date?*

Alia tutted, and then typed back: *Sometime after the 12th.*

Of this month?

Such poor deluded optimism.

Of never.

Peasant.

Nerd.

Smiling, Alia pocketed her phone.

She collected the printout – three pages of A4 – and laid them side by side on her desk. The list contained over a hundred names, each with a phone number and an address, though something struck her as fishy from the start. Several of the addresses were repeated. Some were to a postal box. One had even listed his place of abode as: The Grand Hotel, Barcelona. She found the entry for Erec Dubois and marked it with a highlighter pen. The address he'd given was an apartment in Sitges, not Banyuls, which was odd given he would still have been living with his mother at that time. A few entries above it was Jorge Moreau; he'd been a member a year longer than Erec and, curiously, the address he'd given was the same apartment in Sitges.

Alia thought about that for a while and then emailed Gégé again:

Could you check if anyone on this list has a criminal record?

Five minutes later he replied: *I can, but if they're Spanish nationals it may take some time.*

Do what you can. Why do so many of the addresses look fake?

The rules are you have to give an address in Spain when you join. If you're not Spanish I'm guessing people put down any old address.

And no one checks?

Such is life.

On a hunch, she typed back: *how difficult would it be to cross reference the names on the list with your missing persons?*

You do realise I have other things to do?

I might reconsider about that date ...

It would not be easy.

The time period I'm interested in is seven years ago. Would that narrow it down?

I've lost count of the number of favours you'll owe me when this is done.

Alia left that without a reply and sat waiting. Several minutes passed during which her inbox remained inactive and she began to fear she'd reached the limit of Gégé's goodwill. A notification popped up. SPAM. She immediately deleted it. Then finally a reply:

I need to go and check manually. I'll get back to you.

She responded with a text: *thanks*.

She'd been so engrossed in what she'd been doing she barely registered the sound of her father's van going by and only looked up when she heard the click of the gate. It was ten-thirty and she'd been at her desk for three hours solid.

There was his usual little groan as he took off his shoes by the back door. Alia's spine tingled as she heard him enter the kitchen. The elephant in the room was back.

He called out to ask if she wanted something to drink. Alia leaned in closer to her computer screen, pretending she hadn't heard. She assumed he would get the message and back off, but when she didn't give him an answer he came into the hall.

"Alia – I asked if you wanted something to drink."

Every nerve in her body was set in a state of alarm. How dare he talk to her? Her father, the thief. She tutted. Could he not just go away?

Her father sighed. "Look, Alia. I'm sorry. I truly am. I've thought it through and you must take whatever action you think is necessary. And if that means reporting me then so be it."

She pointedly angled away. Finally, after an excruciating few moments, he took the hint and left.

To avoid the awkwardness of having her father make lunch for her, Alia went into the kitchen at eleven-thirty and made herself a sandwich of cheese, spring onion and cucumber. She left the knife and the crumbs on the breadboard. Back at her computer, a reply had come through from Gégé:

I've found some old missing persons reports. Remind me again why you're doing this.

It's confidential. If I told you I would have to shoot you. And the mood I'm in, you wouldn't want to tempt me. I'm guessing it was a waste of time ...

Just the opposite.

How do you mean?

Are you ready for this?

Losing patience, Alia was tempted to pick up the phone and call him. Instead, she typed back: *WHAT?*

I sent the list of members to my friend in Marseilles. So far, we've checked seventy-five names and found missing person reports on two of them. Along with Erec Dubois that makes three. All three lived within a 50km radius of Perpignan. What are you onto here?

"Bonjour."

Alia looked up as the postman came in. He dropped a bundle of letters onto the counter. "Is Didier around? I wondered if he might want to go fishing at the weekend."

Alia rolled her eyes. Could he not see she was busy? "He's out." She snatched the mail from the top.

"Could you tell him I asked?"

"Maybe."

The postman went off in a huff. Shaking her head, Alia went back to her computer.

Not sure what it means yet. Could you send me all the info you have on them please?

Five minutes later six attachments landed in her inbox. Alia set them to print and soon had thirty-seven pages laid out before her. She was running out of space on the desk so she transferred everything to the floor. Photographs, ages, approximate heights and weights. The other two missing men were Tristrand Lamar from Béziers and Nicholas Blanchard from Narbonne. Aged thirty and thirty-two respectively at the time they'd gone missing. Alia retrieved the photo of Erec Dubois and placed all three in a row. Three missing men, all of them members of the Naxos. Something was definitely going on here.

On a roll, she went into the cupboard with the filing cabinets and pulled the file on the villa Belle Époque murders. The folder with the mortuary reports was still on top, and although she knew most of the stats from memory, she checked them against the figures on the missing persons' reports. And suddenly everything around her turned a little bit surreal. Maybe on some level it she already expected it, but Alia was still amazed when the evidence popped out in front of her.

The stats on the other two missing men matched two more of the victims.

19

It looked at first as if Alia had gone out and a winged intruder taken over the office – that would explain the rustling Margot could hear coming from the other side of the counter. But when Margot peered around the corner she found Alia instead, down on her hands and knees, adrift in a sea of papers.

"It looks like someone's been busy."

Alia blinked, red-eyed and weary. She looked at Margot as if she were the first human being she'd seen all day. "Sorry. I got distracted." She began picking up the papers.

Margot worked her way through to the chair. "What have you been up to?"

"I think I've found something."

"Ooh, go on. Don't leave me in suspense."

Together, they made some space on the desk. When Alia had found the papers she was looking for, Margot watched her line them up in a row.

"I asked my friend Gégé to do some checks on the cannabis club. He managed to get hold of a list of members." Alia picked up one of the sheets of paper. "It's four years out of date but it seems genuine. Look who's on there."

Margot took the sheet and glanced through. The name Erec Dubois had been highlighted, along with Jorge Moreau. She set the paper down. "Go on."

"So, then I asked him to cross-check these names with any missing persons he could find. These two—" Alia indicated two headshots "—were both reported missing during a period of seven to nine years ago. Tristrand Lamar and Nicolas Blanchard. Along with Erec Dubois that makes three young men, all of whom went missing during the time period we're looking at. And all three were members of the Naxos."

Margot looked at the information more closely. "How many members are on this list?"

"One hundred and seventeen."

"Well that can hardly be a coincidence."

"No. And I've checked their vital statistics against the mortuary reports of the Belle Époque victims. Tristrand Lamar matches victim two and Nicolas Blanchard victim five." She rubbed her head. "I know it's not conclusive proof but it looks like something is going on, doesn't it? And the dates fit. Look." Alia passed her yet another sheet, this one written in her own hand, where she'd plotted out a timeline.

"Have you checked to make sure neither of them has turned up since?"

"Not yet. But I've got the phone numbers of the people who reported them missing."

There was silence while Margot considered everything Alia had presented to her, her mind taking time to process what this meant. Could this be the breakthrough they'd been hoping for? She gave Alia a look of mild astonishment.

"But if this all checks out, that's three of the victims you've identified."

"I think so."

"This is inspired work, Alia."

Alia looked away, suddenly bashful. "Gégé helped a lot."

"But you figured it out." Margot couldn't resist giving her a hug. "Okay. Well, we'll need to do some background checks."

"I'll see what Gégé can find out."

"And this club, the Naxos ..." Margot tapped her fingernail on the counter. "What else do we know about it?"

Alia located another file. "It's owned by a man named Farooq Al-Said. He has a wife and three children. He started the club fifteen years ago. Before that it's believed he was a loan shark, though he was never prosecuted."

"A loan shark?"

They were interrupted by Didier coming in through the front door. He paused on the threshold, wiping his feet on the mat. "Bonjour."

Margot tipped her head, but Alia turned away and busied herself with her papers. Silence fell like a huge great weight.

"Lémieux gave me some of his cheese." Didier held up a small package. "I thought we might have some for lunch."

Margot gave him a sympathetic look. "I think Alia's already eaten, and I'm still full from breakfast. Sorry."

"Oh. Well, never mind," Didier nodded slowly. Having seen the lie of the land he retreated to the kitchen.

The silence remained in his wake, killing any prospect of regaining their high spirits. Margot looked up at the ceiling, and exhaled. If there was one thing she hated it was a bad atmosphere. She got to her feet and nudged Alia's arm.

"Come on, you. Let's go and sit by the river for a while. You look like you could do with a break."

They picked a few apricots on their way out and then went down to the river via the gap in the screen of tall grasses. For a while they just sat on the bank and ate, entranced by the sound of the water. After perhaps five minutes Margot turned to look at her young companion: hunched up, eyes down, gnawing the last few strands of flesh from her apricot stone.

"How long has your father been a policeman?"

"Thirty-five years."

"And in all that time has he ever broken the rules?"

Alia stopped gnawing. She drew back her arm and lobbed the stone into the river. "You think I should forgive him? Just turn a blind eye and let him get away with it?"

"No, that's not what I think. But what do you suppose would happen if you did report him? Handling stolen goods – he could go to jail for that. And do you think people would believe that *you* didn't know what was going on?"

"But I didn't," Alia protested.

"I know that, and your father knows that, but the *Police Nationale* might not see it the same way. What effect do you think that would have on your career?"

Alia picked a blade of grass and twirled it around her finger. "What career?" she mumbled gloomily.

Margot sighed. "It's your decision, Alia, but think of yourself in all of this. Tell him what you feel, make sure he knows how disappointed you are, and then move on. Life's too short."

Alia drew in a long breath, and nodded.

———

It was too nice a day to go straight back to the office so they went for a stroll upstream. When the grassy bank ended, they stepped down into the water and picked their way through the shallows. Margot's thoughts quickly came back to the case. The cannabis club could be the key to all this and she was itching to do something more hands-on.

"Why don't we go and check out this club ourselves?"

Alia looked surprised. "To Barcelona?"

"Mm-hmm."

"Shouldn't we report it to the police?"

"We can, and we will, in time. But since we haven't got any hard evidence yet they might not do a great deal. The bodies will have to be formally identified, they'll have to liaise with the Spanish police. All of that could take months. And in the meantime, whoever's responsible might just take note and disappear." Some rocks were blocking the way forward so Margot paused and looked for a route to climb up. She crossed a slippery slope, and then leapt onto a nice sturdy boulder. She waited for Alia to catch up. "But besides that, you did all the detective work. Why should you let someone else take the credit?"

"But we have no jurisdiction."

"I know. But there's nothing to stop me going there as a civilian."

"But you have to be a member to get in. And you need an existing member to propose you."

Margot faced her. "That's very true," she smiled. "And we know just the place to find an existing member, don't we?"

The speed with which Alia blushed suggested her thoughts had already galloped on ahead.

Not wanting to ask Didier to look after the station while they were gone, Alia said they would have to wait until after work before going to the winery. She bolted the front door at six o'clock sharp, hurried upstairs to change out of her uniform, and was ready to go at six-fifteen.

The sun was dipping behind the mountains when they

drove into Banyuls. The winery was closed; the car park empty. As soon as they were out of the car, Margot paused to light up.

"So where's this van of his?"

"It's just up here."

"Does he live on his own?"

"I think so."

An image came into Margot's head: a tatty old transit with a grubby mattress in the back. She could imagine the kind of entertaining he got up to in there.

The road was deserted so they walked along the centre of the tarmac, surrounded by the chirp of cicadas. Once past the gate that led down to the vines, they continued into open countryside. It looked like they were heading into the middle of nowhere, but soon the sound of soft music drifted by. A small light was flickering on the other side of a hedgerow, and the aroma of burning charcoal suggested a barbecue. Alia turned to go through a gap in the hedge, but Margot touched her arm. Sniffing the air, she picked out another odour: the woody scent of marijuana. She held a finger to her lips and then quietly took the lead.

They walked quickly through the long grass, honing in on the van in the corner, but despite Margot's attempt at subterfuge there was no way they could approach without being seen: Jorge was relaxing on a deckchair beside his barbecue, happily smoking a joint while he watched them draw near. When they reached the light cast by the glowing coals, he clamped the roll-up between his lips and gave them a jokey salute.

"*Bon soir, Madame. Mademoiselle.*" He took the reefer from his mouth and slowly exhaled. "How nice to see you both again."

Margot gave him an up-and-down look, unimpressed. He was wearing pink flip-flops, a flowery vest, khaki cargo shorts. "Quite the hippy vibe you've got going on."

"Thank you."

"You do know smoking cannabis is illegal in France?"

He tutted theatrically. "Well, what can I say – you've got me banged to rights." He clamped the roll-up between his lips and offered up his wrists for handcuffing. "Are you going to arrest me right here or drag me down to the station and beat a confession out of me?"

Margot narrowed her eyes at him. She moved round to the opposite side of the barbecue and looked in through the open side door of the van. It wasn't quite the slum she'd expected – in fact, far from it: he'd got a comfy bed in there, pretty little lights, all the mod cons. Still, the bed was big enough for two. No doubt the rear suspension had been given a good workout in its time. The music was coming from an integrated speaker system: a kicked-back version of *Wild Horses* by The Rolling Stones.

She turned back to his cooking area. He'd made up some skewers of vegetables and meat and was laying them on the grill. An open bottle of red wine sat on the table at his side along with one mug, a citronella candle, an open book, face down. "So this is how you spend your evenings: smoking weed and reading—" she picked up the book and looked at the open page. Seriously? "—Tolstoy?"

"That's not illegal as well, is it?"

It would be if Margot had her way.

"And as for smoking weed," he went on. "It's far less harmful than those things." He pointed at the cigarette Margot was still holding between her fingers.

Margot looked down on him, in no mood for a debate. She replaced the book on the table.

"Perhaps we should have a look inside your van. See what else we might find."

"How about a truce instead?" Jorge said. He had a long pull on his joint and then tossed what was left onto the charcoal. His eyes moved pointedly to her cigarette.

Margot really wanted to dislike him. There had always been something about hippies she found irritating, despite admiring many of their values. Life just wasn't that simple. But after a little consideration, she had another draw on her cigarette and then tossed it onto the hot coals. She smiled wryly. "I hate to think what your food's going to taste like."

She gave Alia a small nod and they made themselves more comfortable. Margot sat down on the sill of the van door while Alia settled on the log. Jorge got up and switched off the music.

"So, are we straight now?"

"That depends."

"On what?"

"On how cooperative you decide to be."

He took a bottle of beer from the fridge and then dropped back down into his deckchair. He flipped off the cap and had a swig. "I'm listening."

"The Naxos."

"What about it?"

"How often do you go?"

He shrugged. "Once a month; once every two months. Depends."

"Do you know the owner?"

"Farooq? Yeah; he's usually around."

"How well do you know him?"

Fat from the beef on the skewers started dripping onto the coals, filling the air with fragrant smoke, so he leaned forward to give them a turn. "Not that well. We have a chat every now and again. Why?"

"What kind of person is he?"

Jorge took another swig of beer. "Never really thought about it."

"Friendly, cheerful, morose," Margot prompted.

"Business-like. Kind of serious. I think he owns a couple of other clubs in the city."

"Would you trust him?"

He seemed to find that amusing. "Not with my last euros, I wouldn't. But then, like I said, I don't really know him. I'm not one to judge."

"Did Erec know him?"

"No better than I did. Although ..." He broke off, looking like a lightbulb had just gone off inside his head.

"What?"

Jorge put down his bottle, smiling cheekily. "Actually, yes. Erec had a bit of a run-in with him." Out of habit, he reached into the side pocket of his shorts and took out a worn leather tobacco pouch. Catching Margot's eye, however, he had second thoughts and put it on the table instead.

"What kind of a run-in?"

"He went out with his daughter for a while."

Alia leaned in. "Erec was dating Farooq's daughter?"

"I wouldn't call it dating. She was engaged to someone else at the time."

"How did that pan out?" Margot asked.

"They still got married in the end so I suppose you could say no harm was done."

"But did Farooq know?"

"Oh yeah. It all got a bit unpleasant for a while, but then Erec met someone else and it seemed to fizzle out."

"How long was this before Erec went missing?"

He puffed out his cheeks, thinking. "It was not long after we first started going down there so, dunno, about a year. Six months."

Margot pondered that. Darkness had fallen and the midges were starting to bite so Jorge flicked his lighter and lit the citronella candle.

"Alia's been doing some background checks." Margot looked over and gave her companion a nod.

"Does the name Tristrand Lamar mean anything to you?" she asked.

Jorge thought about it, then shook his head.

"Nicolas Blanchard?"

Another blank look. "Can't say I've ever heard of them. Why?"

"They were both members of the Naxos. At least, they were, seven years ago. They and Erec all went missing during the same two-year period."

For the first time Jorge looked concerned. "And they've not been seen since?"

"No."

"You think they're linked?"

"It's possible they're—"

"That's all we know at the moment," Margot interrupted. She didn't want to reveal too much. Not until they'd got their facts straight.

There was quiet for a moment. The skewers were spitting again so he took them off the heat and moved them to one side. Margot leaned forward. "I'd like to go down there."

"The Naxos?" He sounded surprised.

"Yes."

"What for?"

"To have a look around. Find out what kind of man Farooq is."

The light from the barbecue was casting shadows on Jorge's face. It was impossible to see clearly but he appeared to be frowning. "You mean you really think Farooq had something to do with Erec's disappearance?"

"That's what we'd like to find out."

"As in, go undercover?"

"Nothing as official as that."

"Both of you?"

"Just me. If anything goes wrong I don't want Alia getting into trouble."

"Goes wrong ... what are you expecting could go wrong?"

Margot leaned back and exhaled. He was more astute than he looked. "Do you always ask so many questions?"

"When someone's asking me to put my neck on the block then yes."

"You don't need to get involved. All I want is for you to get me in."

"The kind of people who run these clubs aren't the kind of people you want to mess with."

"I thought you said the Naxos was legitimate."

"It is, but they won't take kindly to people snooping around."

"I know what I'm doing."

He sat back in his seat and picked up his beer bottle. During the pause, his eyes flicked back and forth between the two of them. "Okay. Say I do get you in; what's in it for me?"

"If you get me in then maybe Alia will overlook what we found you smoking when we came up here just now. If you don't, then, well ... who knows?"

He laughed sardonically. "I like this: good cop/bad cop."

"Is that a yes?"

"Maybe."

"So how does it work?"

"I'd have to make an appointment with Farooq."

"And then?"

"And then we'd go down there and fill in the membership form."

"Farooq makes the decision?"

"It's his club."

"And if he agrees?"

"If he agrees, you pay the membership fee and you're in. But you can't just go round asking questions."

"I'm not stupid."

"If Farooq finds out you're working with the police it's me who'll suffer."

"It won't come to that."

"I hope not."

There was a pause.

"Well?" Margot said. "Do we have a deal?"

He picked up one of the skewers and placed it on a plastic plate. He looked Margot in the eye while he licked his fingers, seeming to relish making her wait. "Don't suppose I have much of a choice, do I?"

Smart boy.

"How soon can you get an appointment?" Alia asked.

"Give me your number and I'll text you."

Alia reached for her phone but Margot gave him her number instead. She hadn't missed the furtive glances between the two of them. She got to her feet.

"Thank you. We'll let you get back to your Tolstoy."

He reached for his tobacco pouch and leaned back in his chair as they departed. "Mind how you go."

"We will," Margot said, and soon all they could see of him was the glow from his barbecue coals.

20

After dropping Margot at the gate, Alia drove down to the end of the track and parked the car. Switching off the ignition, she looked across at the garage. All this time she'd been manoeuvring in and out of this space with those stolen goods right under her nose. How could she have been so stupid?

It was eleven o'clock and the moon lit her way through the garden. The moment she stepped into the kitchen, Margot handed her a note.

"I found it on the counter."

I made ratatouille. The pot's in the oven and there's some homemade bread under the tea towel.

Signed: her father, the thief.

Normally he would stay up whenever she was out late, but there was no sign of him downstairs. Alia went into the hall and sent a glance up the stairs. The light was on in his room, though she couldn't hear him snoring.

Returning to the kitchen, she took the ratatouille out of the oven. It had been made with care, the slices of tomatoes, aubergine, courgette and squash laid in perfect concentric rings.

They both instinctively inhaled as Alia set it down on the counter. It did smell nice, but she had no appetite.

"That was sweet of him," Margot said as Alia moved away to the table.

"Have some if you like. I'm not hungry."

"You sure?"

Alia took a seat. All she wanted to do was go to bed and hide under the covers.

"It looks too good to cut into," Margot said, but nevertheless scooped some onto a plate. She cut a slice of bread from the loaf and then brought it to the table with one of the bottles of wine they'd bought on their way back. "I can see now why you were so keen to go back to the winery." Her eyes were twinkling mischievously.

Alia straightened her back. "I don't know what you're talking about."

Margot looked sceptical. "I saw the way you were looking at him."

"I wasn't!" Alia protested, but couldn't help giving herself away with a grin.

"He certainly liked you."

"You think so?"

"He couldn't stop smiling at you."

"I think he smiles at everyone."

"Don't put yourself down. You're an attractive young woman – why wouldn't he be keen on you?"

If only it were that easy. Alia laid her hands flat on the table and rested her chin on her knuckles. She always felt clumsy around men she liked, never knew what to say.

"He only lives in a van because he chooses to."

Margot blew on her forkful of ratatouille. "And why's that?"

"His family own a wine estate near Bordeaux. He could have inherited it, but he chose to let his brothers run it instead."

"I suppose that's admirable, if it makes him happy." The food must have been too hot because Margot spoke in a strained voice. She swallowed, and then had a drink of water. She tutted wryly. "Handsome, talented, kind to boot – some people are so perfect it makes you want to scream." She smiled. "I'm joking. I'm sure he's very nice." She poured some wine into each of the glasses and then leaned across the table. "Listen. We need to stay focussed for now, but when this is over why don't you ask him out?"

Alia's heart began to pound. "I couldn't do that."

"Why not?"

She'd never really had a proper boyfriend. A couple of casual ones at uni, a boy at the lycée who'd only wanted to hold hands. "I never know what to say."

"Just say whatever comes into your head."

Usually that was something silly. Or gibberish.

"Don't look so glum!" Margot chastised. "You've got a lot going for you."

"It's easy for you, you're so stylish. And you know about wine and things."

"I'm also twice your age."

"You don't look it."

"That's very kind but trust me, while youth's on your side you need to make the most of it."

"I suppose so."

"There's no suppose about it. And as for knowing about wine …" Margot slid one of the glasses towards her. "The best way of learning about it is by drinking it."

She raised her glass and they clinked.

———

But Alia should have known better. Twenty minutes later the wine had gone straight to her head and the room was spiralling without mercy. Surprised to find so little wine had been put into her glass, Alia had knocked it back in two swift swallows – did Margot really think she couldn't handle a quarter of a glass?

"You might want to go easy on this one," Margot had said, pouring another mouthful into the empty glass. "I probably should have explained – Banyuls is a dessert wine. You usually only sip it."

"Oh." Was that why her bones had turned to jelly and she was currently sliding out of her seat?

In her entire life Alia had only been drunk on three occasions. This time she took one sip and returned the glass to the table.

She reached for her bottle of water instead, but in doing so her forearm caught the edge of a pile of books. As it toppled, a domino effect spread across the table. Much silliness ensued as they flailed like octopuses trying to stop everything from falling.

They must have been making too much noise to hear her father come down the stairs and Alia was startled when she turned to find him standing on the threshold. He seemed bemused to see her in such a state.

"What's going on here?"

"Sorry," Margot replied, picking up a fallen book. "We didn't mean to disturb you."

He shook his head. "It's all right. I couldn't sleep." He went to the sink to fill a glass with water.

Silence trailed in his wake. For a while Alia kept her eyes on the table, but as the anger grew inside her she stared at the back of his head. Her father, the thief.

"Did you like the ratatouille?"

Even when he turned around, Alia stared back at him. How

could he talk of ratatouille after what he'd done? Conscious of the fact they were both now looking at her, waiting for an answer, Alia faltered. "I wasn't hungry," she mumbled.

"No problem. It will keep for a few days."

He wished them goodnight and started to leave, but this time Alia wasn't letting him go. Now they'd been stirred, the emotions that had been brewing inside her needed venting. She slid her chair out from the table. The legs scraped the floor so harshly that Didier stopped dead in his tracks, spooked like a deer.

"Did you really think that cooking a ratatouille was going to make this better?" Alia made an exaggerated sweeping gesture with her arm that probably made her look quite silly but she was too steamed up to care. Her father shuffled nervously.

"No. Of course not. I just—"

"I looked up to you, Papa!" Emboldened by the sound of her own raised voice there was no stopping her now. "All my life you've been the one I turned to for advice. How many times have you said to me: 'Oh no, Alia. The law is the law. There can never be any exceptions.'" The booming voice she put on was a poor impersonation of him, but so what?

"Alia—"

"And then I find out you've been doing *this* behind my back."

"If you'd just lis—"

"And for all these years! How can I ever trust you again?"

"I've let you down. I know that. But if you could ju—"

Alia held up her hand. "So no, Papa! I'm not going to report you. I'm not going to tell the mayor. But first thing tomorrow you'll take everything out of that garage that doesn't belong to you and you'll return it to the villa. And if the mayor finds out and I lose my job, then so be it."

"Al—"

"That's my decision."

He stood there, considering for a few moments, before dolefully nodding his head. Eyes down, he left the room without another word. And not a moment too soon – thirty seconds later Alia was throwing up in the sink.

21

At noon on Saturday Jorge messaged to say he'd made an appointment at the Naxos for nine o'clock. Deciding it too risky to use the police car, Margot called a rental firm and had them bring a car to the police house for five.

Didier had spent the morning clearing out the garage and returning the stolen goods to the villa. The air between he and Alia had thawed somewhat, but life in the household was far from back to normal.

"Have a good night," he said when Margot came downstairs after getting ready. She'd only told him the bare bones of what they were up to, presenting it more as a Saturday night out.

"Don't wait up," Margot said.

Alia conceded a small smile on their way out.

It was dark when they got to the winery. The air pressure was falling and a string of *tormentas* – thunderstorms – were forecast to move in overnight. Ominous black clouds were already gathering in the west.

Alia parked so that they could sit in the car and still see the road. Two minutes after sending him a text, a shadowy figure appeared, flinching when Alia flashed her headlights.

Thankfully he'd smartened himself up: untucked cotton shirt, a pair of designer jeans. A smell of sandalwood came in with him as he got into the back of the car. His head popped up between the two front seats. "You both look nice."

"I take it Farooq had no objections?"

"Nah, he was cool."

"Who did you say I was?"

"I told him the truth: I said you were a couple of undercover cops checking out a string of missing persons, all of them linked to the club."

He managed to keep a straight face almost long enough for Margot to be taken in. But then he grinned. "Only joking. I said you were a friend of my Mum's."

Margot rolled her eyes. She got the feeling it was going to be a long night.

They took the route north and looped around to pick up the autoroute at Le Boulou. The Saturday night traffic was light, making progress swift. The bright lights of the city soon drew near and by eight o'clock they were cruising one of the great thoroughfares, six lanes of traffic and pavements lined with plane trees.

Jorge navigated. He claimed to know a quick route into the centre and took them along a confusing series of back streets. When he finally told Alia to pull up, Margot had lost her bearings completely.

"We'll have to walk it from here," Jorge said, clicking himself out of his seatbelt. "The streets around the club are pedestrianised."

The bright white lights of a deli shone through Margot's window. She took out her phone and studied Maps. They were parked just a few streets away from the cathedral, and no more than a block from La Rambla. The Naxos was located a few hundred metres to the south, in the maze of tiny streets that made up the Gothic Quarter. It was still only eight-thirty so they remained in their seats.

"What's Alia going to do?"

"Stay in the car," Margot replied.

"I'm your getaway driver," Alia said and the two of them shared a sneaky smile. Oh, the joys of infatuation.

"Have you got a friend-finder on your phone?"

Alia dug it out of her pocket. "I think so."

"Let's add each other. Then you can track us."

A few taps and they were done.

"What about me?" Jorge asked.

"Don't worry," Margot said, dropping her phone into her purse. "I won't be letting you out of my sight."

She bent her neck to look up through the windscreen. So far, the rain had held off, but the sky didn't look promising. According to the forecast, *las tormentas* were due to hit in less than an hour. She checked her face in the mirror and then cast one final look at Alia. "You will be all right on your own, won't you?"

Alia nodded. "How long do you think you'll be?"

"No more than an hour or two."

"We'll bring you back a cookie, if you're good," Jorge said and Margot promptly got out of the car.

She paused on the pavement to light a cigarette and then shook out the match as they walked.

"There's to be no fooling around when we get there." She maintained a brisk and business-like pace. "You'll do exactly what I say and let me do the talking."

"So what exactly do you want me to do?"

Shut up and look pretty, Margot was tempted to say.

"Just do what's needed to get me in and then we'll play it by ear."

He clearly wasn't used to moving so fast and Margot was

forced to slow down. When she turned to look back at him, he gave her a discontented look.

"Are you always this strict on a night out?"

"Lucky for you you'll never find out."

They turned a corner onto La Rambla. The famous thoroughfare was awash with people enjoying the warm evening air. Astute street vendors had switched from selling knockoffs and glowsticks to umbrellas and ponchos. A noise that could have been thunder grumbled in the distance.

They paused to let a scooter go by and then turned into a side street. Margot was still leaving the navigating to her companion. "I presume we're going straight there?"

"You mean you still don't trust me?"

A decision on that was pending.

They entered a small square, crowded with palm trees. Margot had only ever been to the Gothic Quarter once before and that had been in daylight. At night it was a completely different beast: a labyrinth of long shady streets and dark unmarked alleyways. Every other property was either a bar, an eatery, or some kind of club. Exiting the square via an old stone archway, Jorge steered her down another narrow street, the buildings on either side six storeys high. And they all looked so similar that after two or three turns Margot was lost completely.

They arrived in a small inner courtyard, away from the hustle and bustle. Facing a pair of big black doors, Margot eyed him dubiously. "Is this it?"

It was all rather anonymous. Nothing about it said cannabis club. But then perhaps that was the point. Margot stepped back to gaze up at the façade. A line of washing was drying on the wrought-iron balcony above. Higher up, the reflected image of a TV flickered on the inside of a glazed door. It was a duality of life that had intrigued her in Paris: family life going on in apartments above the seediest of establishments.

"You ready?"

Margot stubbed out her cigarette and crumpled the butt into her portable silver ashtray. "Never been readier."

He checked over his shoulder and then pushed the buzzer.

A girl with a face-full of piercings came to the door. She opened it just wide enough for Jorge to show his membership card and then, everything apparently being in order, welcomed them in.

They entered a small lobby. Soft music was playing in the background, and a screen of floor to ceiling banisters separated them from the main space. The girl and Jorge greeted each other with some kind of elaborate fist bump whereas Margot got a polite nod. Margot couldn't help counting the girl's piercings: a small silver bar in her nose, a stud in each eyebrow, a gemstone in her bottom lip. Why did she suddenly feel a hundred years old?

"I'm Gina. This your first time?"

"Is it that obvious?"

"Margot's a friend of my mum's," Jorge said and the two of them grinned.

"Yes, we go way back, Jorge and I," Margot countered. "He was still in nappies when his mother and I first met. He had the cutest little bottom even then."

Happily, that shut him up.

Gina showed them through. In contrast to the unwelcoming exterior, the décor inside was vibrant and modern: orange and yellow walls, reclaimed wooden floorboards, groupings of floppy low sofas. Six or seven people were lounging around, reefers in hand, while a big screen played chilled house music videos. If she'd been expecting the atmosphere to be intimidating she couldn't have been more wrong: the vibe was laid-back and homely. Less opium den, more hipsters' kindergarten.

"Is Farooq around?" Margot asked.

"He'll be in his office. I'll take you up."

"Thank you."

They ducked their heads through a sparkly bead curtain and entered an inner lobby where the walls were decorated with glass-framed movie posters. Gina led them up two flights of stairs to a long wooden landing with only one door. The movie posters continued on every wall: many of them vintage sci-fi, others classics of French cinema. Gina knocked, leaned on the door as she opened it, and said a few words in Spanish to whoever was inside. Gaining an affirmative response, she took a step back.

"Come and see me downstairs when you're ready."

"We will."

Jorge closed the door behind them.

Farooq sat in a large leather wing chair, elbows on the desk, eyes on the screen of his phone. He didn't look much like the photo Alia had unearthed. His eyebrows seemed bushier, his face more worn. According to the file, he was forty-one years of age but the man before them looked more like fifty. The office was lit by a classic green desk lamp, and was sparsely furnished. On the wall to their right, agent Lemmy from *Alphaville* targeted them with his pistol. Without smiling, Farooq laid down his phone and indicated two chairs by the wall.

"Take a seat."

Jorge pulled them over.

"Nice place you have here," Margot said, settling in.

Farooq gazed at her but said nothing. One look at his expression was enough to tell her he wasn't going to be drawn into smalltalk.

"It's a simple procedure."

"Jorge explained it all to me."

"Can I see your ID?"

"Of course."

Margot delved into her purse. She took out her passport and handed it over. Farooq studied the photo for a few moments, scribbled something on a notepad, and then handed it back. He opened a drawer in his desk and took out a form, turned it around and placed it in front of her. He handed her a pen from his shirt pocket. "We just need a few details. Your name, and a local address."

Margot wrote down her real name. She used the address of Jorge's cousin in Sitges, as they'd agreed. She handed it back with a smile. "That was easy."

"The fee is fifty euros."

"Cash okay?"

Naturally he agreed.

She handed him some cash which he put away in a drawer. From the same drawer he took out a small plastic membership card. "The rules are printed on the back, but just to remind you, this is a social club. Our members are entitled to meet on the premises and smoke the cannabis we provide for them. Everything that goes on here is legal. The cannabis you'll be smoking has been prepared exclusively for the use of our members. Please don't take any photographs. Don't attempt to buy or sell, and don't take any of the products away with you. There's no charge for the cannabis we provide, but if you would like to leave a donation on your way out it would be very much appreciated." Like leaving a tip at the museum. "Any questions?"

"Yes," Margot said. Three people from this club went missing and ended up dead in an underground chamber – had that been a simple procedure? "You grow the marijuana yourself?"

He nodded.

"It must be a full-time job, keeping a place like this going."

Farooq continued to stare at her. There was a pause which quickly became awkward, prompting Jorge to shift on his seat. Realising she'd perhaps overstepped the mark, Margot cleared her throat. She turned to the *Alphaville* poster. "I see you like your French cinema."

He'd hardly taken his eyes off her since they'd come in but his face still gave nothing away. "They belonged to the previous owner."

"Ah, I see." Yet he'd been at this address for fifteen years. She would probably have got more joy out of a stone.

Farooq handed her the membership card. "Welcome to the Naxos."

———

Gina gave her the tour: a spiral staircase went down to a 'playzone' complete with board games and a tyre swing; at one end of the lounge, a half-glazed partition screened off a pool table while at the other end was a bar where Gina took them next. Several large jars were lined up on the counter, each one stuffed with pre-rolled spliffs. Margot read the labels: Kali Haze, Vegas, S.A.P., White Widow … Were there really so many different varieties of weed? If bongs were your thing, a selection was arranged on a shelf.

"What would you like to try?" Gina asked, taking her place behind the counter.

Jorge sat on a bar stool, instantly at home, but Margot remained standing. "What would you recommend?"

"Well, we do a variety of different strains. The Harlequin is pretty mild. It's a good one to start with."

"I think Margot would prefer something with more of a kick to it," Jorge said and Margot gave him a sidelong glance. He'd be getting a kick from her if he wasn't careful.

"I'll let you choose," she said.

"Okay. Give us two of those." He pointed to a jar labelled Cinderalla 99.

Gina took out two spliffs and passed them over. "Enjoy."

Margot held hers between the thumb and forefinger of her right hand. It was probably the largest spliff she'd ever seen in her life and she had no intention of smoking it. When Jorge lit his and reached across with the lighter, she searched for an escape.

"Fancy a game of eight-ball?" She looked him hard in the eye to make sure he got the message. Jorge briefly looked rebellious, but then snapped shut his lighter.

The pool table was in a good spot: far enough away from the other patrons to give them some privacy, but with enough visibility through the half-glazed partition to see the bar, the lobby, and the curtain that led into the back. Jorge unhooked the triangle from the wall and started to set up the balls.

"You going to smoke that at some point?"

Margot realised she was still holding the spliff like it was something she'd picked up off the street. Back at the counter, Gina seemed to be keeping an eye on her. In an effort to blend in, Margot struck a match and held the spliff to her lips long enough for it to catch light, but then set it down on the lip of an ashtray, prompting a bemused look from Jorge.

"So you'll smoke high-tar cigarettes, drink strong wine, but you won't touch cannabis?"

Margot pulled a cue from the rack, ignoring him. She picked up the cube of chalk from the edge of the table and ground it over the tip of her cue, then blew the excess dust over the front of his shirt. "Are we playing this game, or what?"

They tossed to see who would break: Margot called heads and won. She smashed open the pack, full-on, lots of topspin. When a stripe dropped into the left-centre pocket a little voice inside her squealed in delight. Moving to the opposite end of the table, she caught Jorge's look of surprise.

"You've played this game before?"

"Once or twice," she said.

They'd had a table in her sixth-form common room. A boy she didn't like had started bullying one of her friends so Margot had practised, challenged him to a strip version of the game, and got him blushing in his boxers at the next Christmas party.

"Nine-ball in the top left."

Sank.

"Thirteen in the right centre."

It came off two cushions, kissed the black, and dropped in the pocket. She smiled, pleased she hadn't lost her touch.

"Fourteen in the top right."

She leaned down to take it, but just as she swung her arm a red light flashed in the lobby, right in her line of sight. She missed the pot by the width of a ball.

"Damn!"

"Ah, bad luck." Jorge almost sounded sincere.

Margot eyeballed him, but then stepped aside. Chalking her cue, she watched through the glazed partition as Gina went down into the lobby. Jorge missed his shot, but Margot waited, watching to see who would come in. Two scrawny young hipsters appeared in the lobby, though they were not welcomed in with open arms. The sound of raised voices disturbed the laidback vibe, but the altercation was short-lived. Gina came back with the hipsters in tow, and then parted the bead curtain to usher them through.

"What was that all about?" Jorge asked, appearing at Margot's side.

"Have you seen them before?"

"Don't think so."

There was no sign of them coming back out so Margot went back to the game. She missed her intended pot, but luck was on her side and the cue ball tucked itself in behind one of her few remaining stripes, leaving him snookered. "Bad luck," she said flatly.

Jorge shook his head in disbelief.

He picked up his spliff and took his time considering his next shot. Margot did a few sums in her head: assuming each member came in once a week, smoked an average of two spliffs per night, each one containing half a gram of weed, that amounted to ... an awful of cannabis to produce in one year.

"You really think Farooq grows all this cannabis himself?"

"That's what he said."

"Is he always that chatty?"

Jorge smiled. "I suppose you have to be cagey in his line of work. After all, you are here to spy on him."

"Shush!" Margot flashed him a look of irritation. No one was within hearing distance but that didn't mean no one was listening.

Jorge made a total hash of escaping from the snooker and ended up potting the cue ball instead. Over in the lounge, Margot noticed Gina reappear through the bead curtain, alone.

"Your turn," Jorge said. He retrieved the cue ball from the dispenser and attempted to hand it over, but Margot left him holding onto it.

"Be a lamb and go ask Gina for another cube of chalk, will you?" She slipped the one they'd been using into her pocket. "And while you're there, see what that fuss was about."

He tutted. "Anything else?"

"Yes – a little less of the attitude if you don't mind."

He narrowed his eyes at her, but left the cue ball on the table while he went to ask. Two minutes later he was back, bearing a fresh cube of chalk. Margot looked at him enquiringly. "Well?"

"She said they were in last week, trying to sell some of their own gear."

"What's happening to them?"

"She sent them up to see Farooq."

"And what will he do?"

Jorge shrugged. "How should I know?"

Gina looked over from the counter, catching Margot's eye. Margot picked up her reefer and held it between her lips, though didn't inhale. She set it back down on the ashtray and then lined up a shot on the ten-ball. She attempted a cheeky double, and – *damn* – caught the jaws of the pocket instead, leaving him with an easy pot.

"What do you know about Gina?"

"Gina? She's all right."

"Does she work here full-time?"

"I presume so." Jorge got down to take his shot. "She does front of house; Farooq stays in the back."

"Does she have a stake in the club?"

"Sort of. Three-ball in the top left." He missed the easy pot, but the three-ball ball bounced all around the angles and dropped into the bottom left-hand pocket. An outrageous fluke. "She's Farooq's daughter."

Margot blinked. "What?"

He took the fresh cube of chalk and ground a little on the tip of his cue. "Gina – she's Farooq's daughter."

"His daughter?"

"Yes."

"The one Erec was seeing?"

"He's only got one."

Margot gaped at him. "Why the hell didn't you tell me this before?"

He seemed amused. Pausing to retrieve his spliff from the ashtray, he had a long lazy draw while he regarded her. "I'm telling you now, aren't I?"

Margot shook her head in dismay. Gina was still at the counter, serving one of the other patrons. Margot tried to picture the two of them together: the freckle-faced Erec, the tanned and pierced Gina. It wasn't an obvious match.

Jorge called the six-ball for the top right. The weed must have been giving him otherworldly powers because even though he missed it by a country mile the ball bounced off two cushions, kissed the black, and dropped into the bottom left. Margot ground her teeth. If they'd been playing strict rules she could have disallowed it for not going in the pocket he'd named. Her mind should have been on other things but she couldn't lose, not to him. Her eyes quickly appraised the table: he had two balls left, she had three. His were out in the open whereas hers were bunched in one corner. The only fly in the ointment from his point of view was the black which was tight against the side cushion and would require pinpoint positioning to get onto. He sank his second to last ball, smiled to himself as he got down for the one remaining. The thought of nudging his elbow briefly crossed Margot's mind (when had she become such a bad sport?) but there was no need – the ball rattled in the jaws of the pocket and stayed out.

"Ah, bad luck."

Was her sarcasm too obvious?

Margot sank the fifteen-ball, separated her final two with a containing shot that also got him snookered. He escaped, but left her with two sitting ducks, both of which she rocketed. As a final flourish, she pulled off a fantastic pot on the black – sending it spinning along the cushion for almost half the length of the table. It had just enough momentum to fall into the near-side corner pocket. Game over.

"Well done." Sportingly, Jorge shook her hand. "Another one?"

Margot smiled. All was right with the world again. "Set 'em up, Joe."

She checked her phone while he was gathering the balls.

The signal was weak, but the friend locator showed Alia was still in the car, right where they'd left her.

Someone new came in while she was chalking her cue. He must have let himself in because the red light hadn't flashed and Gina was still busy at the counter. Tall and weaselly, a look complemented by his black leather jacket, he went straight to the counter. Since Gina was still busy, he let his eyes wander, and spotting Margot at the pool table he gave her an up-and-down look.

"Who's he?"

Jorge turned to look. "The guy at the bar?"

"Mm-hmm."

"That's Marc. Gina's husband."

Margot's brain started to tick a little faster. "The one Gina was engaged to when Erec went out with her?"

"Yes."

Their eyes met again. Margot knew his type only too well – that thin opportunistic smirk on his face as if every woman he chose to look at was fair game. It made her skin crawl. She turned her back and moved out of his line of sight.

Jorge made a defensive break, glancing the cue ball off the side of the pack and bringing it back down the table. Margot played him at his own game, only she got the pace just right and left the cue ball tight on the top cushion. A perfect shot, even though her mind was on other things.

"Did Marc know Erec was the one Gina was seeing?"

Jorge paused to think about it. "If Farooq knew then Marc did. The three of them are pretty tight. Why – what are you thinking?"

Margot made sure they were still out of sight and then indicated he move closer. "Gina and Erec have an affair. Marc gets jealous. Erec disappears."

"You mean, Marc makes Erec disappear?"

"Plausible, isn't it?"

He shrugged.

"What do you know about him?"

"Nothing really. He's not the chatty sort." Now that she'd put the idea into his head, however, Jorge seemed to want to give it his full consideration. "But how would that explain the other two?"

They hadn't played a shot for a couple of minutes so Margot gave him a nudge. "Come on. Your turn."

He fumbled his next shot, leaving her with at least three easy pots, but just as Margot lined up her cue she was distracted by a movement at the counter. Marc had risen from his seat. For one alarming moment it looked like he was going to come over, but then Gina came out from behind the counter and accompanied him into the back. Having an idea, Margot returned her cue to the stand.

"Where are the toilets?"

"Down the corridor by the stairs."

"Wait here."

Leaving Jorge frowning, Margot slipped quietly through the bead curtain. The sign for the toilets pointed straight ahead, but as no one was around she paused at the bottom of the stairs. By craning her neck, she could see that the door to Farooq's office was closed. The young hipsters could have gone out the back, but something told her they were still inside. Another short corridor lay to her right at the end of which an open door was spilling out light. Margot took a few steps closer. It sounded like two people were inside, talking in low voices. Easing closer still, she was able to see in via the reflection in a poster on the opposite wall. Marc was seated in a low chair; Gina on her feet. They were speaking in Spanish, but she knew enough to understand:

"What time did you say I'd be there?"

"Ten."

"I'll go in a minute."

"You don't want to be late. You know what they're like."

"I won't."

Gina had her back to the door so Margot couldn't see what she was doing, but four soft *beeps* suggested she was opening a safe. A few moments later she turned to her side, and through the reflection Margot saw her counting a bundle of cash.

"It's all there," she said, handing it to her husband.

A noise behind her made Margot look round. She hurried back to the foot of the stairs just as a woman came out of the toilets. They passed with a smile, and Margot took cover in the ladies.

There was only one stall. She locked the door behind her and then sat down on the closed lid. It would be nice to know where Marc was going with all that cash, but equally she wanted to know what happened to the two young hipsters. Reinforcements were needed. She took out her phone and messaged Alia:

Everything okay?

Bored but ok

Would you like a small task?

Yes please

F's son in law Marc is here. He'll be leaving soon. Could you follow him and see where he goes?

Of course. What's happening

Not sure. F's daughter just gave him a bundle of cash. She's the one Erec 'dated'.

Give me a description

Tall, black hair, thin face. He's wearing a black leather coat. Looks like a weasel.

I'll wait outside and watch for him

Don't engage. Just watch from a distance.

Ok

22

The rain was falling in spits and spots when Alia got out of the car. She opened the back door, reached inside for her waterproof coat and quickly put it on. Thunder rumbled in the distance.

Ear-buds in, she followed the directions on her phone, and fifteen minutes later arrived at the pair of anonymous black doors she'd seen on her internet walkthrough. Music was spilling out of a nearby window, but there was no one in sight. The pulsing orange beacon on the friend-finder showed Margot's phone located just a few metres inside. Alia looked around. The concrete concourse offered no shelter so she ducked into a darkened recess, and waited.

Fifteen minutes later, one of the doors opened and a man came out. Everything about him said 'weasel' – *la fouine*. After glancing up at the sky, he unfolded the collar of his coat and set off. Alia counted to ten and then took up pursuit.

Wherever the man was going he was in no hurry. The rain didn't seem to bother him and he walked with his head uncovered, eschewing the shelter of the overhead balconies. After turning two corners he stopped outside a bar. He bumped fists with a man seated at a table and they chatted for a while. A little farther on he stopped again, this time in the doorway of a ramen shop. Each time, Alia tried to blend in, but with so few people on the street it wasn't easy. At one point he glanced round and seemed to look right at her, though he showed no suspicion. A few minutes later he was moving again.

They came to a larger street, and as the traffic drew to a halt the weasel nipped in front of a bus. Alia ran to catch up, and then followed him down a dark alley into a large open square. The signs told her they were in the Plaça Reial, though the square itself was deserted, the crowds having shifted to the surrounding arcades. Out in the empty square, pale yellow light from the lanterns reflected on the smooth wet slabs, while in the bars and restaurants it was standing room only. Alia stayed close as they weaved a way through, but when the weasel exited via an archway she hung back. Just around the corner he went up some steps to a door shaded by a green canopy. Above it, a neon sign spelled out the name: Hotel Santa Clara.

Alia paused at the foot of the steps, debating whether to go in. She waited half a minute and then couldn't resist.

Despite its grand location the hotel's interior was nothing to write home about. A worn carpet ran from the front door to a dark behemoth of a staircase that rose up through the bowels of the building, its elaborately curving handrail polished smooth by centuries of use. The potted plants had a layer of dust on their plasticky leaves, and a musty odour filled the air. In the concierge's cabin, a bored-looking man sat watching TV.

The only sign of life came from an opening to her left; Alia looked in to find a cosy bar, its tall windows facing one of the arcades. Two men were standing at the counter, while the weasel sat alone at a table in the corner. He looked up when Alia went in, but again showed no surprise. She ordered a beer and took a seat next to the window.

For two minutes nothing happened. Then a phone pinged on the other side of the room and Alia tilted her eyes to see the weasel tapping his screen. Five minutes later a man came in. He went straight to the weasel's table, tossed the bag he was carrying onto the empty seat between them, and then sat down. They chatted casually for a while. Alia was probably the only one to notice when a small brown package was passed between them under the table. Two minutes later, the man got up and left empty-handed. Shortly after that, the weasel followed suit, picking up the bag, casual as anything.

Alia counted ten seconds and then followed him out.

He was twenty metres away and striding purposefully along the arcade, heading towards a street full of bright lights, but when he reached the exit he halted and gazed out. The rain was coming down heavier now, pelting the footpaths with a vengeance. A crowd of noisy people walked by so Alia hid in a shop doorway. She quickly tapped out a text:

I followed him to the hotel Santa Clara near Plaça Reial. He exchanged the cash for a bag

A reply came straight back: *Where is he now?*

Back on the street. Shall I keep following?

If you can. But be careful.

ok

Alia put away her phone, but when she looked round *la fouine* had gone.

―――

Margot was 2-0 up and just about to beat him in the third when a boom outside made her think a bomb had gone off. She cocked her head. "Was that thunder?"

"Sounded like it," Jorge replied. Even through the closed front door they could hear the sound of the rain coming down.

Margot potted the black, taking the score to 3-0, but stepped aside when her phone pinged.

Jorge racked the balls. When he went break, however, Margot called him over. "Have you heard of the Hotel Santa Clara? Near the Plaça Reial."

He shook his head.

She showed him the screen of her phone. Jorge gave her a concerned look.

"You think he's buying drugs?"

Margot held a finger to her lips. She looked across at the bead curtain. There was still no sign of the two young hipsters. They'd been in Farooq's office for almost half an hour.

"We can't risk talking here," she said. "Gina keeps giving me funny looks." It wasn't her break but Margot leaned over the table and smashed open the pack. She left him with an easy pot, though Jorge didn't move. The seriousness of the situation was starting to sink in.

"Shouldn't we tell someone?"

"Like who?"

"The police."

Margot shook her head. She still hadn't told him about the link with the villa Belle Époque murders and was mindful of the fact she had no right involving him. She drew him to one side, out of sight of the counter.

"You don't have to be part of this now. You can leave if you want to."

"What about Alia."

"She knows what she's doing."

"And you?"

"Don't worry about me."

He gave it some thought. At last, a smile came back to his face.

"No, you're good," he said. "I mean, I couldn't leave a friend of my mum's to fend for herself, could I?"

Fifty metres down the street *la fouine* was walking rapidly away from her. Alia raised the hood of her coat and went after him.

The downpour had sent people scurrying for cover but the traffic on the street was still nose-to-tail. When a gap opened up, the weasel ran across. Caught unawares, Alia was slow to catch up and by the time she'd crossed over he'd gone down another short street. They walked under some scaffolding; crossed La Rambla where the crowds remained undeterred. Alia tried not to look spooked when he paused at the end of a line of parked scooters and stared back at her. Head down in her waterproof coat, he surely couldn't have recognised her.

He crossed the wet road and disappeared into a gap between two tall buildings. When Alia reached the same corner, she watched him stride away down a long dark passageway. Fearing a trap, she paused. She waited until he'd gone all the way to the end and then ran after him, pausing again when she emerged. Across the street, the weasel had reached a parked car. He glanced over his shoulder, opened the rear door and got in. Feeling suddenly exposed, Alia took shelter in the entrance to a pizzeria.

Despite being parked under a street-light the car's blacked-out windows made it impossible to see in. Alia memorised the registration, expecting it to pull away, but the car didn't move. She wiped the rain from the dial of her watch. It was nine-forty-five.

Another ten minutes went by. On the other side of the glass door, the pizzeria was busy and the staff were starting to give her curious looks. She was considering moving on when the weasel emerged, minus the bag. After re-crossing the street, he returned to the alley they'd come through. Alia gave him a short head start and then went after him.

They retraced their route to the Plaça Reial. Back in the cover of the crowded arcades, his pace slowed right down. They completed a full lap of the square at little more than a stroll and Alia began to wonder what on earth he was up to. Every now and again he stopped to look round, never turning his head quite far enough to see her. And every time he did so Alia was forced to stop and look for a place to blend in.

Finally, he took a seat on the edge of a pavement café and casually pulled out his phone. Alia hid behind a large potted fern and sent a message to Margot: *he met with someone in a car and dropped off the bag he picked up at the hotel. Shall I keep following him?*

Follow him for another ten minutes and then come back to the club. We'll meet you outside.

ok

Soon the weasel was back on his feet and off they went again.

After reading the message, Margot turned her phone around for Jorge to see.

"I think we should go and find her," he said.

Margot thought about it, but was promptly distracted by some activity in the lounge. She moved closer to the half-glazed partition. Gina had reappeared through the bead curtain, and following close behind were the two young hipsters. They didn't appear to have been harmed. When the three of them reached the front door, they bumped fists and said their goodbyes in a friendly manner. Margot mentally shrugged. Perhaps she'd been reading too much into it.

The game wasn't yet over but Jorge was right. Margot returned her cue to the rack. "Come on, then. Let's go and find Alia."

They'd just stepped away from the pool table when the red light flashed in the lobby. Gina had been on her way back to the bar so she turned right around and returned to the front door. A man came in, shaking the rain from his red umbrella. The lobby was too dark to see any detail in his face but as he came into the light his features were revealed. And Margot's heart skipped a beat. It was one of those rare moments when she literally could not believe her eyes. Standing before them, putting away his membership card, was Pascal Deveraux.

23

Despite there being at least a dozen other people in the club, Pascal's eyes immediately snapped onto Margot's. At that moment he froze, his face mirroring what Margot was feeling inside: total surprise. For a second or two he didn't appear to know how to react as if he couldn't quite believe what he was experiencing. As he carefully fed his umbrella into the stand, he didn't seem to hear the question Gina must have asked him, waiting expectantly for a response. His cheek twitched, though there was no smile.

"Are we going then, or what?" Jorge asked, bringing Margot back to life.

Rather than answer his question, she pulled out her phone: *You won't believe who's just walked in – Pascal Deveraux.*

After exchanging a few quiet words with Gina, Pascal strolled towards the pool table. He wore an immaculate grey suit which, despite the laid-back setting, looked quite chic. He produced a smile when he reached the opening in the half-glazed partition, though his body language remained far from relaxed. "Now what are the odds?"

Margot put away her phone. "Pretty slim, I'd say."

"I never realised you were a member."

"I only just joined."

"But you knew I was coming?" Despite how difficult he was to read he seemed genuinely puzzled.

Margot shook her head. "I had no idea." His name had certainly not been on the list of members, though the fact it had been four years out of date might have explained that. "Is this one of your regular haunts?"

He didn't answer. Margot could imagine his mind ticking over, curious about how much she knew. He switched his attention to Jorge.

"And who's this?"

Jorge introduced himself.

The two men shook hands, though Pascal didn't return the courtesy of saying who he was. Was he really so vain to think people still recognised him from his film-star days? His eyes flicked back and forth between them, wondering about the nature of their relationship, no doubt. Margot was happy to leave him guessing.

"You weren't leaving, were you?"

Suddenly Margot was in two minds. The prospect of spending time with this man made her skin creep, but this was too big a development to ignore. What were the odds, indeed?

"I suppose we could stay a little longer." She turned enquiringly to Jorge. He nodded uncertainly.

"Excellent. Let me just visit the little boys' room then I'll come and chat."

There was nowhere to sit in the pool table area so they wandered into the main room. Margot indicated the sofa in front of an exposed stone wall and they sat. Every nerve in her body was tingling.

"So who is this guy?"

"You don't want to know."

"A friend of yours?"

"Hardly."

Margot was craving a cigarette. She reached into her bag and closed her hand around the packet but didn't remove it. She turned to look Jorge in the eye, and realised she couldn't keep him in the dark any longer. "His name's Pascal Deveraux."

"Should I have heard of him?"

"Does the name villa Belle Époque ring any bells?"

He thought about it, but then shook his head.

Some people walked by so Margot waited. When they'd moved on, she continued in a lower voice: "Six years ago, five men were found dead in an underground vault. They'd all been brutally murdered."

Finally, the penny dropped. "Oh, yeah. I remember that. But wait a minute …" He swallowed hard. "Wasn't Deveraux the name of the family who lived there?"

Margot nodded. "Pascal grew up there."

"So this guy—"

Margot nodded again. "At one point he was the prime suspect."

"Holy shit."

"My thoughts exactly."

"What are we going to do?"

"You keep schtum. Leave the talking to me."

"And what about Alia?"

Margot took out her phone and typed with her thumbs: *change of plan. We're staying here for a while. I'll keep you posted.* She showed the screen to Jorge.

The way the sofa was positioned meant she had to keep turning her head to see the bead curtain. Gina had abandoned the counter and gone into the back. It was impossible to see through, but Margot had little doubt she and Pascal were back there together, discussing this unforeseen development. Her mind continued to race. His surprise at finding her here had clearly been genuine. So what was the connection? Was there any way he could have found out what she was up to and followed her? Unlikely. Alia's friend Gégé was the only other person who knew of their interest in the club, and from what Alia had said he could be trusted. There was no way anyone could be onto them. But now that he had turned up, maybe she could get something out of him.

The curtain moved and Pascal emerged, Gina hot on his heels. They both looked over at the pool table. Seeing no one was there, Pascal appeared alarmed, but then relaxed when he spotted them on the sofa. Gina handed him three spliffs from one of the jars and he came over. "Room for a little one?"

Margot shuffled to make space, making sure Jorge would be between them, but Pascal changed his mind and dragged over a chair instead. He handed out the spliffs though made no attempt to light them, keeping his clamped between his fingers like an unnecessary prop. Margot had left her first smouldering in the ashtray by the pool table and Jorge had put his out, no longer in the mood.

"Do you come here often?" Margot asked.

He returned her smile. "When I'm in the area. What about you?"

"It's my first time."

"So what prompted you to join, tonight of all nights?"

"Oh, I'm always keen to try new things." Margot fired back that glint in his eye. If this was going to be a duel she was well and truly up for it. "Are you here on your own?"

He gave a small nod.

"And how was Roselyn, after your little 'accident'?"

His mouth twitched. Here she was again, tempting. "Funny you should mention Roselyn – she used to love coming to Barcelona."

"Really? Why was that?"

"The art and the architecture. And the Picasso connection, of course. We used to come here all the time." He leaned forward, elbows on his knees. "Have you been to the Carrer d'Avinyó?"

Margot shook her head. The name did sound familiar but she couldn't quite place it.

"That's just around the corner from here, isn't it?" Jorge said.

"Indeed it is."

"So what's there?" Margot asked

His expression softened, disappointed perhaps. "You know *The Young Ladies of Avignon*?"

Margot nodded. She was familiar with the painting: five nude female prostitutes painted in flat splintered imagery. Picasso's first foray into Cubism.

"Number forty-four, Carrer d'Avinyó is the brothel Picasso used for his five subjects." He sat back. "We could go and take a look, if you like."

"To a brothel?"

"It's not a brothel now. The last time I was here the place was all boarded up. But it's an interesting piece of art history."

Margot shifted her gaze. She was keen to keep him talking, but the idea of walking these streets in his company was in no way appealing, even with Jorge by her side. "It's getting rather late."

"Late?" He almost choked in surprise. He turned his wrist over. "It's only ten o'clock. The evening's barely begun."

"We've got a long journey home."

"Then stay over."

Margot eyeballed him. Why was he so keen to get them away from the club? "You haven't smoked your joint yet."

"Neither, I see, have you."

"We were just about to go and meet our friend," Jorge put in, attempting to come to her rescue, though Margot gave him the smallest shake of her head. Keeping Alia at arm's length could prove useful.

"Actually, she just sent a text. She had to cancel."

"Did she?"

Margot winked.

Pascal parried like a pro. "Well, that's settled then. Let's go and see the brothel."

He grinned triumphantly. It seemed they'd come to the end of round one.

24

Opening his umbrella, Pascal stepped into the street. The storm had closed in and lightning was sheeting through the clouds, illuminating the sky with strobing white light.

They walked quickly, navigating between puddles. Pascal clearly knew his way around and led the way without hesitation, turning corners without even glancing up at the street signs.

Carrer d'Avinyó was not quite the artistic landmark he'd implied. Number forty-four, the site of the former brothel, turned out to be an anonymous archway in a rather dingy street. A security grille and a boarded-up door covered in graffiti prevented any chance of gaining entry, though there was nothing to hint at what once lay inside. Margot regarded it from the shelter of a balcony while the two men stood chatting.

"So what's so great about this painting?" Jorge asked.

Pascal exchanged a glance with Margot, perhaps wanting to give her the chance to explain, but this was his stage and she let him take it.

"You're familiar with cubism?"

"A little."

"*The Young Ladies of Avignon* is probably the most famous

example in art. It caused an uproar when it was first exhibited. Picasso's genius was to deconstruct the five figures and represent them using geometric shapes, completely devoid of perspective. In doing so he created an entirely new language of painting."

Margot looked it up on her phone just to remind herself. These days, the painting was not quite so highly regarded by all. To some, the desire to depict hacked-up bodies of naked females gave a rather more insightful view into the artist's mind than he'd probably anticipated. He'd certainly had his issues with women.

Rainwater was dripping from the balcony, wetting her head. Pascal had made no attempt to share his umbrella. When he'd finally finished droning on about the painting he turned to face her. It had taken him a while but at last he picked up on her state of displeasure.

"All right, I concede, it's not the most impressive of sights."

"You'd make a rotten tour guide."

"In that case allow me to make it up to you. Have you eaten?"

Margot unfolded her arms, not quite the development she'd been expecting.

"What were you thinking?"

"I know a rather nice tapas bar near here."

She looked at Jorge. Rain was running down his face, making him scowl. "Whatever we do can we do it inside?" he said.

Margot returned her gaze to Pascal. Her appearance at the club had clearly got him worried. If she gave him enough rope then maybe he might just hang himself. She gave him the nod. "All right. Lead on."

Margot scanned for landmarks as he took them deeper into the maze, trying to memorise the route they were taking, hoping at least some of it would be familiar to Jorge, but she soon gave up. Most of the streets were only a few metres wide yet they still had alleys and passageways branching off them, leading to who knew where. The shutters were down on many of the doorways, the steelwork providing canvasses for modern-day Picassos. Had the esteemed artist been alive today, Margot could just imagine him stalking the streets in the dead of night, armed with a beltful of rattle-cans.

The tapas bar was crowded. A fug of hot sweaty air hung over the assembled bodies, fragrant with the aroma of frying foods and rain-damped humans. Margot stayed at the back as the three of them squeezed through to the bar.

"What would you like?"

Adrift in a sea of noise, Margot had to read his lips.

"You choose," she shouted back.

The food came quickly and was delicious: fried anchovies on little pieces of tomato bread; Fuet served on a layer of boiled sweet onions; Serrano ham with Manchego cheese. He ordered the drinks: a Mojito for Margot, a beer for Jorge, a straight red vermouth for himself. While Jorge was keeping him occupied, Margot sent a message to Alia:

We're with PD in a tapas bar on Carrer del Regomir. Where are you?

Still following. I've no idea where he's going

Five more minutes then come back

Ok

A cold hand touched the flesh on her forearm, making her jump. Pascal had leaned across to pass her another dish of food. Margot caught his eye, and in that moment was struck by what a bizarre thing she was doing here, eating food with this man.

One thing was for sure: if Jorge hadn't been with her she would have run a mile.

They'd barely got through the first dish when Pascal excused himself to go to the gents. As soon as he'd gone, Margot tapped Jorge's arm and pointed at the door. He followed her out.

It was a relief to get back into the open air. The rain had eased and people were returning to the streets. Ears ringing from the relative quiet, Margot lit a cigarette. "Thanks for keeping him occupied."

"That's okay. But what exactly is going on here?"

Margot puffed out her cheeks. "I wish I knew."

"Have you heard from Alia?"

"She's coming to find us."

Some others smokers were clogging the doorway so Margot stepped to the other side of the street. When Jorge joined her, she leaned in closer. "Remember those other two other club members we asked you about?"

"The ones who went missing?"

"We think all three were killed at the Belle Époque."

Jorge blinked in surprise. Margot reached out and touched his arm.

"It's not certain yet. The bodies were so badly injured it'll take time to identify them, but I'd be happy to lay money on it."

"But if you're right, then that guy in there ..."

Margot nodded. "It's a distinct possibility. We had no idea he was a member of the Naxos until he walked in just now, and that's the strongest link we've established so far. But there's also Farooq and Marc to consider."

Jorge ran a hand through his hair, dazed. Margot felt bad. She'd been treating him far too casually.

"I'm sorry," she said. "I should have told you sooner."

He shook his head. "It's all right."

"We can walk away right now if you want to. Slip off while he's not looking. I really don't mind."

Jorge looked across at the bar. It was impossible to see through the mass of bodies but it seemed Pascal had not yet come out. They still had time.

"But if he did kill Erec ..." Jorge said. "And we've got a chance to find out. We should do that, shouldn't we?"

"He likes to play games. If we play along with him for long enough then maybe he'll let something slip. At least, that's what I'm hoping."

"What about Alia?"

"I'll try and get her to shadow us. In the meantime, if the two of us stick together we'll be fine. But *shush* – here he comes now."

Pascal had emerged from the bar and was looking around. Spotting them, he crossed the street, grinning like a loon. "There you both are."

"It was getting a bit crowded in there," Margot said.

"It was a bit, wasn't it? Why don't we move on?"

The change him in was subtle but Margot spotted it: the glaze of sweat on his top lip; the tiny white specks in the hairs of his nose. The little trips to the bathroom suddenly made sense.

Margot stubbed out her cigarette. Whatever game they were playing the stakes had just got a little bit higher.

They played bar roulette: took turns picking a number, drank a round in whichever bar they landed on. Pascal went first; chose number six. They turned corners at random and the sixth place they came to was a cocktail bar. A house wine for Margot, a beer for Jorge, another red vermouth for himself. They'd barely been there fifteen minutes when Pascal decided it was time to move on.

"Your turn, Jorge."

He chose two.

The route Jorge selected took them into a dimly-lit area. They passed a seedy bar, walked on until the flashing neon lights of a dance club beckoned. Inside, the walls pounded to the beat of Hip-Hop music while strobing yellow spotlights roved a packed dance floor. Half-naked women strutted on podiums next to the DJ's bench. The music was so loud Margot could barely hear herself think, but Pascal got them into the VIP area where things were a little more relaxed. He ordered more drinks: shots of red vermouth all round followed by cold beer. When the waitress brought them to the table, Pascal lined up the glasses. He downed his shot, waited for Jorge to do the same, then looked at Margot with challenging eyes. She wasn't in the mood for drinking games but a challenge was a challenge. She knocked back her vermouth in one gulp and then tilted the beer bottle to her lips.

"You know what?" Pascal said while she was still guzzling. "I still can't get my head around it."

Margot finished swallowing. "Around what?"

"You turning up at the Naxos."

She took a breath, then looked deeply into his eyes. He was determined to find out, but the more he pushed the more certain she became they'd hit a nerve. "It came as a surprise to me, too."

"Funny, though. I mean, I've been a member for ten years; you only joined tonight. That's one hell of a coincidence."

"How come your name wasn't on the membership list?"

"How do you know it wasn't?"

"Ways and means."

"I use an alias."

"Why would you do that?"

His eyes said: *No comment.*

Margot waited, but he still didn't come up with an answer. Instead, he got up and went to the bathroom.

They breathed a sigh of relief. Jorge was looking a little worse for wear, his hair mussed up, his pupils dilated. He'd downed his shot in one, but when he reached for his beer, Margot stayed his hand.

"Try to stay sober."

He puffed out his cheeks and put the bottle back down. "You guys certainly know how to put it away."

"It's taken years of practice."

What had happened to Alia? Margot checked her phone. Her location hadn't updated in the past half-hour and it seemed the friend-finder had developed a glitch. She was about to send a text when Pascal reappeared, buzzing with energy. He chivvied them out of their seats, having decided it was time to move on.

Back on the street, he pointed a finger at Margot. "Your turn."

Margot was growing tired of the game but she picked three, her lucky number. She turned left at the next two corners and took them into a small square. Of the three visible exits, she picked the one that looked the most salubrious. The first two bars were closed, but at the far end, La Blue Girl looked very much open for business.

They went down some steps, into a tunnel of blue light. A doorman gave them the once-over before waving them through. One long bar, a dozen or more semi-circular booths, a faint blue tinge colouring the air making it feel like they'd stepped into an alien world. As they ordered the drinks, the theme quickly began apparent: the waiting staff were covered from head to toe in blue body paint, naked apart from the tiniest of colour-matched thongs.

"Good choice," Pascal smirked, staring unashamedly as a naked blue woman jiggled by.

At least it was champagne night. Margot ordered a bottle and sought out a vacant booth. They'd barely shuffled into their spaces when a blue man appeared, bearing an ice bucket and three glasses. Margot watched as he poured the champagne, wondering how long it took him to apply that paint every night and, perhaps more importantly, how long to remove it. As a job, it must have taken some commitment.

"Margot."

"Sorry?"

It seemed Pascal had been saying something.

"I said, why don't we liven things up a little? Make the night a little more interesting."

Margot recalibrated. "How?"

He shifted his gaze. Margot followed his line of sight and found herself looking at the booth one row down. The backs of the seats were so high it was difficult to see in but she counted four female heads.

"See the one in the tiny black dress?" Pascal said. "See how she's left her bag lying on the seat?"

Margot saw it. From the amount of giggling that was going on it was obvious they were drunk, but she disliked where he appeared to be going.

"So what?"

"Isn't that asking for trouble?"

"Not really."

"I bet I could go over there and take the wallet from her bag without her even noticing. What do you think?"

Margot shared an uneasy glance with Jorge. Given a free rein, who knew how far he might go, but she couldn't just sit here and watch.

"So now you're a pickpocket?"

"It's just a matter of distraction. Like a magic trick. Give them something to look at while you put your hand where they least expect it."

"And if you get caught?"

"I'll give it right back. Say I found it on the floor."

Margot looked him in the eye. He wasn't seeking her approval. All he wanted was an audience; the way his life had been all along, no doubt. After a few moments of holding her gaze, he downed his glass of champagne.

"Watch."

"You'd better give it straight back."

With one finger he made a cross over his heart.

Jorge shuffled over to let him get out. Neither of them could quite believe it when Pascal walked up to the four young women, bold as brass. He tugged his shirt cuffs, leaned down to their eye level, said something that caused a fresh eruption of laughter. But the merriment morphed into cries of alarm as it appeared a glass had got knocked over. Pascal was full of apologies; offered to clean it all up; and in the ensuing confusion, his hand slipped unnoticed into the girl's bag.

Even without his act of misdirection they were probably too drunk to have noticed. A blue woman came over to help clean up so Pascal stepped away. Making sure Margot was looking, he carefully slid a ladies' wallet from his inside jacket pocket.

"Go on, then. Give it back," Margot urged through gritted teeth.

But Pascal just smiled. He slid the wallet back into his pocket, turned on his heel, and headed for the door.

There was no logic to the route he was taking. Alia was certain they'd circled the block at least once during the past half-hour.

Walking with his hands in his pockets, like someone with no particular place to go, *la fouine* hadn't once looked back. She began to suspect he knew he was being followed and was leading her on a wild goose chase and if that were the case she needed to keep up her guard.

The rain had brought a special kind of smell up from the pavements but now that the storm had passed a different odour was being carried on the air: Alia could smell the sea. They emerged from the side streets onto a busy main road, two carriageways separating them from the marina. A pedestrian crossing lay just down the street, but the weasel ignored it and walked all the way down to the next set of lights. An ornate red bridge conveyed them across the first carriageway. From there, a footway spiralled down to the promenade. The paving expanded to join the concourse of the marina, and soon they were walking through the land of the mega-yachts.

And still he kept going: on around the side of the marina, past hardy street vendors still touting their wares from mats on the pavement. When they went up some steps to the footpath that fronted the beach there seemed nowhere left to go. Ahead of them, the sea was an invisible dark mass, just a few white crests catching the glow of the city's bright lights.

La fouine went down onto the sand but Alia stayed put. Only a few others were out there. The suspicion he was trying to lure her into a trap suddenly became real again.

And so she waited, watching the blackness swallow him up. Maybe a sixth sense told him he was no longer being pursued because a few minutes later he reappeared, fifty metres on, walking through a cone of light cast from one of the streetlamps.

Alia shadowed him from the safety of the promenade, in two minds whether or not to turn back. The beach was so long she couldn't even see to the end. If he went much further she decided she would quit.

As if reading her thoughts, the weasel ran up the next set of steps and re-joined the footpath. Just as he'd done earlier, he stared straight back at her. Only this time Alia was certain he recognised her. She froze. It seemed for a moment that the tables had turned and he was going to come after her, but then a car pulled up beside him. He snatched open the door and got in.

Ten seconds later the car raced by, *la fouine* turning to look at her from the passenger seat, sneering triumphantly.

———

They had little choice but to go after him. Margot strode past the doorman, went through the tunnel of blue light, and back up the steps to the street. Pascal was down at the next intersection, looking back as if to make sure they were following. When he was happy they'd seen him, he ran on.

They eventually caught up with him in a triangular Plaça, next to a children's playground surrounded by small trees. Even at midnight, the air was a sultry twenty-five degrees.

"I told you I could do it." He threw back his head and laughed.

Margot bore down on him. "You promised you would give it back!"

"She was so drunk she didn't have a clue."

"Then it was hardly a challenge."

"No, but it was a hoot."

Margot glared at him. Finally, he got the message.

"All right," he sighed, the amusement draining out of him. "Wait here while I go and give it back."

They watched him set off down the street.

Jorge puffed out his cheeks. "Is this the point where we do a runner?"

"Don't tempt me."

Margot checked her phone and found a message. "Alia's down by the beach. Marc got into a car and drove off."

She typed back: *get into a taxi and come to* – "Where are we?"

Jorge looked round. "Plaça de George Orwell."

Plaça de George Orwell. Keep your distance when you see us. We're still with HIM.

Two minutes later Pascal was back. "Happy now?"

"Hardly."

Thunder grumbled in the distance. Either the storm had moved on or another was on the way. Margot was about to suggest they call it a night but Pascal, unsurprisingly, wasn't yet ready to quit.

"All right," he said. "One final throw of the dice. The next place we come to will be the last."

"Fine by me."

A jazz club, slotted between a bank and a Chinese restaurant. Past a small bar, a singer in a sequined dress was singing *The Girl from Ipanema* on a blacked-out stage. It was all rather intimate: petite round tables; candles in jars. Pascal bought yet another round of drinks, cocktails this time, but when his phone rang he stepped outside to answer it. Jorge helped Margot carry the drinks to a table, but then he too abandoned her, excusing himself to go to the gents.

"Don't be long," Margot said, reluctant to let him go. The prospect of being left alone with Pascal gave her the chills.

The singer finished her number and a trumpeter came on. He was just about to start playing when Pascal came back.

"Where's our friend?"

"Gone to the little boys' room."

Something about him was different. His movements were less fluid as he sat down, his body language less open. Like something had knocked him off kilter. Margot looked at the window, tempted to ask him who he'd been speaking to on the phone.

But then the band struck up. Face covered in sweat, the trumpeter poured his heart and soul into a pumped-up version of *Mambo No. 5*. He was really very good. By the time he reached the final chorus, half the audience were up on their feet, dancing away. He took a bow to uproarious applause.

The band went off through a door into the back. People began migrating to the bar, but Margot and Pascal remained in their seats, uncertainty filling the air. Pascal stared at the empty stage just like he'd stared at the non-existent view from his apartment window. Margot sent a glance back to the door to the restrooms. People were coming and going, but there was no sign of Jorge. She was tempted to go herself. Her bladder was quite full.

Pascal moved on his chair, angling his body in a peculiar way: spine bent, head turned fractionally towards her. Finally, he came right out with it. "I take it you've been investigating the club?"

The candle on their table had gone out so Margot struck a match. "The name did crop up."

"How do you suppose it's involved?"

When the flame came to life, she blew out the match. She stared at him for a few moments before lightly shrugging her shoulders. "This is hardly the time."

"On the contrary." He turned to face her properly now. "I'd say this is exactly the time."

The look in his eyes was really quite unnerving at times. It was amazing how he'd suddenly sobered up, how in control of his faculties he appeared to be. Margot began to wonder if it had all been an act: he'd been buying the drinks; she hadn't actually seen him take any cocaine.

"What's your connection with Farooq?"

"Farooq owns the club."

"He's also a loan shark."

"And?"

"Have you ever borrowed money from him?"

He twitched a smile. "So that's what you think – Farooq was lending me money?"

"You were a heavy gambler. You must have been getting your money from somewhere."

His face continued to smile though Margot doubted he was feeling it inside. He leaned across the table, fingers laced. "This is a very interesting theory you've come up with. Anything else?"

Margot bit her bottom lip. Her brain was tired. Part of her was willing this night to be over. Adrenaline was about the only thing keeping her going.

"Erec Dubois."

"What about him?"

"He was a member of the Naxos as well."

"So you suspect Farooq?"

"We did."

"But?"

Margot hesitated. "There's one common thread running through all of this and that's you. You knew Erec Dubois. He disappeared seven years ago. And now we discover you were both members of the same cannabis club. How's that for a coincidence?"

Pascal had no immediate comeback. Margot feared she'd said too much but it was too late now. The band came back to the stage. The trumpeter took his instrument off the stand and started playing another lively number. It was far too loud to continue talking so they sat back in their seats, trading suspicious looks, wondering at the state of play. Margot's heart was pounding. Had she finally cracked him?

During a lull in the music, Pascal stretched to speak into her ear. "Let me get us some refills." He took the glasses with him.

Margot was glad of the break, but she didn't let him out of her sight. His manner remained subdued as he went to the bar and ordered the drinks. He stood, one hand in his pocket, head slightly bowed, almost – dare she believe – looking defeated.

Margot switched her gaze to the door to the restrooms. Where the hell was Jorge? He must have been in there ten minutes by now. She had half a mind to go in and find him, though now she had Pascal on the ropes she was reluctant to let up.

The band was playing the bossa nova as Pascal returned with the drinks. The singer stepped up onto the stage, the sequins in her dress twinkling as they caught in the beams from the spotlights rotating gently over their heads. Pascal went back to ignoring her, chair angled slightly away, eyes on the singer. Margot had no idea what he would do next. His unpredictability was perhaps the most dangerous thing about him.

She swallowed a mouthful of her cocktail, then glanced at her watch. Twenty-to-one. Jorge still hadn't come out. Maybe the food had disagreed with him. There was probably a simple explanation. Come to think of it, she wasn't feeling too good herself: her face felt hot, her stomach bloated. When she moved her head, the room took a moment to catch up.

But then her eyes continued to go out of focus and it was obvious something was very wrong. Margot stared down into the bottom of her glass. She licked her lips. The cocktail had tasted off. Why hadn't she noticed immediately? When she looked across at Pascal and found him grinning slyly, she realised too late. How could she have been so stupid?

The bastard had spiked her drink.

25

Standing outside La Blue Girl, Alia stared at the screen of her phone. According to the friend-finder app, Margot was inside, but her location hadn't updated in the past forty-five minutes. She looked down warily from the top step. *Keep your distance,* Margot had said. Then her phone buzzed in her hand, startling her.

"Jorge?"

"Alia – where are you?" He sounded like he'd just stepped out of a boxing ring.

"Outside La Blue Girl. Where are you?"

"I'm in ... Carrer dels Escudellers. You need to get over here."

"Why?"

"Margot's gone."

"Gone where?"

"I think Pascal's taken her. I'll explain when you get here."

Alia's hand shook as she looked up the address. It was only a few streets away. She ran all the way there and found Jorge hunkered down against a wall, nursing his head. When Alia squatted beside him he held out his hand, fingers wet with blood.

"What the hell happened?"

"I got hit from behind."

"Who by?"

"I'm not sure."

He tilted his head forward so Alia could examine him. His hair was matted with blood but the wound looked superficial. "It's stopped bleeding. I think it's okay."

"Someone jumped me when I was in the toilets." He eased himself to his feet. "We were in there." He indicated the nearby jazz club. "When I came out they'd gone."

"You sure she's not still inside?" Alia looked in through the open door, but the club was crowded and full of noise.

"The waitress said she left with two guys. I think the other one was Farooq."

Alia called Margot's phone but it went straight to voicemail. Her mind was galloping. She needed to pause, and think.

"Could they have taken her back to the Naxos?"

Jorge gave a small nod. "Maybe. It's worth a try."

It wasn't far. Ten minutes later they were outside the anonymous black doors. Lights were still on in the windows above, but the doors were locked.

"I think they close at midnight," Jorge said.

Alia looked at her watch. Twenty-past-one.

"Is there a back way in?"

"There must be. Let's try down here."

Jorge hurried down an alley a short distance to their right. They turned left at the end and moved along another dark passage. It was difficult to get any bearings, but it seemed they were working their way along the rear of the buildings. The doors and shutters were plastered with graffiti, and few of them had signs.

"This could be it."

Jorge halted next to a plain steel door marked with the letter

N. A chain-link fence hemmed them in, but leaning against it Alia looked up to see a silhouette move in a first-floor window. It was too dark to see any detail.

An intermittent buzzing sound came from inside. Realising an alarm had been set, Alia grabbed Jorge by the arm and pulled him into the cover of a wheelie bin. A young woman emerged, talking on the phone:

"They want me to take the G Wagon ... Okay ... Yes, I'm leaving now. Pick me up in fifteen minutes."

She locked the door and set off in the opposite direction.

They waited until she was out of earshot and then rose to their feet.

"Who's that?"

"That's Gina; Farooq's daughter," Jorge said. "Shall we follow her?"

Alia glanced up at the window. The light had gone out, and if Gina had set the alarm then there couldn't be anyone left inside. She'd already spent half the night traipsing the streets of this city but she gave Jorge the nod.

They waited for her to reach the end of the passageway and then raced after her. Rounding the corner, they spotted her go through a door twenty metres down. It turned out to be the entrance to an underground car park.

Gina was already one flight down, skipping lightly on the concrete steps. Peering through the gaps, Alia watched her go all the way down to the bottom and then disappear through a door.

They hurried to catch up. Emerging on a dimly-lit car deck, all was quiet. Vehicles were crammed into every space so they spilt up, scanning the ranks of vehicles for a G Wagon. Just as Alia was venturing up the ramp to explore the next sub-level a car engine started. Down at the far end, a silver-grey Mercedes G Wagon was reversing out of a space. Alarm bells rang in her head.

"Jorge!"

They ran back to the stairs. Jorge got their first, but Alia overtook him on the way up. Bursting through the door to the street, she paused. Right on cue, the G Wagon emerged from the exit ramp fifty metres down. Jorge hailed a taxi.

"Follow that car!" he said as they climbed into the back.

The driver couldn't have been less impressed, but then Alia flashed her badge, something she'd always wanted to do. "Police!"

It wasn't much of a pursuit. The traffic was slow-moving, and after less than ten minutes the G Wagon pulled into an access at the side of a hotel. The taxi dropped them in the street, and when Alia stepped out onto the pavement she was surprised to realise she knew exactly where they were. Down the alley at the side of the building lay the bright green awning of the Hotel Santa Clara.

26

Margot came round to find a pillow resting on her face. Dust was getting in her nose, making her want to sneeze. But her nervous system must have been on a go-slow because when she tried to remove the pillow her forearm crashed into it instead, cushioning the blow to her face. She felt more intoxicated than she'd ever been in her life.

With a second attempt, she managed to tug the pillow away. Bright light stung her eyes. She was lying on a bed in a high-ceilinged room. The air smelled of old carpet, and furniture polish. She pinched shut her eyes and reopened them, hoping she might wake somewhere different. But alas, it was not to be.

She wasn't the only one in the room. Standing in the corner were two men, their backs to her, talking in low voices. An involuntary groan must have escaped from her lips because both men turned at the same time. Side by side, Pascal and Farooq stood silently regarding her.

Sparking with adrenaline, Margot tried to get up, but her limbs wouldn't coordinate and she ended up knotting herself in the bedclothes. Pascal came over, put one knee down on the floor, and reached across to try and untangle her.

"Try to lie still," he said, his voice soft, seemingly full of compassion. "You'll do yourself an injury if you try to get up."

Margot froze. "Where am I?"

"You're safe."

"What the hell's going on?"

"You were feeling unwell, remember?"

Her limbs may have turned to jelly but there was nothing wrong with Margot's memory. It all came back to her. "You spiked my drink."

He smiled. "Now don't be silly."

"We were in the jazz club."

"Hush now." Pascal tried to cover her with the bedspread but Margot batted his arms away. She had to get up. With a concerted effort, she freed herself from the bedclothes and rolled to the edge of the mattress, but the moment she leaned on her arm her elbow gave way and she fell flat on the floor with a thud. Farooq strode over and the two men lifted her up.

"You'll feel much better if you just lie still," Pascal said. "Try and sleep it off."

They got her back on the bed, waited for her to settle and then returned to the corner.

For now, Margot gave in. She explored the room with her eyes. She was lying on one of twin beds, a nasty blue carpet covered the floor, cheap flat-pack furniture was pushed against the walls. Stains marked the ceiling, and heavy brown curtains covered the only window. A fire notice on the inside of the door told her she was in a hotel room. She was still fully clothed; had on the same outfit she'd been wearing all evening, even her shoes. She returned her gaze to the men in the corner.

"What did you do to Jorge?"

Pascal spoke from over his shoulder. "Jorge?"

"He went to the restroom and didn't come back."

"You must be getting confused. You and I were the only ones

there."

"That's not true."

"Perhaps you were hallucinating."

"You're lying."

"You had had rather a lot to drink," he smiled.

Fuelled by another burst of adrenaline, Margot tried to get up. She managed to wriggle her head up the headboard, but the effort made her go dizzy and she soon had to stop. She slumped back down.

"Where's my purse?"

"Right there on the table."

"And my phone?"

Pascal came back to the bedside. Hands in his pockets, he looked down on her in a conquering way. "You must have dropped it when we were leaving the club."

Margot gritted her teeth. "I want to leave. *Right* now."

"We brought you here for your own safety. I couldn't leave you walking the streets, the state you were in."

"You won't get away with this."

"We're only trying to help."

"Let me go."

"Go where? You can't even get out of bed, let alone walk."

Margot glared back at him. In that moment she could have driven a knife through his heart. "Let me go or I'll scream this place down."

It was Farooq who snapped. He charged over from the corner and went to the other side of the bed. Grabbing her by the chin, he glared into her eyes. "One more word out of you and you'll regret it."

The look in his eyes suggested it wasn't an idle threat.

There was a knock on the door. Farooq shoved her chin to the side and went to answer it. Margot looked up to find Gina entering the room.

"Any problems?" Pascal asked.

Gina shook her head. "It's parked around the side." She held out a car key and dropped it into his hand.

Pascal put the key in his pocket and the two men went back to the corner. Gina stayed put. Her gaze drifted to Margot, a look of uncertainty flickering across her face. Margot pleaded with her eyes. Surely a fellow woman would help her out. Gina turned back to the men. "Are you sure about this?"

"Go back to the club," Farooq said. "We'll take it from here."

Gina lingered for a few more moments, but then went to the door and left.

Silence fell. The men began moving with a renewed sense of purpose: Farooq went to the window to make sure the curtains were fully closed; Pascal checked the door. Margot eased herself up to try and see what was so interesting about the corner. A small table was pushed against the wall with a black cloth spread over it. On top of the cloth was a small tin, a padded envelope, and a stainless-steel kidney dish. Finished with the curtains, Farooq came to the bedside. At the table, Pascal opened the tin, took out a vial and a hypodermic syringe. Margot's heart raced as she watched him insert the needle into the top of the vial. He drew out a measured amount and, turning it upside down, squirted some colourless fluid into the air. The eyes of a madman turned to look back at her.

"Just a little something to take away the pain."

Farooq pounced before she had time to cry out. Right hand over her mouth, left knee in the centre of her chest, he pinned her to the mattress with ease. Pascal set the kidney tray down on the bedside table and settled himself on the edge of the bed. He grabbed her right arm and tapped out a vein.

"Don't worry," he smiled. "I've done this before."

Then, with delicate precision, he inserted the tip of the needle into her vein.

27

Alia crouched while she snapped a photo of the G Wagon's registration. She checked through the windows, but there was no one inside. The only place Gina could have gone was through a gate in the wall at the back of the hotel.

Jorge was looking up at the side of the building where all but one of the windows were unlit. "You reckon Margot's in there?"

"There's only one way to find out."

He moved to go around the front but Alia called him back. Finding the gate unlocked, they went through to a small courtyard. Alia activated the torch on her phone, shining her light over a trio of overstuffed wheelie bins. A short flight of stairs led up to the back door where a wedge stopped the panic latch from closing. They crept inside.

A short corridor. Light was spilling out of an opening, and heavy machinery was making the walls vibrate. When they reached the opening, Alia peered in to find several large washing machines on the go. No one was around. A laundry room from the zombie apocalypse.

Jorge whistled softly – Alia turned to see he'd moved to the next corner. He pointed upwards, indicating someone was coming down the stairs, so they ducked through a metal fly curtain and into a room that turned out to be the kitchen. Footsteps approached. The dangling chains were still tinkling when Gina walked by, but she paid it no heed. The back door opened and then closed.

Alia dashed back to the laundry room. Jorge turned out the light and they moved to the only window. Together they watched Gina emerge from the back gate, walk straight past the G Wagon, and head towards the street.

"Where's she off to?" Jorge said, craning over her shoulder.

Alia looked up into his eyes. "Perhaps Marc's picking her up."

"So where's Margot?"

She looked around the humming dark space. Who'd have thought, when they started out this evening, this was where they would end up?

"Let's try upstairs."

The corridor turned a corner and took them to an open door. Stepping through, Alia found herself midway along the lobby she'd visited earlier. The staircase lay to her right; the bar and the concierge's office to her left. The lights were off in the office, and the bar was dark and empty.

She moved to the other side of the hall and looked up from the foot of the stairs. Gina had been told to bring the G Wagon; Margot had to be here somewhere. Jorge regarded her expectantly. Alia swallowed, and then cautiously went up.

The landing revealed a row of equally spaced doors, with another corridor continuing through a door behind them. Peering through a glazed panel, Alia counted at least six more rooms. The building was old; its walls thick. It was clearly much larger than it had looked from outside.

"We should split up," Alia said.

Jorge nodded. "I'll go this way. You carry on up."

Alia climbed the next flight of stairs. The floor above was identical in layout, though the carpet had changed colour to blue. She listened at each door in turn, but no sound escaped from anywhere.

The scene was repeated on the next level, and one more turn of the stairs took her to the top. It seemed unlikely they would have brought Margot all the way up here; she certainly wouldn't have gone willingly. Alia was just about to head back down when a hinge squeaked below.

She froze. Someone was huffing and puffing; heaving and straining. She leaned over the bannister and looked down. Two floors below, the heads of two men jostled as they struggled with a large black bag.

"Hey!" she called out.

Pascal's face turned to look up at her. His companion heaved the bag over his shoulder and they ran.

Alia ran after them. Jorge emerged from the corridor just as she reached the first-floor landing but they were both going so fast they almost collided. Precious seconds were wasted as they sorted themselves out. By the time they got down to the hall, the door to the fire escape route slammed shut in their faces. Jorge threw his shoulder against it, but to no avail.

"They've blocked it."

"This way."

Alia ran to the front door. The key was in the lock, but the bolts took some shifting. As Jorge heaved it open, she raced down the steps just as the G Wagon came speeding towards her. Alia put one foot into the street, foolishly thinking she might stop them, but the car raced by. After rounding the corner, it pulled into the stream of traffic, and quickly disappeared.

———

The police sergeant must have been having a bad day: he barked orders at his two constables; shouted to someone on the phone. Lights spinning, they were driven to the Naxos at high speed.

Half an hour must have gone by while Alia and Jorge had sat in the back of the police car, explaining what had happened. In that time, the G Wagon would have been well away. Jorge reached over and squeezed her hand.

"They'll find her. Don't worry."

If only she could believe him.

They bounced in their seats as the sergeant drove the car over a kerb. He braked millimetres short of a bollard. The five of them got out, and with Jorge directing, trooped along the series of narrow streets that led to the Naxos. The sergeant sent his constables around the back and ordered Alia and Jorge to stand to one side. When everyone was in place, he pounded on the door.

"Police! Open up!"

Gina appeared in her nightclothes, backing away as the sergeant barged in. Moments later, Marc was being escorted in from the back. The sergeant took charge of the questioning. They spoke rapidly in Spanish, and Alia could barely keep up, but the body language spoke volumes. With Marc by her side, Gina put up a fight, but the sergeant was relentless and soon had her defeated. He turned his attention to Alia.

"She admits it. Her father and this man Deveraux took your friend to the hotel."

"Where are they now?"

He fired more questions at Gina.

"She says the same place he took the others."

Alia looked into Gina's eyes. "The villa Belle Époque?"

No translation was required. Gina just nodded, sombrely.

The *Policía Nacional* arrived a few minutes later and the scene turned chaotic. There was too much noise inside the club so Alia stepped into the concourse. It was three o'clock in the morning and she wasn't expecting her father to answer quickly, but after just two rings he picked up.

"Papa?"

"Alia – is everything all right?"

"Margot's been kidnapped."

"What!?"

Alia could barely believe her own words but she continued. "Pascal's taken her. He's bringing her to the Belle Époque."

"What for?"

"We don't know. But we need to keep him out as long as possible. Could you go over there and lock the gates?"

"Of course."

"Pascal has a key so you'll need to use a padlock."

"How long have I got?"

"Maybe an hour. They left over an hour ago."

"I'll go right away."

"Don't get involved. Just lock the gates and go home. The police should be there soon."

"Don't worry about me."

"No, Papa. I don't want you—"

But it was too late. Her father had already hung up.

28

The autoroute was an eerie place at three a.m.. With her head lolling against the passenger window, her body as weak as water, Margot watched the world go by. Every now and then, headlights flashed by on the opposite carriageway, bleaching her retinas. There was little feeling in her limbs. Either she couldn't muster the willpower to move them or whatever he'd injected her with had left her paralysed.

Sitting at the wheel, Pascal drove without speaking. From time to time he hummed a happy tune to himself. They could have been heading off on their holidays. Margot pulled her eyes round far enough to look in the back, but no one was there.

"It's just you and me now, Margot," Pascal said, a bizarre touch of whimsy in his voice. "The way it was meant to be from the start, don't you think?"

He smiled across at her. He'd changed out of his suit and into a dark, turtleneck sweater. They must have stopped somewhere along the way but she had no memory of it. The last thing she could recall was being flat on her back in the seedy hotel room, him coming towards her with a needle.

The engine note climbed as they accelerated to overtake a truck. Once they'd eased by he pulled back into the inside lane.

"How are you feeling?"

Her face may not have been capable of showing it but Margot regarded him in astonishment. *How was she feeling?* She rolled her head back to the window, physically and mentally drained. It felt like her heart was pumping molten lead rather than blood. She needed to keep her mind active, work on finding a way out of this, but all she wanted to do was sink into unconsciousness.

"You know," he went on, "from that very first day we met I had an inkling we'd end up like this. We're so alike. Two sides of the same coin."

Margot finally found her voice. "We're nothing alike."

"Oh, come now. We both like to stand on the edge. Tempt fate. See how far the boundaries can be pushed."

He was completely and utterly deranged. Totally insane. There was no point trying to reason with him. Nothing she might say would have any effect.

Silence fell. The constant hum of the engine, holding a steady 120, was hypnotic, and every few minutes Margot's eyelids grew heavy and started to pull shut. Oh to wake up and find this had all been a horrible nightmare.

"This is actually quite nostalgic," Pascal resumed. "It's just like old times."

Curiosity got the better of her and Margot heaved her head off the window once more. "What is?"

"Taking this road, at this time of night. A passenger slumped in the seat beside me."

"So it was you?"

"Who killed all of those men? Oh yes, of course it was. Did you really suspect anyone else?"

A flashing blue light appeared in the mirrors. Margot

watched his grip on the wheel tighten as a vehicle approached from behind. He moderated his speed, fidgeting in his seat, but the lights raced by. Just an ambulance.

"I was genuinely surprised," he continued. "You finding me at the Naxos like that. That was an excellent piece of detective work."

"What really happened with Erec?"

"Erec? Oh, he was a fun one. My first. And probably the best." He looked across at her, but appearing to realise she lacked the energy for conversation, continued on his own: "You were on the right track, though, with that incident in Sète. Cheeky little sod he was. It started with this woman at the Naxos I had my eye on. One night, Erec comes along and starts giving her his spiel. I hate people like that, don't you? They've got practically nothing going for them yet women fall at their feet, just because they've got the gift of the gab.

"Anyway. A few weeks went by, and then there he was at the casino with this woman in tow. I thought he deserved a little payback so I waited for him outside in my car. I would happily have run him over. Oh yes, probably reversed, too. But the little sod jumped out of the way at the last moment ... Margot, are you listening?"

She nodded her head.

"Anyone else would have taken the hint, but do you know what he did instead? Gate-crashed one of my parties. Can you believe it? And then he started coming on to Roselyn, and that really was the final straw. So I slipped something into his drink. I thought he'd crashed out upstairs but I must have given him too small a dose because when I went to find him the little shit had gone."

"Was that the night he was seen in the village?"

"He'd escaped over the fields. Roselyn was the one who spotted him. I tracked him down and took him back to the villa.

I didn't have a plan. I put him in one of the outbuildings and slapped him around a bit. And then I hit him over the head with a hammer." He laughed. "Now don't look at me like that. It was fun. You should try it sometime."

If Margot could have thrown something at him she would have done.

"It wasn't enough to kill him. He just lay on the floor, groaning. I realised I had to get him out of the way so I stripped him of his clothes and took him down into the chamber. And yes, to answer your earlier question, of course I knew it was there. Roselyn and I found it when we went off into the woods one day. No one else seemed to know about it so it became our den."

They overtook a car. Margot looked in their windows as they cruised by: a young family, a child asleep in the back. Could they imagine they were sharing the autoroute with such an absolute monster?

"The next day I went down there and he was still alive. Only he wasn't so cocky now. I think the hammer must have damaged something in his brain because he kept slurring his words and drooling. It was revolting.

"I left him for another day. The third time I went down he looked like he'd given up. He barely moved when I stuck the knife into his throat. Oh, the blood that came out – you wouldn't believe it. Yet he still wouldn't die! So I cut him a little bit more, stabbed him here and there. It was exhilarating. And then I sat down and watched him expire."

He looked across, smiling. Margot averted her eyes.

"After that it became rather easy. I mean, once you've killed one person what difference does it make if you kill one more? I tried to make each one's death a little more unpleasant than the one before, see how far I could go."

"Where did Farooq fit in?"

"Farooq? Oh, Farooq was my supplier. My source of fresh

meat. He deals with all sorts in his line of work and from time to time he needs someone disappearing. I owed him money. It seemed an ideal arrangement."

Margot blinked in disbelief. "You mean you killed them to pay off a debt?"

His grin widened. "Genius, don't you think? All I had to do was get rid of some piece of lowlife and he would knock twenty thousand off what I owed. He didn't seem to realise I'd have done it for half the price."

"So why stop at five?"

His eyes sparkled with mischief. "Who said I stopped?"

A chill crept through Margot's bones as she stared back at him. She had no doubt she was looking into the cold-hearted eyes of a psychopath.

The signs for Girona passed by. Margot's mind had been so fogged she'd given no thought as to where they might be headed. If they carried on up the autoroute they would soon reach Perpignan, but something told her that wasn't what he had in mind. She squirmed in her seat, fearing she was running out of time.

"And Roselyn?"

"What about her?"

"How was she involved?"

Pascal looked at her without speaking. Margot went on, "She must have been down into the chamber at some point. I saw her initial carved on the wall."

He continued to remain silent, just stared at the road. After a full minute had gone by, he finally gave in.

"She watched me kill Erec. I wanted her to help with one of the others, too, but it all got a little too much for her."

"And the man in the swimming pool?"

"That was a joint effort. I smashed the bottle, Roselyn

pushed him into it. Lucky for him he fell in, otherwise she'd probably have scratched out his eyeballs."

"Just because he got friendly with her?"

He tutted. "You must think we're a family of incorrigible deviants. He touched her up and Roselyn didn't like it. Perfectly reasonable, I'd say."

"You're not your father's son, that's for sure."

"You don't know anything about my father."

"I know you were a disappointment to him."

They were the first words Margot had spoken that appeared to get through. But after a few moments of silently regarding her, he turned his eyes back to the road.

"You're wasting your time. Mind games won't work on me."

"You're a monster."

"Demonise me all you like, I have no regrets. Everyone I killed deserved it. And you should be happy, too. You've done your job, solved your case. You've found your murderer." He flicked the indicator as they approached a junction. "It's just a shame you'll never get to tell cousin Célia."

They peeled off into the exit lane and looped around a full 270 before arriving at a tee-junction. A dark and empty road greeted them, but he remained at the junction for a few extra moments, listening to the *tick-tack tick-tack* of the indicator. The road signs told Margot they were still in Spain, though she was not familiar with any of the place names. She gripped the seat-belt to raise herself up.

"Where are we going?"

"Haven't you guessed?"

He pulled out of the junction and turned left. The dark mysterious shapes of mountains loomed in the distance.

"I always used to take the back way in. For the sake of completeness, I thought I would show you exactly how it was done."

The clouds parted and the moon came out. The storms must have missed this area because the tarmac was dry, the trees unruffled. The hustle and bustle of Barcelona seemed very far away.

He slowed as they entered a small village. Perhaps a dozen houses lined the street, the blinking green cross of a *Farmacia* the only sign of life. Despite the complete absence of traffic, a light turned red as they approached. There was quiet in the car while they waited for it to change. Margot looked down at her door handle. Would her legs carry her if she tried to make a run for it? She could flex her right foot, but there was little feeling above her knee. Her arms moved better: she could yank on the handbrake, elbow him in the face, lean on the horn until someone came out. But the lights changed before she could decide on a plan.

They climbed a steep hill and entered a forest. The trees were so tall and packed so densely that even with the moonlight there was little to see by. Pascal slowed down and began searching for something through the side windows. He pulled up at a gap. It wasn't what he was looking for so he drove on. A little further down the road he repeated the manoeuvre, and on the third such occasion he slammed on the brakes.

"Ah! Here it is."

He reversed. Through her window, Margot saw the entrance to a track.

"What's down there?"

"You'll see."

He hauled the wheel hard to the right and eased past a damaged gate. The track was unpaved and heavily rutted, but the G Wagon handled it with ease. The trees thinned as the route began to climb and here and there views opened up to them: heavily-forested hills in one direction; rocky mountains in the other. Soon they were zig-zagging up the side of a narrow valley.

"Is this the smugglers' trail?" Margot asked.

"Bravo! The final piece of the puzzle slots into place."

Margot recalled the route she'd taken when she'd walked to the villa. The landscape was starting to look familiar. The ridge they were approaching looked very much like the one she'd seen when she'd scrambled up the rocks. Some feeling was coming back to her legs. She could wriggle her toes; rotate her left foot.

"I used to look forward to it."

"What?"

"Getting that call from Farooq. I don't know about you, but you reach a stage in life when you think you've done everything there is to do, seen everything there is to see. Yet there has to be something more, doesn't there? Otherwise what's the point?"

They crested the ridge and began the descent. The way down was much more perilous with numerous hairpin bends and rocks littering the route. Tackling it with gusto, Pascal picked up speed. They raced along the straighter sections, rolled heavily as he steered around the bends. The G Wagon bounced over small rocks, throwing them up in their seats.

Somehow, they made it to the bottom in one piece. The track cut directly across the valley floor, the only hazard being a river. It didn't look deep. Gravel bars split the flow into multiple channels and they forded it at speed, spraying water into the air. They sped over a gravel bar, plunged into deeper water, but as they neared a cluster of boulders he had to slow down. The water bubbled and frothed around their tyres as Pascal picked a way through, aiming for two ruts that marked the exit point. The wheels spun as he steered them up onto the bank, but then the tyres found traction, the four-wheel drive kicked in, and the G Wagon pulled itself up with ease.

And then they were back in the trees, bumping along a narrow defile. They were on the home stretch now. They couldn't be far from the section of trail she'd accessed from the lay-by. Margot felt panic rise within her.

"You won't get away with this."

"Why not?"

"I hope you rot in hell for what you've done!"

Losing concentration, he failed to notice a large rock. The front end bucked violently when they went over it, and a nasty cracking sound came from the rear. He slammed on the brakes.

After sitting still for a few moments, he tiredly exhaled. When he turned to her again, it seemed his patience was wearing thin. He exhaled. "Now look what you've made me do."

He got out to inspect. It didn't seem much damage had been done, however, and he was back in less than a minute. He put it into gear, but paused before letting out the clutch.

"You're becoming rather tiresome now. I think I'm going to enjoy killing you as much as I did Erec."

The scenery looked different in moonlight but Margot was certain they'd reached the section of the trail she'd walked just a few days earlier. Branches scraped the bodywork as they squeezed through; fingernails raking a blackboard. That, together with the bumpy ground, reduced their progress to little more than a crawl. They rocked and rolled for another few minutes before a grinding sound came from the underside. Pascal pushed hard on the accelerator, but the wheels on the G Wagon spun uselessly.

He cursed as he opened his door, having to force it against

the vegetation. He squeezed through to the rear of the car and stooped to inspect the underside. Returning after just a few seconds, he turned off the ignition and snatched out the keys.

"We'll have to walk. Get out."

Some feeling had come back to her legs but Margot remained seated. "You injected me, remember?"

"It should be wearing off by now."

"I still can't walk."

"Well, it's up to you. You can either walk, or I can drag you along by the hair. Which would you prefer?"

He returned to the rear of the truck and opened the door. Margot adjusted the rear-view mirror to keep him in sight. She watched him take out a flashlight, a coil of rope, and a handful of cable ties. Something that looked very much like a knife glinted in the moonlight as he held the blade up to his face.

She couldn't quite believe what she was doing but Margot opened her door. She pivoted in the seat and eased her legs out. There was hardly any space. When her feet touched the ground, her legs turned to jelly and she had to grab hold of the door to stop herself falling.

Pascal pushed through to join her, but a branch sprang back, whipping him in the face. He cursed loudly.

"Hold out your hands?"

"Why?"

He grabbed them himself and forced her wrists together. Margot tried to keep her hands slightly parted as he looped a cable tie around, but he wasn't to be fooled. He pulled it so tight the plastic dug into her flesh. Switching on the flashlight, he pointed it straight in her eyes.

"Keep up. Otherwise I'll end this right now." Coil of rope over his shoulder, he set off.

Margot blinked, waiting for her retinas to recover.

Without the aid of the torch it was difficult to see where she was going. Even with the moon out, the trees were so dense they sucked all light from the air. Her foot caught a fallen branch and she stumbled; Pascal barely glanced back. They reached the section above the lay-by and Margot paused, looking down. She could lie on her side; roll down that barren slope, head for the road.

"Margot."

She looked up. Pascal was walking towards her. Margot recoiled as he again shone the light into her eyes.

"I told you to keep up."

"My legs are still numb."

"Yet you were just thinking about running away, hmm. Somehow I don't believe you." He removed the coil of rope from his shoulder and searched for the end. "Anyway, we're almost there. It's time I put you on the leash." He fed the end of the rope around the binding on her wrists and started tying a knot. Margot could do nothing but watch.

"You realise you're walking into a trap."

He made no comment.

"The people I was with will have called the police."

He pulled the knot tight.

"And Gaston and Madame Baudet will be down there. You've got no chance."

Pascal looked into her eyes. "Do you know what – I've grown rather tired of the sound of your voice." He cut a short length from the other end of the rope. "From now on we'll continue in silence."

He forced the rope between her teeth so quickly that Margot had no time to react. She struggled, but he'd soon tied a knot.

They walked on. Soon they came to the fork in the track and took the left-hand route. Margot held back as they approached the field gate, her chest growing so tight she had difficulty breathing. She couldn't believe he was actually going to go through with this. He was just trying to scare her, go out with one last hurrah. Even in his deranged state, he surely knew he wouldn't get away with it.

The rope had gone tight so he gave it a tug. Margot stumbled a few steps forward. The light from his torch roved the undergrowth before settling on the fencing around the entrance to the passage. The steel sheet was still in place. Margot went cold remembering what lay below.

A noise down at the villa distracted him. Pascal moved to the field gate, and Margot looked, too. Lights were on in the house. Cocking her head, she could hear people shouting, calling her name. A figure appeared on the footpath to the side – could that be Didier? And following a short way behind was what appeared to be Gaston, brandishing a shotgun. Margot's heart rose in relief.

But Pascal wasn't done yet. He tied his end of the rope to a tree and then approached the entrance to the tunnel. It didn't take long to kick down the fence. There seemed no way he would move the steel sheet on his own, but Margot watched in amazement as he squatted down, eased his wiry fingers beneath an edge, and raised it a millimetre or two. Spreading his legs, he shifted it far enough to expose a corner. He reached into the hole, pulled out the short ladder and threw it into the undergrowth.

Mesmerised, it took Margot a few seconds to realise that with the rope now loose she could pull out the gag. She cried out as he approached, but she'd left it too late. Pascal grabbed her around the waist, dragged her to the hole, and then dropped her in.

29

Her legs gave way and Margot fell down, hitting her head against the brick arch. Too stunned to move, the darkness quickly swallowed her up. Cold air was draughting up out of the tunnel, tickling her ankles, while above her head the steel sheet had been moved back into place, sealing her in.

Fighting nausea, Margot hauled herself up. The sheet was only a few centimetres above her head, but with her wrists still bound it was impossible to get a grip. Behind her, the dark void of the tunnel seemed intent on sucking her in.

Exploring with her flattened palms, she discovered a corner where a little of the earth had fallen in. She made claws of her hands and scraped away. The dirt was dry and crumbled easily. Uncovering a plant root, she pulled until it snapped. Soon she'd made an opening wide enough to see out.

A gun went off, the blast so loud it carried all the way up through the trees.

With renewed vigour, Margot clawed desperately at the ground. As soon as the hole was wide enough, she burrowed out and wriggled up onto the grass. She rose to her feet and staggered to the field gate. The lights were still on in the villa, but there were no signs of movement. If it were Gaston who'd fired the shot then why were he and Didier not out looking for her?

Margot climbed over the gate. The meadow was so steep she dropped to her rear and slid most of the way. At the bottom, she stumbled forward and fell against the wall below the kitchen window. Her pulse hammered in her ears while she recovered her breath.

A second shot rang out, startling her. What the hell was going on?

She picked up the rope that was still attached to her wrist binding and set off around the east wing. The pool lights were on; a window was lit in Gaston's cottage. But the mystery was short-lived: rounding the house's front corner Margot came upon a scene of horror. A bloodied mess that could only be Gaston lay on the edge of the lawn while Pascal towered over him, shotgun in hand.

He didn't seem surprised by her sudden appearance and his feet remained rooted to the spot as he turned slowly towards her. Staring at his blood-spattered face, Margot was struck dumb.

"Madame Renard!"

Madame Baudet stepped out from the front door, armed with a poker. She ventured a few steps onto the drive, but when Pascal turned again she panicked and threw the poker at him. She missed by a mile.

Margot dashed to the front door and, grabbing the housekeeper's arm, hustled her inside. She slammed the door and shot home the bolts. Moving to the nearest window, she saw Pascal hunched over Gaston's body, searching his pockets with careful, unhurried movements.

"He's gone mad!" Madame Baudet shrieked. "Stark raving mad!"

Margot grabbed her by the shoulders. The housekeeper was shaking all over, almost hysterical. "Where's Didier?"

"He was outside. With Gaston."

"Have you called the police?"

"Y-yes."

Margot's mind was racing but she needed to calm down. Think. "Okay. Help me with this."

They hurried through to the kitchen. Madame Baudet took a knife from the drawer, and although the cable tie was tight against her skin, Margot let her cut it. The rope dropped to the floor.

"Are all the doors shut?"

"Yes."

"And the windows?"

"I think so."

Margot rubbed life back into her wrists. The police would surely be on their way, but doors and windows wouldn't keep him out for long. Not with a shotgun. "Are there any weapons in the house?"

"Weapons?"

"Anything we can use to against him."

Madame Baudet shook her head.

Margot returned to the window in the hall. Shadows were moving on the drive, but Pascal had gone. A scream from the kitchen made her turn sharply back. Margot ran in just as a hand reached up and tapped on the glass.

"Come out, come out wherever you are."

Through the kitchen window, she glimpsed him heading around the back, shotgun in hand.

"Quick! Slide this over to the door."

Madame Baudet grabbed one end of the kitchen table while Margot took the other, but it was far too heavy to shift. A crash and a clatter came from nearby – tins falling, a thud and a squeak. Surely he hadn't got in that quickly. Margot and the housekeeper watched in disbelief as the kitchen door opened. Moments later Pascal looked in, smiling when he saw them.

"There you are." He casually closed the door behind him. "You must have forgotten about the window in the pantry. It always was the easiest way in."

Madame Baudet screamed. She grabbed a piece of majolica from the dresser and threw it at him. Pascal ducked, and braved the onslaught as she continued to hurl objects at him like a woman possessed. But the moment he got a chance, he raised the shotgun and pointed it at her head.

"One more and I'll blow your head off."

Madame Baudet turned to a statue.

"Now, you." He swung the barrel towards Margot. "Pick up that rope."

Margot didn't move. Every second she delayed could prove vital.

"I won't say it again."

Would he really blow her head off? He'd had umpteen chances to kill her already. Something told her that wasn't the way he wanted this to end but she wasn't quite brave enough to risk it. She crouched and picked up the rope.

"Now both of you, walk to the front door."

Margot gave Madame Baudet a nod of reassurance before leading the way out. Pascal shadowed them, the gun on their backs, but as they neared the front door he overtook and backed them against the wall.

"You." The barrel was aimed at Madame Baudet. "Open the door and get out. And you." He turned the gun on Margot. "Stay right where you are."

Madame Baudet didn't need telling twice. Hands fumbling with the bolts, she couldn't get out fast enough. She flung open the door and fled onto the drive, just as flashing lights appeared in the distance.

Pascal spotted them. A car was approaching at speed, siren wailing, but he didn't seem alarmed. He calmly closed and bolted the door.

"What are you doing?" Margot said. "You may as well give yourself up."

He moved to the dining room door, opened the secret panel, and took out the key. He unlocked the rim-lock and pushed the door wide open.

"On the contrary," he said. "The show's not over yet. Inside."

Margot stepped cautiously into the dining room. Pascal switched on the lights and then locked the door behind him. He completed a rapid circuit of the room, checking the shutters were all in place, the curtains properly drawn. Satisfied they were safely sealed in, the tension seemed to go out of him. Standing at the head of the table, he put down the shotgun.

"Give me the rope."

Margot hesitated. She couldn't help but glance up at the beam in the ceiling.

She threw him the rope, aiming short. It landed on the back of one of the chairs making him step forward to retrieve it.

"Well, here we are," Pascal said, coiling the rope in his hands. "Like nothing's ever changed."

He moved to the other side of the table, a faraway look in his eyes. It was impossible to imagine the effect of the memories that were stirring inside him, being back in this room, after all this time.

"We'd been playing hide and seek in the garden. Roselyn and I." He smiled fondly. "I was annoyed because she kept cheating. Kept coming to look for me before she'd finished counting."

He pulled out one of the chairs and used it to step up onto the table. The hook was still too high to reach so he took the chair with him and stepped up again. He placed one end of the rope over the hook, adjusted it for length, and then secured it with a knot. He stepped back down onto the table and began tying a noose.

"So I ran back inside to tell my father. And this is where I found him. Standing right here, about to string himself up."

Margot's eyes switched to the gun. He'd left it at the far end of the table. She was closer to it than he was; she could easily grab it while he was distracted.

"He hadn't noticed I was there," Pascal went on. "Not that that was anything new. He cared more for his blasted museum than he ever did for me. I stayed quiet as a mouse. At first, I didn't understand what he was doing. I thought perhaps it was something only grownups got up to. To a six-year-old boy, adults are mysterious things. But when he put the noose around his neck I began to comprehend."

Out in the hall came a loud crash. Shouting voices appeared on the other side of the door, but if Pascal had heard he remained unconcerned.

"I wasn't sad, or scared. I didn't feel sorry for him. All I can remember is being fascinated. I wanted to see if he would actually go through with it. I wanted to know what it would be like to watch him die.

"He stepped off the edge. A short clean drop, though it didn't kill him outright. He went very red in the face. Kept swinging his legs. He must have been hanging there for a good few minutes before he finally stopped moving. And all the time I stood and stared."

Someone banged on the door.

"In here!" Margot cried. "I'm in here!"

Margot took it as her cue to run for the gun. She grabbed it from the table, put a finger to the trigger, and took aim. Pascal remained unruffled.

"Shoot if you like," he smiled. "It's not loaded." He tugged the rope to test it was secure and then slipped the noose over his neck. "I just wanted you to watch."

Eyes glazing over, he looked at Margot one last time. Whatever madness was within him seemed to briefly disappear and all she could see was a cold empty man.

"Thank you for a lovely evening," he said. "I've had a ball."

And then he stepped off the edge.

30

Blue and orange lights were flashing in the trees as Alia sped up the drive of the villa Belle Époque. She pulled on the handbrake, skidding to a halt just metres short of one of the two police cars.

"That's Madame Baudet."

The housekeeper was standing with a female police officer. Alia unclicked her seat-belt and was out of the car before Jorge could even open his mouth.

The officer was trying to console her but Madame Baudet was in shock. Hands shaking, teeth chattering, she reached out as Alia approached.

"Oh, Alia!"

"What's happened?"

"They're inside."

"Who is?"

"Pascal and Madame Renard. He's got a gun!"

Two policemen ran out of the house. They opened the boot of their car, took out a battering ram, and then ran back in. Everything was happening so quickly that none of it seemed real.

"Oh hell!"

Jorge had moved off to one side. The other car was blocking her view, but when Alia moved round she found him pointing at a body lying on the edge of the lawn. The face had been blown away, but she recognised the clothing in an instant. Alia clapped a hand to her mouth.

"It's Gaston."

"Pascal's shot him!" Madame Baudet cried out.

But where was Papa? Alia moved numbly back to the housekeeper. "Have you seen Didier?"

"He was heading that way." She pointed towards the west wing. "I don't know what happened to him."

The moon was out but that side of the garden was in shade. For a few moments, Alia didn't move, paralysed by a vision of her father lying dead in a shrubbery. She looked at Jorge. Jorge looked at her. This wasn't the way things were meant to be.

Sparking back to life, Alia ran across the gravel, into a sea of amorphous grey blobs. The summer house was the only definitive object, caught in a glow of moonlight. And the unmoving figure lying on the steps was plain to see. Once again, Alia froze.

"Papa?"

The word very nearly didn't come out of her mouth. It couldn't be him, could it? Not her father. She'd told him to lock the gate and go back home. Alia gritted her teeth as emotion welled up inside her. The foolish old man. Why couldn't he have just done as he'd been told?

Jorge held onto her arm, but Alia snatched it free. The short walk over there was the longest journey in her life and Alia didn't wanted it to end. Her father was lying face down on the woodwork, limbs set at an unnatural angle, a matt of bloodied hair on the back of his head. Two metres was as close as she could bear to go.

Jorge moved past her. He knelt down and reached to the side of his neck. And in the very same moment, her father let out a groan.

———

Didier slowly came round. They helped him get up on the step where he slumped against the newel post, dazed but very much alive. But there was no time for elation – all hell was breaking loose inside the villa.

"You go," Jorge said. "I'll stay with him."

"You sure?"

He nodded.

A small convoy was speeding up the drive. Alia pointed an ambulance crew in the direction of the summer house and then carried on running.

Three officers were already inside, targeting the dining room door with a battering ram. Two swift blows and the rim-lock buckled and fell to the floor.

Alia was forced to stand back as the officers stormed in, weapons drawn. Several seconds of organised chaos ensued, but it quickly transpired the threat had already been neutralised: Pascal was swinging by the neck from the end of a rope; Margot was sitting on the floor.

But he wasn't yet dead. Face bulging, cheeks turning purple, he looked like his head was about to explode. One of the officers grabbed him by the shins while the other jumped up onto the table. As the rope was released, the three of them collapsed into a heap on the floor.

Alia rushed to Margot's side. She was dazed but conscious. "Are you okay?"

Margot nodded. "Have they found Didier?"

"He's fine."

More bodies rushed in as Alia helped her to get up. And in the centre of it all, Pascal looked up from the floor, an air of disappointment slowly escaping through his eyes.

31

Margot set her travel bag down by the door and did one final sweep of the room, just to make sure she hadn't forgotten anything. Moving to the window she enjoyed one last view of the garden. She'd been here less than a week yet the place felt like home.

The door to Didier's room was ajar. Margot knocked lightly, but found him fast asleep. He'd needed five stitches in the back of his head and had had to spend the night in the hospital, but apart from a mild concussion, he'd come away pretty much unscathed. For whatever reason, Pascal had chosen to spare him.

Margot stepped quietly to his bedside and left her thank-you note on the table.

Down in the kitchen, Alia was busy tidying up. She seemed to have developed a new obsession and had spent most of the previous day cleaning the house and reorganising the office. Her way of coping, perhaps.

Margot set her bag down on a chair. "That's me all set." She smiled as Alia came over and they kissed on both cheeks. Reluctant to let her go, Margot pulled her in for a longer hug. She always found it difficult saying goodbye to newfound friends. "Thank you for putting up with me."

"It was a pleasure."

"And I'm sorry the way things turned out."

The car hadn't arrived yet so they went outside and sat on the bench. It was a beautiful summer's morning. "So what are your plans now?"

Alia picked a pink Marguerite from the pot beside her and twizzled the stem between her thumb and forefinger. She looked older than when Margot had first met her, more mature.

"Oh, there's plenty that needs doing in the garden. Papa's not going to be back on his feet for a while yet."

"And after that?"

"You mean about a career?"

Margot nodded.

Alia sighed. "I probably will join the *Police Nationale* one day, but not yet. Papa needs me here."

Margot nodded again. Family bonds were a hard thing to break.

"Besides," Alia smiled, "I think we've seen enough excitement in Saint-Clair-de-l'Ouillat to last a lifetime."

A car horn hooted.

"That'll be for me." Margot nipped into the kitchen to collect her bag and then gave Alia one more hug. "Anyway. I hate long goodbyes."

"Me too."

"Give Didier my best."

"I will."

"And do keep in touch. You're welcome in Argents any time."

Alia waved her off from the gate. With a heavy heart, Margot set off, warmed by the sight of the candy red Bentley waiting at the end of the track.

"Has she gone?"

Alia removed the flannel from her father's forehead and rinsed it in the bowl of cold water. "Yes, she's gone. She left you a note to say thank you."

"That was nice of her."

Didier rolled onto his side so she could check the back of his head. The wound was healing nicely. After tidying up the dressing she replaced the flannel.

"Thank you, Alia. That feels much better."

"You're welcome."

"Do you think you could bring me some fresh apple juice later? And perhaps one of those avocados for lunch? You know how I like them, with a little bit of balsamic vinegar and olive oil."

Alia narrowed her eyes at him. There was nothing wrong with his legs. Couldn't he at least go downstairs to eat? But she dutifully promised she would bring him his lunch and seconds later watched him sink into a deep and contented sleep.

She cleared away some of the detritus that had accumulated at his bedside in the past few days and then paused for a rest in his armchair. His sturdy old armchair, the one that used to be in her room, where he would sit night after night, with Alia on his lap, reading a bedtime story. How the tides do change.

He'd blamed himself for Gaston's death. Following her phone call, he'd gone straight round to the villa, and after locking the gate had enlisted Gaston's help in patrolling the grounds. Papa didn't remember much about it. It was all still hazy. The only thing he could clearly recall was Pascal springing out of some bushes, taking him by surprise. And he hadn't seen Gaston get shot. When they told him, he went very quiet and insisted upon seeing the body. The image of Gaston's blown-out face would surely live with them both forever. But her father wasn't to blame. If anything, it was her fault: if she hadn't phoned him in the first place then none of it would have happened.

"*Salut?*" said a voice from downstairs.

Alia came to her senses. She went down the stairs and found Jorge standing in the front doorway, a chicken clutched to his chest.

"I don't suppose this little lady's meant to be wandering around."

Alia tutted. She relieved him of the troublesome bird. "Honestly. If we put a two-metre high fence around the run this one would still find a way out."

She led him out through the kitchen and returned Henrietta to the chicken run. When she turned, she found Jorge casting an appreciative eye over the garden. "Nice place you have here."

Alia folded her arms. He wasn't wrong. It did look nice at this time of the morning with the sun appearing over the tops of the trees and the air sweet with the scent of roses. It had never really occurred to her before that perhaps one day all of it would be hers.

"Papa did all the planting. The garden's his thing really."

"How is he?"

"Oh, he's fine. Enjoying being a patient a little too much."

They shared a smile. His eyes seemed to keep wanting to find hers and Alia was having a hard time resisting. She tucked her fingers into the front pockets of her jeans. "So, what are you doing here?"

"I came to see how you all were. And say goodbye to Margot."

"You're too late. She left yesterday."

"Oh, that's a shame."

"Don't worry. Now she knows you work in a winery I'm sure she'll become a regular visitor."

He threw back his head and laughed properly this time. Alia felt a tingle inside. How wonderful that she could make him laugh like that.

"Can I get you a drink?"

"I thought you would never ask; I'm parched."

They went into the kitchen. It felt a different place with everything clean and tidy. And this was how it was going to remain, Alia resolved. She might even make a few changes; buy some new furniture; paint some of the door fronts; get herself a proper coffee machine. She filled the kettle with water.

Jorge pulled out one of the chairs and took a seat at the table. After so many years of being just herself and her father it felt odd seeing a young man there, feet under the table. Alia wasn't quite sure how to feel about it. She remained on the nearside of the counter and busied herself with making the coffee.

"Need a hand?"

"No thanks."

"Are you back at work now?"

"Not yet. The mayor said I should take a week off, but I'd rather keep busy." Alia turned to face him. "What about you?"

"Ah, we'll be starting the harvest soon. It'll be non-stop for the next few weeks. All hands on deck."

Alia nodded. Then after that he would no doubt be heading off in his van, going wherever the road might take him. Now she looked into his eyes. What kind of relationship would that be? Always on the move. Never settling down. Would she ever be able to admit to herself that actually she quite liked the idea?

Jorge got up from his seat and came to the counter.

"You know," he said, leaning down on his elbows, "you could always come round and give us a hand. Take that week off, after all."

Everything did indeed feel shiny and new, but Alia rather liked it. The kettle started to whistle.

32

"I must say, I feel rather ashamed by the impression this affair must have given you of the Deveraux family," Célia said, seated at her desk in her office at the *Palais de Justice*. "I can assure you, my side of the family are rather more staid."

Margot reached for her coffee. She held the cup with her left hand, having still not recovered full use of her right. Célia had helped enormously with her recovery and had insisted on getting her access to the very best medical care. Her neurologist hadn't been able to conclusively determine which drug Pascal had injected her with, but he remained optimistic the problem would resolve itself. The mental wounds, however, would take longer to heal.

"I think that would be a very slippery slope," Margot replied. "I certainly wouldn't want to be held accountable for the things my family have done."

"Quite."

The judge's mind appeared to wander. Underneath that calm exterior she clearly remained troubled. She went on, "I can't help feeling I should have done something sooner. If I'd intervened, perhaps some of it could have been avoided."

"From the brief time I spent with Pascal I don't think it would have made any difference," Margot said. "He seemed totally unmoved by the feelings of others."

Weren't psychopaths born rather than made? Without professional intervention early on it's unlikely any of his crimes could have been prevented. Apart from the five dead men, it was perhaps Gaston Margot felt most sorry for. Shunned by the village for most of his adult life, and then shot in the face whilst attempting to come to her rescue. Florian had been trying to trace his next of kin but so far had found no living relatives. His family had hailed from Normandy, and Célia had arranged for him to be buried in the same churchyard as his parents.

"I take it there's enough evidence to prosecute him for Gaston's murder?"

Célia had just taken in a mouthful of coffee so she nodded. "The *procureur*'s already appointed a new JI. We're still deciding what to do about the original five. A confession would be nice, of course, but given Pascal's condition I hardly think it's likely."

Pascal had spent the past few days in the intensive therapy unit at the hospital in Toulouse. His prognosis was good, but the fact he would be spending the rest of his days in a different kind of hospital didn't seem in doubt. No additional bodies had been found; his claim not to have stopped at five had probably been fantasy, like so many of the words that had come out of his mouth. And two of the five remained unidentified.

"Has Roselyn been informed?"

Célia nodded. "I telephoned her ex-husband in Lyon. He's going to see she's taken care of."

"Will she face any charges?"

"I don't think so, given her mental state. From what you've said we would have a hard time proving she was an accessory."

A coughing fit came on from nowhere. When it showed no

sign of abating Célia quickly got up and hastened into the bathroom.

Margot sat still. She hadn't mentioned what Pascal had said about her illness; she still couldn't decide whether to believe him or not. When Célia didn't come straight back, Margot got out of her seat and took her coffee over to the window. Down in the park, some workmen were trimming the summer growth from the pencil cypress. Sometimes, when you got stuck in one of life's dramas, it was easy to forget that life goes on, the world keeps turning, the postman keeps delivering the mail. Right now it was nice to have some mundanity back. Margot turned as the door to the bathroom opened.

"Sorry about that."

"Is everything all right?"

Célia picked up her coffee and came to join her. "It's just a cold, that's all."

Margot doubted that were true.

"You know," she said, "when he stepped off that table and I saw him hanging there, part of me was glad. I hoped he would die."

"That's entirely understandable."

"After the terrible things he'd done I thought it was the least he deserved."

"Of course. I'm sure many would share that opinion."

But Margot remained troubled. "What's been bothering me most of all though is, had the police not come in when they did, would I have saved him?"

Célia looked as if she had an opinion to give but she waited, allowing Margot time to get it all out.

"He was right there in front of me. All I had to do was grab hold of his legs. Or even climb up and cut the rope. If you see someone in danger shouldn't your instinct be to save them?"

"You were in shock."

"Yes, but it wasn't just that. There was a moment when I thought about saving him. When I could see what I ought to do. But in the end, I did nothing. And I think I would have just sat there and watched him die. Does that make me a bad person?"

Célia gathered her thoughts. "I've been a *magistrat* for over thirty years: sixteen as a *juge d'instruction*, a further fifteen as a *procureur*. The judgements I've made have decided the fates of thousands of people, and for my predecessors that would have meant sending many of them to the guillotine. But what gives us that right?"

"You're a member of the *magistrature*. Your function is to uphold the law."

"In a technical sense, yes, but I'm talking morally. I'm just a human being. I'm always questioning my right. And I can't honestly hold up my hand and say I've never made a mistake." She reached out to Margot's forearm. "You have no reason to rebuke yourself, Margot. Your actions were entirely understandable."

Perhaps, but Margot couldn't help seeing the similarities with how Pascal had watched his father die. Two sides of the same coin, he'd said.

The telephone rang, breaking the mood. Célia crossed to the desk to answer it. She replaced the receiver after a single *Merci*.

"I'm afraid that's our time up. My next appointment has just arrived."

"Of course." Margot returned her cup to the tray. "I'm glad we had this little chat."

"So am I." Célia walked her to the door. "My son's coming down from Strasbourg at the weekend. It would be nice if you could meet him."

"I'd be happy to."

"You'll like Stéphane. He's fun to be around, despite being a human rights lawyer."

"Not the most exciting of professions, I imagine."

"No, he's good. We could go for a picnic on the beach."

Margot took a breath, her mood lifting. "Yes. Thank you. I'd like that."

The sun came out as she walked home along Rue Voltaire. A small white yacht was heading out of the harbour, preparing to set sail. The afternoon light had a magical quality, just right for imbuing the sea with that impossibly deep shade of blue. Perhaps she would get out her easel.

THE END

PLEASE REVIEW THIS BOOK

Please don't underestimate how important reviews are to authors, particularly independent authors who don't have the backing of a huge marketing machine. If you enjoyed **FIVE DEAD MEN** please consider leaving a review on either Amazon or Goodreads, it will be very much appreciated.

WHAT NEXT?

Margot Renard will return in:

No Tears for Sandrine

For updates, sign up at: www.rachelgreenauthor.com

FOLLOW:

https://twitter.com/AuthorRachelG
https://www.instagram.com/authorrachelg/
https://www.facebook.com/AuthorRachelG
https://www.bookbub.com/authors/rachel-green?follow=true

Printed in Great Britain
by Amazon